PENGUIN BOOKS
STRANGE OBSESSION

Shobhaa Dé describes herself as an 'obsessive-compulsive writer'. Columnist, commentator, and author of fourteen books, she lives with her family in Mumbai, a city that she considers a 'character', not just a locale, in her work.

She is currently planning her next book, a novel.

Strange Obsession

SHOBHAA DÉ

PENGUIN BOOKS

PENGUIN BOOKS
Published by the Penguin Group
Penguin Books India Pvt. Ltd, 11 Community Centre, Panchsheel Park, New Delhi 110 017, India
Penguin Group (USA) Inc., 375 Hudson Street, New York, New York 10014, USA
Penguin Group (Canada), 90 Eglinton Avenue East, Suite 700, Toronto, Ontario, M4P 2Y3, Canada (a division of Pearson Penguin Canada Inc.)
Penguin Books Ltd, 80 Strand, London WC2R 0RL, England
Penguin Ireland, 25 St Stephen's Green, Dublin 2, Ireland (a division of Penguin Books Ltd)
Penguin Group (Australia), 250 Camberwell Road, Camberwell, Victoria 3124, Australia (a division of Pearson Australia Group Pty Ltd)
Penguin Group (NZ), 67 Apollo Drive, Rosedale, North Shore 0632, New Zealand (a division of Pearson New Zealand Ltd)
Penguin Group (South Africa) (Pty) Ltd, 24 Sturdee Avenue, Rosebank, Johannesburg 2196, South Africa

Penguin Books Ltd, Registered Offices: 80 Strand, London WC2R 0RL, England

First published by Penguin Books India 1992

Copyright © Shobhaa Dé 1992

All rights reserved

25 24 23

ISBN 9780144000487

This is a work of fiction. Names, characters, places and incidents are either the product of the author's imagination or are used fictitiously and any resemblance to any actual person, living or dead, events or locales is entirely coincidental.

Typeset by Vans Information Limited, Mumbai
Printed at Anubha Printers, Noida

This book is sold subject to the condition that it shall not, by way of trade or otherwise, be lent, resold, hired out, or otherwise circulated without the publisher's prior written consent in any form of binding or cover other than that in which it is published and without a similar condition including this condition being imposed on the subsequent purchaser and without limiting the rights under copyright reserved above, no part of this publication may be reproduced, stored in or introduced into a retrieval system, or transmitted in any form or by any means (electronic, mechanical, photocopying, recording or otherwise), without the prior written permission of both the copyright owner and the above-mentioned publisher of this book.

To my husband Dilip—
for all the caring and sharing

One

'Mrs Aggarwal, you are spoiling your daughter. What nonsense this is! How can you allow such a young girl to go to Bombay all by herself?'

Amrita's mother smiled indulgently. She told her neighbour politely but firmly that Amrita was no longer a child. She was twenty years old and a very responsible young lady. Besides, what future did she have in Delhi, anyway? The neighbour wasn't convinced. The two women sat knitting companionably on the small patch of lawn behind the Aggarwal's Vasant Vihar bungalow. There was a mild sun rising high into the winter sky as the aroma of paranthas soaked in ghee wafted out to where they were seated.

'It's not as if there are no models in Delhi,' Mrs Sethia continued.

Amrita overheard the remark and snapped, 'Yes there are . . . third-rate models posing for Ludhiana Woollen Mills. That's not my style.'

Her mother stared with pride at her beautiful daughter and gently silenced the neighbour by placing a finger on her lips. Amrita's suitcase on the veranda was already crammed to the brim with clothes. Her mother wondered what else she was going to stuff into that bag. Amrita was crazy about clothes and could not have enough of them. But then, thought, Mrs Aggarwal, wasn't it natural for an attractive, ambitious, glamorous model to want the best? Besides, Amrita had always been touched by good luck. From the day she was born. Everybody said she was blessed, even the pandit who drew up her kundali. When she was born Amrita's two older brothers had stared at their brand-new baby sister with awe and told their mother, 'She is so pretty. So perfect. She is going to be the most beautiful woman in the world someday.' They'd been joined in their admiration by Amrita's father who had agreed wholeheartedly with them. He had gazed at his little daughter lying contentedly in her mother's arms and told his wife, 'This child is special.'

Mr Aggarwal, who had begun his career as a babu in a lowly government office, had quit his job and started a small business on borrowed capital. By the time Amrita was five years old, the family had prospered sufficiently for her father to move them all out of a crowded basti in Old Delhi, to their present home: a neat, well-maintained bungalow in Vasant Vihar. Now he was the hard-working owner of a processed foods factory in Gurgaon with over two hundred people working for him.

Amrita had breezed through school. With two doting brothers to escort her and a beaming father to cater to her every whim, Amrita was certainly someone who aroused envy in her classmates. But, as her mother often reminded her, the envy had more to do with the way she looked—stunning!—at a time when other teenagers were uniformly gawky and awkward.

Even though Amrita was no more than an average student, there was something exceptionally bright and compelling about her. Perhaps it was the golden glints dancing in her tawny eyes or the radiance and freshness she exuded each time she turned her head to face someone. Or, perhaps, it was the litheness of her magnificently structured body, with its long, toast-brown legs, narrow waist, and breasts that stood out—proud, high and firm. If there was one slight imperfection it was a suggestion of a squint in those wide-spaced, feline eyes fringed with unnaturally dark lashes. It was also in the tip-tilted nose that gave her oval face an elfin charm but was a problem to photograph. What attracted most people was the deep cleft in her chin. Without it her face might have been too pretty, too symmetrical, too boring. However, it was when Amrita laughed, throwing back her head and allowing her rich mane of hair to flow around her face like the sea, that she was irresistible. The laugh, open and throaty, would gurgle its way up and emerge in a cascade of uninhibitedly happy sound that would fill the room with infectious joy. Amrita knew the effect it had on people . . . and that always made her laugh some more.

*

'Time to go,' said her brother Amrish as he tossed the car-keys at Ashish, the younger one. Mrs Aggarwal couldn't stop hugging Amrita and crying, as the sound of the Maruti 1000 reversing out of the garage reached them.

Amrita was dressed in her favourite attire—well-worn Guess jeans and a black Gap T-shirt.

Her father looked disapprovingly at her and said, 'Isn't this a bit too . . . a bit too . . . .'

Amrita completed his sentence for him by saying brightly, 'Casual? Shabby?' before rushing into his arms and clinging to him.

'We trust you, beti,' her father said. 'Bombay is different from Delhi. You already know that. Take care of yourself. Don't go out alone at night. Keep in constant touch. Eat well and sleep well. And, remember, if you are ever in any kind of trouble, no matter how small, call home.'

Amrita was too overcome to respond. She buried her face into her father's shoulder and was suddenly beset by all sorts of fears. It would've been so easy to say, 'I've changed my mind. I want to stay.' But she didn't. It had to be Bombay. She wanted the big time. And she wanted it bad.

Two

Meenakshi was buying a pack of imported cigarettes from the paan-wallah in Colaba when she spotted her for the first time. Amrita was getting out of a taxi and rushing into a building across the street. She was carrying heaps of clothes on hangers in one hand and an ungainly make-up bag in the other. Meenakshi watched the flustered girl as she made a last minute dash from the road divider. A sharp screech of tyres and she saw Amrita sprawled across the street, her clothes all over the wet, slimy road, as a taxi-driver abused her lustily and the crowds gathered, as if out of nowhere, to watch the impromptu street-show.

Meenakshi put the fiver back into her jeans' pocket, slipped the pack of Cartiers into her unconstructed linen jacket, and strolled over to see what was going to happen next. Anything could. Bombay was like that. She found Amrita in tears, attempting to pick up her scattered belongings while the people in the crowd heckled, 'Woh Shampoo walli ladki ' and the taxi-wallah continued to curse, encouraged by the large audience.

The traffic had come to a standstill and there were even people looking out from the windows of the adjoining buildings. Meenakshi's heart melted. She strode up to Amrita briskly and held out her hand, 'Here . . . let me help you up.' Amrita grabbed the proffered hand gratefully and began babbling something incoherent about being late for her assignment. 'Relax,' Meenakshi said, as she took charge. She walked determinedly up to the cabbie and fixed him with a steady stare. 'I am Inspector General V.S. Iyengar's daughter. You want to act funny with this girl?' The cabbie looked at her, uncertain whether to believe her or not.

Suddenly, a traffic policeman strolled up, late as usual, and noticing Meenakshi, saluted smartly before asking, 'Any problem, madam?' That was the cue for the crowds to disperse. Meenakshi shook her head and waved him off.

Amrita's face was streaked with smudged eye make-up and her carefully blow-dried hair hung in rat-tails down her back. Meenakshi burst out laughing, 'You aren't going to get too many modelling assignments if you go around looking like that,' she said, taking her by the elbow and escorting her to the entrance of the building which housed a well-known ad agency on the fourth floor.

Amrita, still flustered, stared gratefully at her. 'You've been so sweet. I don't know how to thank you,' she said. 'I'm still new to Bombay and I often lose my way going to my photo-sessions.'

Meenakshi stared into the most beautiful eyes she had ever seen and forgot what she wanted to say. Recovering swiftly she held out her hand. 'Minx Iyengar. Don't bother to tell me who you are. I know. So do all these thousands of people who just saw your pretty pink panties.'

Amrita flushed crimson and tugged at her short skirt. 'Oh, my God!' she said, covering her face with her hands.

Meenakshi grinned and reached over to tousle her hair, 'Come on, I'll see you upstairs. My uncle owns the agency.'

*

Minx was waiting for Amrita when she emerged three hours later. It was dark outside. Strange how Colaba transformed itself once the sun went down. All sorts of weirdos—bleached out beach bums, drug-pushers, drug-users, whores who looked like good girls and good girls who looked like whores, local toughs, familiar drunks—everybody crawled out from the bylanes and thronged the Irani cafés notorious for serving more than just their specialities of bun-pao-maska with over-sweet tea. Amrita was delighted to see Minx hanging around in a black jeep, chatting with what looked like a bunch of sleazy drug dealers.

'Hi!' Amrita called out to her.

Minx flicked her half-finished Cartier expertly into the nearest gutter and got out of her jeep. 'At your service, Highness,' she said with a sardonic laugh. The thugs moved off respectfully and watched.

Amrita stared quizzically at them. 'Who are they?' she asked Minx in a whisper.

Minx looked around, stuck her fingers into her mouth and let out a sharp whistle, 'Abbey saalon . . . come here,' she shouted. The men approached. Amrita suppressed an involuntary shudder as Minx introduced them one by one. 'This is Kallu. That's Kaniya. He's Albert and this is his friend, Pagla.' After a pause, she added, 'Don't worry . . . they're my boys. Safe.' Still puzzled, Amrita let Minx take her things from her and help her into the jeep. 'Local dadas,' she said by way of an explanation, 'but loyal to me.'

Amrita decided not to probe further as Minx gunned the engine and sped down the causeway, full throttle. Amrita relaxed as she felt the rain-laden breeze through her hair. She caught Minx staring strangely at her at the traffic lights. 'You are gorgeous . . . you know that? Of course you do. Everybody must be telling you so.' Amrita blushed. She was used to receiving compliments. She had been receiving them all her life. But, let alone a woman, no man had ever looked at her the way Minx just had. And no previous compliment had affected her in the same manner.

Three

A sharp knock on her bedroom door woke Amrita the next morning. Her landlady was standing outside, clad in a faded housecoat. 'Somebody has sent you flowers,' she said absently, and waddled off towards the kitchen to fight with the cook. Amrita rubbed the sleep out of her eyes, put on her robe and went to the door. She was still feeling groggy. Mrs Pinto had entertained a particularly rowdy bunch of 'friends' last night. Amrita spotted the empty feni bottles stacked up near the fridge. Not that Amrita minded. It was still worth it, considering she was living on a leafy, shaded, quiet road in Central Bombay. It was close enough to most agencies and photographers and yet afforded her the few hours of seclusion she so desperately missed after leaving home. Besides, she couldn't afford anything fancier. Laburnum Road was convenient and reasonably classy. And Mrs Pinto's home, neat and well-kept.

The courier with the flowers was shifting restlessly from foot to foot when Amrita opened the front door. For a minute, she could only stare with wonder at the enormous bouquet he was carrying. It was like nothing she had ever seen before. No, she couldn't describe it as a bouquet, it was really a very elaborate ikebana arrangement, complete with driftwood and Japanese fans. 'Is this for me?' she asked foolishly.

The delivery-man looked witheringly at her and shoved an envelope under her nose. 'Your name?'

'Yes,' said Amrita.

'Then it is for you. Now sign quickly. I'm already late.'

Amrita pulled out the expensive letter-paper from the envelope. She had already guessed who had sent it. 'To your eyes,' read the short message. Amrita dragged the arrangement into the drawing-room. It was a bit too grand for her tiny bed-sitter. Mrs Pinto came bustling out, still bleary-eyed after last night's binge. 'Nice flowers, dear,' she said, 'new admirer?' Amrita giggled. Well, Minx could be described like that, she supposed and nodded.

Mrs Pinto ordered coffee for both of them before launching into her favourite topic—the indecent cost of living. Amrita only half-listened. Her mind was on last night and the long drive home in Minx's smart black jeep. But there was no time to dawdle that morning. She had to report for a shoot at ten sharp. This was likely to be her break-through campaign. Not much money in it. But enough prestige to make up for that. Besides, the photographer was rather dishy. She had met him briefly at the agency when they had both gone across for the initial brain-storming session. It was a jewellery campaign for a new client. The approach was filched (as were most other campaigns), but the treatment was going to be unique. A colour co-ordinated visual. All-red for rubies, gold for gold, green for emeralds and so on. It would involve hours of painstakingly applied make-up, but she knew she was going to be in the best hands. Freddie was the paintbox wizard who remade star faces with a few clever flicks of his wrists. And Karan, the man behind the lens, was the one who shot the most talked-about ads in the business. Amrita was nervous, but not overly so. Her gut feeling told her this was to be her big day. And she was prepared for it.

*

Karan refused to acknowledge her more than perfunctorily, when she walked into the studio. But Freddie more than made up for his bad manners by flapping around her excitedly, running his artistic fingers through her heavy, auburn-streaked hair, marvelling at her flawless skin and large, almond shaped eyes. 'Darling, this is too, too exciting. No falsies for you. Ooh! I just hate them,' he giggled. Karan's face was impassive, almost stony.

Freddie's assistant assured Amrita that the 'falsies' being referred to had nothing to do with padded bras. 'Eyelashes . . . you know . . . synthetic ones,' Pinky explained. Amrita looked relieved.

'Music?' Freddie demanded imperiously. 'Let's have something hot and throbbing.' Pinky giggled. Karan continued to fiddle with his camera equipment and look bored.

Intrigued by Karan, Amrita decided to speak to him. 'Excuse me . . . shall I show you some of the props and clothes I've brought with me?'

He stared at her intensely and said 'No,' before turning back to his Nikon.

Pinky, who was fixing Carmen rollers into her hair, whispered, 'Don't mind him. He's a little nutty. Moody. He doesn't mean to be rude.'

Amrita withdrew into herself and thought about Delhi. How cold Bombay people were by comparison. Just then an assistant flew into the room. 'Is there some babe called Amrita around?' he enquired, holding a remote-controlled telephone in his hand.

'Yes, that's me,' Amrita said.

He walked up and handed the instrument to her, 'Call for you.'

Amrita was startled. 'Me? Can't be. Nobody knows I'm here.'

He shrugged, handed her the phone and sauntered off.

Strange Obsession

Amrita found Karan regarding her coolly. She switched on the button and spoke nervously. Minx's voice came through sounding frighteningly close. 'Startled you, sweetheart? Sorry. Didn't mean to. Just called to check whether you'd got the flowers.' Amrita, flushed and uneasy, did not know what to say after a weak 'thank you'. Minx took care of that for her. 'I know it's going to be a long and tedious shoot today. You'll look fabulous in emeralds. But don't let Freddie go overboard with the eye make-up. You don't need it'

Amrita was about to ask, 'How did you know I'd be here . . .' when she thought the better of it. She had known Minx for only a few hours. But in that short period, she got the feeling that it was probably wise not to look deep into her new 'friend's' affairs.

*

Karan was meticulous, demanding and impatient. Amrita watched him as he worked. He wasn't particularly handsome, and yet there was something about him, a coiled anxiety, an unexpressed rage, a rare kind of sensitivity, that made people around him self-conscious. He rarely laughed. Or even smiled. But his manner was consistently, studiously, almost irritatingly, polite. That was why Amrita found it strange that he had responded so rudely to her innocent question. She decided not to speak to him through out the long photography session. In any case, he gave the impression that small talk infuriated him. She studied his close-set, dark eyes, the aquiline nose, mean mouth and the silky black hair that he wore in a neat ponytail. Beautiful hands, she noted, with well-shaped nails. And fabulous feet in well-worn, one-of-a-kind Kolhapuri chappals. Amrita liked men with well-kept hands and feet. They reminded her of her father who was very fastidious about his own. But that was where the resemblance between Karan and Mr Aggarwal ended. Karan was serpent-like and silent as a winter frog. Poor Mr Aggarwal with his broad accent and his hearty sense of humour still retained his old rural mannerisms, which Amrita found most endearing.

'Turn to the left,' 'That's too much,' 'Lower your chin,' 'Your nose is shining,' 'Tuck your tummy in.' The commands came sharp and quick. Amrita generally obeyed photographers' instructions without demur. But even she was finding Karan a bit too abrupt and demanding. Freddie tried to enliven the atmosphere with silly jokes but not a smile creased Karan's face as all the others cracked up. Finally, between takes, Amrita went up to him with a mug of coffee and said, 'It won't kill you to encourage me. I could do with a compliment or two.'

Karan stared at her unblinkingly before snapping, 'I'm here to shoot you. Not flatter you. You're doing a job and getting paid for it. Same as me. I don't know what kind of photographers you've worked with in the past, but to me, a model is a model—a subject for my camera. Nothing more. You could be a vase of flowers or an ice cube.'

Something told Amrita not to take offence. She switched on her charm and purred, 'Tch! Tch! We are very touchy, aren't we? I was only trying to be friendly. I get the feeling we'll be working together quite a lot in the future.'

Just then Freddie's voice cut through the studio, 'Da-r-r-r-ling,' he trilled, 'come and get the goodies.'

Amrita waved to him and winked. She knew the pictures were going to be great. Absolutely great. And she wasn't going to let Karan get her down. This was going to be the decisive campaign that would take Amrita to the top. She would show those Bombay girls. Those horrible snooty females who treated her like a villager and spoke in a language she was just about beginning to understand, filled with local slang and affectionate abuse that kept outsiders firmly out of the charmed circle. They dressed differently too, in dresses that resembled bandages and weren't much bigger. And they smoked too much. Amrita had heard wild stories about their nights on the town. And she was curious. But so far nobody had bothered to invite her to one of their bashes. Her world was limited to Mrs Pinto's cramped room and cabins in fancy ad agencies. But all that was going to change. And fast. Amrita was not prepared to wait around endlessly for good things to happen. One super campaign would alter everything for her. Just one super campaign. And she had the feeling, this was going to be it.

*

There were no lights on in the narrow staircase as she groped her way out of the building to look for a cab. It was close to ten o'clock. She had been working for twelve hours with only a short break for an impromptu lunch of soggy dosa and lukewarm tea. She was famished and fatigued. Maybe Mrs Pinto would warm up some mutton curry for her. She stepped out into the street. It was slushy and stinking.

A long curl of smoke floated in her direction. Minx was leaning against a shop front, puffing away at a Cartier. Amrita was glad to see her. Quickly, she calculated that, thanks to Minx's efficient transport arrangements, she would be able to save fifty bucks worth of cab fare. Gratefully, she beamed at Minx, who reached out easily and took Amrita's bags from her. 'At your service, beautiful,' smiled Minx and helped her into the waiting jeep.

Four

'Mrs Pinto,' Amrita yelled, 'I can't seem to find one of my panties. A bra is missing as well. Would you ask the new ayah if she's put it somewhere, please?'

Mrs Pinto shuffled over and stood by the door shaking her head. 'No, my dear, they aren't lost. Someone came and asked for them. Said you needed them urgently for your next modelling session. I handed them to her myself.'

Amrita stared at her landlady and then burst out laughing. She should have guessed. It had to be Minx. What was she up to now? Amrita sniffed the air. Yes. The unmistakable smell of stale Cartiers. Hurriedly, she went back into her room to check to see whether anything else was missing. She found a cigarette stub under her bed. She picked up her pillow. It smelt of Minx's shampoo. She had obviously tried out Amrita's narrow divan for size. God! What a strange creature she was turning out to be, this new-found friend of hers. She opened her suitcase. The brand-new one her father had given her and in which she kept all her precious belongings—including her diary. Sure enough, one or two of her boxes had been moved around. And there was a man's hanky with Minx's distinct cologne on it. Armani. Wasn't that the one she always used? The musky, heady fragrance that made Amrita slightly dizzy? Had Minx been careless, leaving a trace of her presence behind? Or had she wanted Amrita to know?

The rest of the room looked undisturbed. But there was an addition on the dresser. A perfectly formed, nearly black, long-stemmed rose in a slim, single-bloom crystal vase. No note. Amrita picked up the flower and smelt it. It had no smell. It could have been plastic. She thought she saw something glistening within its tightly closed petals. Sure enough, nestling near its centre was a sparkling ring. Amrita pulled it out gingerly . . . and gasped. It looked like a diamond. It probably was one. She tried it on and it fit perfectly. Suddenly, she felt cold and afraid, she could not explain it to herself, but she needed to talk to her mother or her brothers. She rushed out of the room and ran straight into Mrs Pinto who was bringing her a cup of coffee.

'What's the matter, my dear?' the landlady exclaimed, 'you look like you've seen a blooming ghost or something.'

Amrita held on to her plump, fleshy arms to steady herself, 'Mrs Pinto . . . I need to make an urgent STD

Strange Obsession

call to Delhi,' she gasped, 'please . . . I know you don't allow that. But I'll pay for it in cash. Right now.'

Mrs Pinto helped her to a chair and waited for her to calm down. 'Is there an emergency, my child?' she asked, her voice full of concern.

'Yes . . . I mean, no . . . I mean, not exactly,' Amrita stuttered, 'it's just that I'm missing my mother and home.' Having said that, she burst into tears.

Mrs Pinto fetched her a glass of water and waited for her to calm down. Amrita noticed through her tears that she was about to light up a Cartier. She stopped crying abruptly and screeched, 'Where did you get that cigarette from?'

Mrs Pinto's throwaway lighter stopped mid-course. She removed the unlit cigarette from her mouth and said casually, 'Your sweet friend gave me a pack. She has promised me a carton . . . God bless her.'

Amrita rushed across and nearly pulled the cigarette out of her fingers. 'Don't . . . don't smoke it . . . please . . . I beg of you . . .' she pleaded.

Mrs Pinto stared at her in surprise. 'You are shaking . . . what has happened to you?' she asked quietly.

Amrita collapsed into an adjoining sofa, repeating, 'I don't know . . . I don't know . . . please . . . '

Mrs Pinto patted her hand and that's when she noticed the ring. 'My, my, dearie,' she said, holding up Amrita's slim fingers. 'Do you have news to give, or what? Share it with auntie also.'

Amrita drew back her hand abruptly and pulled off the ring with a jerk. 'There's no news to give. This ring isn't what you think it is. It's . . . it's . . . nothing. Just some junky rubbish,' she cried.

Mrs Pinto shook her head and figured it was the usual boyfriend problem. These young girls today! My word, how they carried on! She'd seen them all—frisky air-hostesses, hotel girls, corporate secretaries, ad agency executives. All the same. One day this man. Next day someone else. And she had thought this new 'Dilli-walli' would be different, especially as she had been recommended by Lt. Colonel D'Silva—as straight and simple an armyman as any.

Amrita went back into her room and locked herself in. She could hear her sobs. Mrs Pinto dragged herself to the small cabinet near the refrigerator. Just a tiny shot of feni, she told herself. Not too much. For that she would wait for her boys to arrive. Those rowdy, lovable ruffians from her village back in Goa. Oh, how she enjoyed their company.

*

Amrita cancelled her shoot with Karan the following morning. She knew he would be furious, but she didn't care. The thought of leaving her bed was overwhelming. She moped around till mid-day and then she stirred out for something to eat. Mrs Pinto was obviously resting in her room. Thank God. Amrita was in no mood for small talk. She strolled into the kitchen and nearly screamed. There, lying in the sink, was a dead piglet, covered with blood, its eyes still open. The ayah came out of the servant's room when she heard someone pottering around. Seeing Amrita's expression, she began giggling. 'Woh . . . memsaab . . . aapka friend . . . blood is still there.' Amrita backed out of the kitchen. She wanted to throw up.

Her room was getting on her nerves. She had to get out. Breathe the air outside. Clear her head a bit. She had heard someone mention Naaz Café on Malabar Hill. That wasn't too far. She would walk. In any case, she needed the exercise. She had skipped her workout for two days. And she had not been able to resist an extra helping of Mrs Pinto's bibinca pudding. Briskly, Amrita changed into a jogging suit, slipped on a sweat band over her forehead, put on her favourite Reeboks and stepped out.

Halfway up the hill, a car screeched to a stop next to her. She jumped out of the way. Damn! She cursed the narrowness of the footpath which had forced her on to the road. In a flash Karan was blocking her path, his eyes blazing with rage. 'You ditched,' he hissed. She stared at him blankly. 'You ditched,' he repeated, his voice choking with anger.

'Yes,' Amrita admitted softly.

'Why?'

Amrita looked at him wordlessly and shrugged.

'That's not a good enough excuse, I'm afraid,' he said before adding, 'listen to me and listen well! If you want to make it as a model you'd better get your act together. Nobody is going to sit around waiting for you to show up. Girls like you arrive by the train-load everyday. Nobody even looks at them. They come. They starve. And they go back. Get it? Don't fuck with me. Remember, your future is in my hands. I nix you for an assignment and you're out on your sweet little ass. No questions asked. The agencies don't give a shit. We were about to replace you this morning. We had a standby model.'

Amrita asked him quietly, 'Then why didn't you?'

Karan paused and then took her arm roughly. 'You are creating a bloody traffic jam,' he said and pushed her into his car.

They drove silently down towards Haji Ali. Amrita noticed his watch. She did not know what make it was but it looked unusual and impressive. He had not spoken a word since his furious outburst. 'Still mad at me?' she asked.

He turned to look at her. 'No,' he answered briefly and went back to concentrating on the road.

'Where are we going?' Amrita demanded.

'Home,' he replied as he swung his Maruti to the left and drove towards Worli.

*

'I like your place,' Amrita said staring appreciatively around her. 'It's very peaceful . . . and sort of Japanese,' she added, taking in its starkness.

Karan, fiddling around with the music, responded, 'I like Japan.'

Tatami matting on the floor, sliding doors and bamboo everywhere, even bonsais and ikebanas in driftwood, placed strategically around. But what intrigued her most was the collection of swords and weapons lining one wall. Karan noticed her staring at them. 'Ancient Samurai stuff. I got a few when I visited Japan. The rest are from dealers,' he explained.

Amrita was famished but she did not dare ask for anything. Karan finally found the tape he was looking for. The music wafted over the sophisticated sound system. It was a strange kind of music—more like Buddhist prayers being chanted by lamas in a monastery. She asked Karan about it.

'Ritualistic music,' he told her, 'I recorded it when I went to Tibet.' It had a soothing hypnotic effect on Amrita. She rested her head against a leather bean bag which she had gratefully sunk into. 'This is bliss,' Amrita sighed. Karan walked into the kitchen to fix her a cup of fragrant herb tea. He wasn't such a monster after all, Amrita mused, as she heard him moving around the kitchen efficiently.

Minutes later he emerged carrying two steaming mugs with bamboo patterns covering them. 'Also Japanese?' Amrita teased, looking over the rim of hers at him.

'That was a brilliant guess,' Karan said sarcastically and reached for his camera. Amrita immediately stiffened and began to fix her hair.

'Relax,' he snapped, 'these are for me. For us. The light's looking good on you just now.'

Amrita started to protest, 'But, I don't have my face on.'

Karan grinned, 'Why do you think I'm inspired?'

She unwound gradually as he shot away.

'What do you know about Meenakshi Iyengar?' Amrita asked him when they were taking a break.

'Why ask me?' Karan countered. 'I was about to ask you.'

Amrita looked thoughtful before saying, 'Look, I'm new to Bombay. I don't understand all you people. I happened to run into her and I thought she was very friendly and sweet. That's all.'

'Then she must be friendly and sweet,' Karan replied shortly and tried to change the subject.

Amrita was not ready to give up. 'You aren't telling me something. There's obviously more to her. Please, Karan, I must know . . . it's important.'

He looked at her strangely. 'There's nothing I can tell you. She's the daughter of a big-shot cop, that's all.'

Amrita was on her feet. 'Liar! There is more to her story than that! What's the matter with you? Don't you trust me? Why can't you tell me the truth?'

Karan put his hands on her shoulder and forced her to sit down. 'Look,' he said steadily, 'that female is bananas. I don't know what's with her. And, frankly, I don't want to know. All I can tell you is that there was another beautiful girl—a model—whom Meenakshi had taken a fancy to last year. We used to see her hanging around at shoots like she's doing with you these days. Nobody thought much of it till one day this chick disappeared. Just like that. She was expected for a shoot and she didn't show up. We thought she was ill. We called her place. She wasn't there. That's the last anybody saw of her. She was a p.g. like you. From Chandigarh. She came to Bombay to join the movies. You know the story. Got mixed up with some sleazoids. Meenakshi came into the picture. And then, bang! She was gone.'

Amrita's eyes had widened with fear. Slowly she asked Karan, 'Is that why you came looking for me today?'

'Yes,' he answered briefly and walked over to the large windows to stare at the sea outside.

Amrita came up behind him, 'Thank you. I mean that sincerely. But you needn't have worried. I'm not like that other girl. And I won't disappear.'

Abruptly, Karan whirled around and said, 'Come on. Let me take you home.'

Wordlessly, the two of them walked out of his stark apartment and into the car. Amrita wondered, but did not ask, why nobody had thought of going to the police when the other girl vanished.

Five

'Did I scare you off?' Minx's voice over the phone sent a chill down Amrita's spine.

'Not at all,' she lied while trying to think rapidly of the quickest way to end the conversation.

'Karan has a pretty cool set-up, doesn't he?' Minx asked sweetly. 'Especially all those Samurai swords and stuff. Very Zen. Very tasteful.'

Amrita stiffened. So Minx knew where she had been the previous day. She did not reply and there was a long pause.

'Are you there?' Minx enquired and added, 'of course, you are. As I was saying, Karan's quite a guy. Dozens of hungry models will tell you that. Oh yes! He's really something. An absolute hunk, I hear.'

Amrita said nervously, 'Why are we discussing him? Let's talk about something else. I only have a minute.'

Minx laughed, 'You can't fool me. Hey! Loosen up! Has Karan been telling you nasty things about me? Such a wicked boy! He's constantly doing that. I bet he told you that absurd little story about some girl from Chandigarh. He did, didn't he?'

Amrita was too taken aback to say anything.

Minx continued smoothly. 'Strange chap. So many gorgeous girls dying to bed him and he spreads stories about me. Imagine! Don't you think that's crazy? Anyway . . . forget it. Feel like a coffee somewhere?'

Amrita thought quickly. The image of the freshly-slaughtered pie swam before her eyes. She pushed it away as she felt her gorge rise. How could she get out of this? 'I'm sorry . . . but I'm busy right now,' she stuttered.

'Busy?' Minx sounded surprised. 'Doing what? Writing that childish diary of yours? Come on. You can't get rid of me that easily. Let's say . . . twenty minutes? I'll be downstairs. Twenty minutes.'

Amrita put down the reciever just as Mrs Pinto bustled in. 'Aren't you looking sweet,' she exclaimed before adding, 'oh, before I forget, your friend was here again. She has left something for you in the fridge. Didn't Mary tell you?'

Amrita shook her head and walked towards the kitchen. She tried to guess what Minx could've left for her this time. Gingerly she opened the fridge door and looked inside. All she could see was the usual mess Mrs Pinto hoarded—stale food, left-over cake, mouldy cheese, half-eaten jelly and carelessly packed vegetables. Amrita summoned Mary, 'Where is my stuff?' she asked the surly maid who was busy picking nits out of her matted hair as usual. She pointed to the freezer compartment and stood around scratching, a wicked smile on her face.

Amrita opened the freezer warily and jumped back in fright—there, lying amidst the ice-cube trays and ancient Goan sausages, was a frozen heart with a red satin bow tied around it. It looked like a human heart, but Amrita guessed Minx must have got it off a butcher and that it probably belonged to an illegally slaughtered calf. She stepped back from the fridge and walked slowly into her room. The showdown she had decided to have with Minx wasn't going to be easy.

*

'Why did you come to my room?' Amrita asked quietly. Meenakshi had been waiting for her outside Mrs Pinto's house, when she stepped out for her evening walk. She was dressed dramatically in black—a black turtleneck over black trousers. The clinging sweater outlined her figure and, Amrita realized with a start, that Minx had a supple, well-proportioned body and an exaggerated bustline. Strange she hadn't noticed it earlier.

Minx caught her staring and shrugged, 'I can't stand the damn things. They get in the way all the time.' Amrita blushed and looked away. Minx continued coolly, 'I came up to your room to see your etchings.' Amrita looked puzzled. Minx said, 'That's just a joke. OK here's really why I came to your room. I wanted to see how you lived. Where you lived. What your bed looked like. The basin in which you brushed your teeth. The loo in which you peed. The shower under which you showered. Everything.'

Amrita looked coldly at her, 'You also stole some of my things,' she said steadily.

Minx answered easily, 'Of course I did. I wanted a couple of mementoes. Also, I didn't want to go wrong. On the sizes. I have another surprise for you.' She reached into her trouser pocket and whipped out a slim package. 'Silk undies,' she announced. 'Wear them and think of me.'

Amrita whirled around and started to walk swiftly away. Minx took her time, catching up with her under a streetlight. 'Look at you, sweetheart,' she said, tilting Amrita's face. 'Frightened like a cornered rabbit. Why? I'm not going to hurt or harm you. I only want to be your friend. That's all. Allow me to do that and there won't by any trouble. Or any surprises. Promise.'

Amrita slapped off her hand and snarled, 'I don't want to be your friend. Why can't you accept that? We can never be friends. You are weird. Abnormal. I knew girls like you at school.'

Minx did not budge. 'Abnormal? What are you talking about? You think I'm a bloody lesbian, don't you? Well, guess what? You are wrong. And so are all of them who've been telling you that. I'm not a dyke. I'm not kinky. And I'm certainly not crazy. Don't ask me to explain it to you—but I'm in love with you. I love you. I adore you. It is not sexual. I don't wish to go to bed with you. All I want is to be around you. That's all.'

Amrita looked contemptuously at her and spat out, 'Forget it! We can never be friends or lovers or anything. I don't know what it is that you want out of me. But whatever you're after, you won't get it.'

Minx laughed, 'Sweet, sweet, Amrita. You still haven't understood, have you? I'm not one to give up so easily. Whether or not you like it, you'll have to accept my presence in your life. You see, Amrita, you have become a part of me. You live right here in my body. I can feel your presence inside me all the time. Today it's a helpless, dumb animal's heart in your fridge. Who knows, tomorrow it could be mine. Don't play with my life, Amrita. You'll regret it ....'

Amrita spotted a gap in the traffic and started to run blindly across the street. She wanted to get as far away from Minx as she could. She heard the horns blaring and she heard the motorists shouting. But it didn't matter, for the gap in the traffic had closed and there was no way Minx could reach her. Not now, at any rate.

Six

'I think you should change your address,' Karan advised Amrita the next morning. They were between shoots on a location twenty kilometres outside Bombay.

Amrita replied glumly, 'How would that help? She'd track me down anywhere, anyway.'

Karan agreed. Given her police contacts, nobody was inaccessible to Minx.

Amrita continued in a low voice, 'Maybe I should just forget about this whole modelling thing and go back to Delhi.'

Karan stared at her in surprise, 'Are you crazy? You are going to be the most sensational discovery on the modelling scene after our new campaign gets released. You already have half a dozen prestigious contracts in hand. Tomorrow you might get flooded with movie offers. And you want to throw all that away because of some mad woman?'

Amrita confessed, 'I am scared to death of her, Karan. I feel she could harm me someday. I can't go anywhere without the creepy sensation that she is close by somewhere, watching me. It's a horrible position to be in.'

Karan fiddled with his Nikon and then asked, 'Have you spoken to your family about this?'

Amrita jumped up, 'Are you nuts? My brothers will be here on the next flight. They'll probably kill her or something. No way. I can't tell them about her. Mummy will ask me to come back tomorrow if she found out. And as for my father, it will blow his mind. As it is, he was against my coming to Bombay.'

'Yes, well, I see what you mean. But it's crazy to run away just because Minx gives you the creeps,' Karan said.

'Let's see, perhaps it will pass. Maybe I can work it out.'

The art director of the agency walked in to tell Karan that the set was ready. Amrita adjusted her hair and looked at herself in the mirror. What a difference make-up made, she thought, staring at her image. Even her family wouldn't have recognized her today. She patted her freshly gelled hair into place. How sophisticated she appeared. And so much older too. Karan hated her with her hair styled like this, but the ad agency guys were keen on projecting a sleek soignee look for the present campaign. Her co-model was a muscular movie aspirant so completely self-obsessed that he had barely noticed her. The model co-ordinator, a perky Parsi girl called Karina, came bouncing in with a change of outfit for Amrita. It was a ruffled dress in black with a sequinned bustier. She was carrying the accessories with her as well. Enormous, dangling rhinestone earrings à la Madonna and chunky bracelets to match. 'Ooh!' she giggled, 'aren't we looking sexy!' Amrita and Karan exchanged glances as she strolled over to join her mucho-macho hero-in-the-making at a table set for two. It was going to be a long and tiring shoot.

Amrita stared indifferently around the hired bungalow. She saw the pack of cigarettes before she spotted her. It was tossed carelessly on a trolley. Sharply, Amrita surveyed the small crowd of people fussing over wires in a corner. Of course it was her. It had to be! Minx was somewhere on the set. What the hell was she up to now? She heard the art director briefing Karan and then the make-up man came up with a tissue to blot her nose.

Amrita asked him softly, 'Do you know that woman over there? The one in the frayed jeans?'

He looked over his shoulder towards Minx and shrugged, 'New to this unit,' he answered and started on her moist upper lip. 'My . . . you do sweat a lot,' Bhiku said as he mopped up the beads of perspiration gently.

Amrita found herself shaking. She could not control the tears even when Karan began shooting. Obviously he had not noticed Minx in the shadows. He put down his camera and came up to Amrita. 'Listen . . . there's a problem. Each time the shutter clicks, you move. Most of my frames are off. Out of focus. We'll have to repeat this, OK?' Suddenly he noticed the stricken look in Amrita's eyes and asked, 'What's the matter? Seen a ghost?'

She could not trust herself to speak. Silently, she pointed to where she had seen Minx standing. Karan turned around to look. There was nobody there.

'I saw her,' Amrita broke down. 'I swear I did. She was here just a moment ago, Karan. I swear to you. You must believe me.'

Karan tried to calm her down saying, 'It's all right. You must be tired. Let's take a break.'

Mr Macho looked exasperated. Stupid hysterical bitch, he thought, wasting everybody's time. The art director walked up to find out what the matter was. Karan told him, 'Amrita has been pushing herself these last couple of days. It's OK. She needs a short break. A coffee and a sandwich. Let's all take ten.' The art director shrugged. They were already behind schedule. The client was expected any minute to watch them wrap up. It was a new account and Mr Menon wasn't at all pleased with the way things were going.

Amrita stopped him as he was about to stroll away and asked, 'Have you hired some new girl in your technical unit?'

He looked at her as if she was crazy, 'You're asking the wrong man. I'm not the one who hires spot boys or coffee girls. I don't know what you're talking about. All I can tell you is that we are wasting a lot of my client's time and money here. Let's get on with the shoot and we'll discuss crew problems later.'

He stalked off leaving Karan to comfort her, 'Amrita, it's possible you might be seeing things,' he said. 'It happens when a person is very tired.'

Amrita all but yelled at him, 'You don't believe me either, do you? Well, I'll just have to prove it to you. Come with me. I'll show you something.' She walked briskly towards the trolley. The pack of cigarettes was gone. She looked around desperately.

Karan said gently, 'Forget it, baby. Don't make a scene here. As it it, this gang is pretty upset.'

But Amrita wasn't listening to him. She was on all fours, looking for something. Two minutes later she scrambled up, flushed and triumphant. 'See . . . I've found it!' she said.

Karan came up to take a look at what she was holding between her fingers. It was a stubbed out cigarette. 'Her brand,' Amrita announced. 'Now do you believe me when I say it was her?'

Karan laughed and put his arm around her. 'Silly girl,' he said, 'Mr M, the guy who walked off in such a huff, is addicted to these. Everybody knows that. Whoever wants to suck up to him gives him a carton of Cartier. Now get your act together and let's go back to work.'

Crestfallen, but far from convinced, Amrita dragged herself to the tiny table. Minx had been there. She had seen her. The make-up man had confirmed it. And she had found a stub. She did not require further proof.

Seven

'Fooled you, didn't I?' Minx laughed as Amrita walked into her room, mentally and physically exhausted. It was well past midnight. 'Good dinner? Karan's crazy about Chinese. I bet he took you to "Sampan",' Minx taunted from where she was comfortably lolling on Amrita's small bed.

Too tired to fight her, Amrita asked in a low voice, 'What do you want from me this time? Please tell me so that we can work something out. But I can't stand what you are doing. I'll go crazy . . . unless that's what you want.'

Minx drew on her cigarette long and hard. 'Tch! Tch! Come here, you poor baby. You must be exhausted. Don't argue, fight, sulk or cry. I'm here to make you feel good. Feel great. Not to harass you. Don't listen to those fools and their silly stories about me. I'm your friend. And I want you to be mine. That's all.'

Amrita threw down her things and started to go towards the bathroom. She was dying for a hot shower. She knew Mrs Pinto didn't really like her to use the bathroom at such a late hour, but she needed to freshen up. One long leg blocked her way.

'Not so soon. Relax. Talk to me. Tell me about your day. Of course I know how a part of it went. But what about the other? Here, let me help you take off all those sticky clothes.'

Amrita jumped back instinctively as Minx reached out for her. 'Don't you dare touch me,' she said.

Minx stopped her hands from within inches of Amrita's sweater and sat back on the bed heavily. 'OK, sweetheart. No touch. Promise. I was only trying to help. But if you no like, I no do.'

'Thanks,' Amrita said stiffly. Suddenly, she was scared to go into the bathroom for that much-needed shower. What if Minx forced her way into the cramped shower space? She decided to sit down and talk Minx into leaving. In a voice that sounded unnatural to her own ears she said, a bit too loudly and brightly, 'So? How did you manage to get in this time?'

Minx lit another cigarette. 'Easy. Mrs Pinto passed out as usual after a binge with her boys. And Mary is always looking for some extra bucks on the side. She needs new dresses for her novenas every Wednesday. I've promised her one from Dubai.'

Amrita nodded tiredly. The desire for a shower was fading. All she wanted was to catch some sleep. Fortunately she had a relatively free day tomorrow. She looked pointedly at her watch. Minx looked at her own and announced, 'I'm going to the kitchen to fix some coffee. You want?'

'No thanks,' Amrita snapped, 'I don't want coffee . . . but I'd very much like to sleep, if you don't mind.'

'Go ahead,' Minx said cheerfully. 'Don't let me stop you. Ignore me. I'll just hang around or read or something.'

Amrita stared coldly at her, 'I'd prefer it if you left. Right now. And another thing. Stop following me.'

Minx laughed uproariously, 'Just like that, huh? I like the way you said that. Say it again, "stop following me". You're sweet. Really you are, too sweet. So you saw me today, right? Wow! That took some doing. I bribed the technician and when that didn't work, I threatened him. These poor buggers are so scared of the police. I've never been able to understand it,' said Minx, walking out of the room.

Amrita couldn't keep the disgust and loathing out of her voice as she called after Minx, 'No matter what tricks you try, you'll never be able to fool me. I hate you . . . did you hear that? Hate you! Hate you! Hate you!' She heard Minx lighting the gas in the kitchen and slammed the door of her room shut, taking care to lock it from the inside.

Strange Obsession

Amrita tossed around in her bed for more than two hours. In her half-awake state she kept imagining Minx materializing through the heavy, old-fashioned door and looming over her. For the first time, Minx's face swam into sharp focus in front of her closed eyes. And Amrita realized how ugly she really was. Amrita couldn't put her finger on it—was it the flaky, mottled skin that gave Minx a reptilian appearance? Or the close-set, grey-green eyes that never seemed to blink? Was it the lank, cropped hair that looked listless and dull, or the mouth set in a severe line, like a gash carved by a blunt knife? In Amrita's fevered imagination Minx was right outside the door, smoking languorously, menacingly, helping herself to endless cups of Mrs Pinto's precious coffee.

At some point during that long, troubled night, Amrita fell fast asleep. She did not hear the front door slam shut when Minx left, or know when a slim envelope was slipped under her own. She found it in the morning. At first Amrita was reluctant to open it. The sight of Minx's spidery scrawl had started to give her the creeps. She picked it up and took it to the dining-table. An enormous tin of Columbian coffee was sitting on it. She could guess where it must have come from.

Amrita flicked open the envelope and read the words scribbled across the letter-paper inside. It was a love poem, an old-fashioned one. Browning. Minx had signed it with the symbol of Gemini—her astro sign.

The footnote read: 'Last night you met the good twin. Beware of the bad one. I love you. And always will.

Amrita crushed the note in one swift gesture and chucked it away angrily. The phone rang, making her jump. Amrita picked it up warily, fearing it was Minx.

'Are you all right?' Karan asked anxiously.

Amrita relaxed, 'Yes, of course, I am,' she said, 'why?'

There was a pause, 'I don't know. After I dropped you home I had an uneasy feeling . . . it's hard to explain. Somehow I thought your life was in danger. Crazy! Maybe we've both been working too hard. Take it easy today, OK? If you feel like a drive, a chat, a snack, music, anything, call me.' And he rang off.

At that point, the only person Amrita really wanted to speak to was her mother. She went in search of Mrs Pinto. It was an unwritten rule that she had to seek permission before dialling an STD call. She found her landlady still in bed and snoring. A huge bouquet of Easter lilies by the bedside caught her eye. She went for a closer look and noticed the card with Minx's unmistakable scrawl. 'Dear Mrs Pinto . . . you know whom to call if ever you are in trouble,' it said. Below it Minx had very carefully printed out the telephone numbers of the nearest police station with the names of the duty officers. Amrita tiptoed out of the room. It was obvious that she had to move out. Minx had infiltrated this place so completely, that nobody was going to be safe from her. Not even poor, unsuspecting Mrs Pinto.

Eight

'Hey! I like your style!'

Amrita whirled around in her seat to see who it was. The small café in Fort was unusually crowded that night. Amrita was there with three other models. They had been rehearsing late for a fashion show that was being talked about as the most sensational event of the catwalk calendar. India's top designers had got together for the first time and signed the priciest models from Delhi and Bombay to show their collections. Amrita's friends exchanged glances and suppressed giggles as she stared into the eyes of Rover (a nickname he had acquired at Sanawar after classmates combined his first name 'Ranjit' with his surname 'Grover'). Rover the Rogue, as models and starlets knew him. Right now, he was the property of a sprightly divorcée, Sangita Singh, a much-travelled, much-loved woman of the world who put all sorts of dubious deals together and very successfully at that. Rumours were out that the city's best-known toyboy was feeling bored and restless with his older woman. But no model in her right mind would have tried to steal him away from 'S.S.'. Her bulging brown eyes flashed an easy-to-interpret 'hands off' signal each time an attractive female so much as glanced in Rover's direction.

And here he was, gazing boldly into Amrita's eyes, challenging her to take it from there.

'Who are you?' Amrita asked.

Rover guffawed and announced to the entire restaurant, 'Hey guys! You hear that? This chick just asked an asinine question. Does someone care to enlighten her?'

Amrita's friends nudged her urgently. Priya, the girl immediately next to her, kicked hard under the table and whispered, 'Stay cool, and don't fuck with him or we're all gone.'

Amrita continued to stare at him as he towered over her, one leg resting on the edge of her Irani chair, hands outstretched. Others at adjoining tables laughed nervously but nobody dared to say a word. Rover bent low over her and chucked her under the chin, 'If you must know, sweetheart, I am God's gift to womankind,' he said arrogantly, his face inches away from hers.

'Says who?' Amrita challenged.

'Says I,' he replied and brought his mouth down savagely over hers. It was a kiss that sent her reeling.

And it went on and on and on. When he finally removed his lips, she was gasping for breath and blushing deeply. 'Convinced?'

After a minute of stunned silence, everybody in the café went back to what they had been doing, as if the Rover-Amrita incident (as it came to be known) never happened. But the next day, the entire modelling world was talking about only one thing—Sangita Singh was out for Amrita's blood.

*

'Is it true?' Karan was on the line first thing in the morning.

Amrita, sleep still in her eyes and not fully awake, asked irritably, 'Is what true?'

'The Rover business. Bastard. I'll kill him. He's a creep. Don't get mixed up with him.' Suddenly Amrita sat up. It wasn't what Karan was saying that had startled her. It was the all-too-familiar smell coming from the kitchen. 'Just a minute,' she told Karan and ran off to investigate.

'Good morning, doll! My, my, you're looking lovely today!' Minx greeted her cheerfully. 'Breakfast? I thought you might have been missing your mother's alloo paranthas. I called her up last night and got the recipe.'

Amrita stormed out, too agitated to speak, and picked up the phone. 'Karan, I can't talk to you right now. You can guess why.'

Karan shouted back, 'Don't tell me that son-of-a-bitch is with you? I'm coming there right now.'

Amrita laughed dryly before saying, 'Don't be ridiculous. It isn't him. It's her.' And she put the phone down rapidly, sensing Minx standing close behind her, holding a plate with a parantha on it. Mimicking Amrita, she wiggled her bottom and sang out, 'Don't be silly—it isn't him—it's her.' Amrita shuddered seeing the expression in her eyes.

Mrs Pinto had left for her weekly bazaar at the nearby Grant Road Market. Mary was in the servant's bathroom. Minx had Amrita against the wall, trapped in the tiny niche where the telephone table was. Abruptly, she thrust the plate at Amrita and commanded, 'Eat.'

Amrita turned her face away and said, 'Take it away. I don't want it.'

Minx broke off a piece of the parantha and pushed it close to her mouth, cajoling, 'Come on, baby. It's good for you. Just like the paranthas Mummy makes . . . your brother told me you can't resist them. Such a friendly fellow. And so worried about you. I told him, "As long as I am there, you don't have to think about your sister. She'll be safe. I won't let anybody touch her."' Minx paused before adding, 'Anybody. That includes Rover.'

Amrita opened her mouth to say something. Harshly, Minx shoved the parantha piece into it and said, 'Shut up, you slut. Did you think I wouldn't find out? I have spies everywhere. He screwed you, didn't he? Don't lie to me. I know he did. His servant-boy confirmed it. All it took was one slap from my havaldar-driver. You see, baby, it's very easy for me to get information in this city. Very easy. Oh, and it will only be a matter of time before Sangita Singh has a contract out on you.'

Amrita thought she was going to throw up. Hazily, the details of the previous evening swam into her mind. It had been a late and disturbing night. Rover had insisted on her drinking champagne with him. Two or three glasses later the world had ceased to be in focus. They had left the restaurant together. Amrita remembered her mild resistance to Rover as he undressed her in his apartment. And her embarrassment at the presence of a dog in his room. 'He's watching,' she had giggled as Rover stepped out of his crotch-tight jeans and came over to the enormous low bed where she was lying, clutching a sheet to her chin. 'Don't worry, good old Champ is trained to keep secrets. He won't tell any one,' Rover had said before covering her body with his and entering her rapidly, roughly. Amrita had not experienced any pleasure. Just a dull pain which had receded into the background as curiosity took over. She recalled thinking, 'So, this is what it's all about. How disappointing.' Rover's face, above hers, had looked almost grotesque. Yes, she had admired his body with and without clothes, but 'the act' itself was almost comic. Amrita had tried to concentrate on her own feelings and then given up. She couldn't take her eyes off the boxer who was sitting barely six inches away from her face, staring unblinkingly at their heaving bodies.

Minx snapped her fingers in front of her face. 'Hey! Wake up! The dream is over. This is reality, OK? Come on, wash up and get dressed. I have to take you to my gynae. Hurry. You have twenty minutes.'

Amrita looked at Minx. Gynae? What was she talking about. 'I'm not going anywhere with you,' she said and tried to walk away.

'Not so fast,' Minx said and caught her arm savagely. 'That man is an animal. He fucks anything that moves. I want you to be medically examined. We'll have to do a blood check. Who knows what sort of bugs he's distributing these days? Sangita Singh doesn't know this and she won't believe it anyway, but her private stud happens to swing both ways. I know guys he crosses with. My cops have told me they've spotted him at the Gateway walls picking up truckers.'

Amrita covered her ears. 'I don't want to hear any more. You and your filthy mind. Instead of spying on other people, why don't you see a doctor yourself? You are the one who is sick.'

She felt a sharp sting across her cheek as Minx's hand came own swiftly. 'You talk too much. Just watch your words. The sickos in the world are people like you. Bloody sex-starved nymphos, ready to fuck the first man they can lay their hands on. I have no such problems. I'm pure and clean. Ask my doctor when you see her . . . as you will in a few minutes. She'll tell you.' Minx pushed Amrita in the direction of her room and went and sat down on a chair right outside. 'Don't be long . . . or I'll have to come and get you.'

'You have no right to intrude into my life like this. No right to talk to my family. No right to interfere. How dare you!' Amrita screamed.

Minx smiled, 'What are you planning to do about it? Kill me? Sorry, darling. You are stuck with me. You don't get it, do you? I love you. I have to protect you. It's my duty. And now go get dressed before you make me really angry.'

'Get out, get out, before I scream again,' Amrita said, half-sobbing.

Minx gave a short, sharp laugh. 'All right, if that's the way you want to play it. But I won't let you off so easily next time. So, darling, get your life together. Now!'

Nine

Rover was in no mood to listen to Amrita. 'Shit, man! Why are you screwing everything up?' he said, running his fingers through his thick, gelled hair. They had been seeing each other on and off for a month. 'I like you . . . yeah . . . I really do. But we'll have to break off. My old lady is possessive, see?'

Amrita bit her lip as she held back her tears. 'I thought I was special, that the first night wasn't just any night for you. I've been through so much myself.'

Rover lit a cigarette and blew smoke rings at the ceiling. Amrita gazed at him, noticing everything about him and feeling powerless. Of course he was maddeningly handsome—the most attractive man she'd ever seen. But she was beginning to realize that it was something more than his looks that had made her abandon her innate caution and good sense when they were together. It was his utter lack of interest in anybody other than himself that she found disturbing and fascinating at the same time. She had never met anybody as self-absorbed, who lived only to indulge his body and its needs. And yet, his sheer physical presence overwhelmed Amrita. The way he strutted across the room, his slim hips moving to their own rhythm, with his well-muscled torso in perfect control. She liked his easy way of dressing—faded jeans, invariably tighter on the crotch, combined with freshly laundered white T-shirts. He looked like a Ralph Lauren ad—with cowboy boots and a rugged worn leather belt setting off the 'Rover Look'. Amrita found it difficult to understand her passion for him. Yes, he was her first man, but she had had boyfriends in the past for as long back as she could remember. Yet, it was Rover with his narrow, close-set, Richard Gere eyes and his full wide mouth who turned her on. And she wasn't alone. He had this effect on most women, irrespective of their ages. And he knew it. 'Listen, lady,' he had drawled after making love, 'you are pretty. Like I said, I dig your style. You are new and different. But that's all. I'd like to see you again—but when it suits me. You know the old line, "Don't call me. I'll call you," that's the way it works with me.'

Amrita had nodded her head, cursing herself. God! he had said, irritated by something as he walked to the fridge to get himself—not her—a glass of water. But even in the half-light of the darkened room, Amrita had taken in her breath sharply at the sight of his naked body moving gracefully away from her. She recalled her friends telling her in the restaurant, 'He treats his women like dirt. Forget the guy. He'll use you and discard you. S.S. will chew you up.' Amrita had known they had meant to warn her. But she had also been equally sure they were wasting their time. As soon as she recovered from the shock of his first kiss, she knew she was hooked and nothing could break the spell.

The small, ferocious world both of them belonged to was already buzzing with the news of their affair. If Sangita knew, she had chosen to keep quiet. Amrita figured it was not the first time she'd had to deal with such a situation, and, going by Rover's track record, it certainly wasn't going to be the last. He had made that pretty clear himself. She also knew she would be the loser in the end. Rover made it a point to rub that in at each encounter. 'Nobody wins with me, lady,' he would remind her, as he watched himself in the enormous mirror near the bed. Amrita was so used to being stared at herself that this was a completely new experience for her. Here was a man who had eyes only for himself. She had tried teasing him about it a couple of times but had retreated swiftly—Rover did not take very kindly to such jokes. When the other girls said to Amrita that the general opinion was that Rover the Rogue was really quite a dud, Amrita bristled, 'Oh no, he isn't! In any case, why should I play his defence counsel?'

It was true and she was only too aware of it. The man was a narcissistic bore whose conversation did not extend beyond his next assignment and his latest clothes. In her saner, quieter moments Amrita acknowledged all this to herself and longed for Karan's company. But he had chosen to withdraw after his initial outburst. Funny, she mused, he was acting almost like a jealous lover. These days she saw him infrequently, briefly, while waiting around at a studio or in the lobby of some agency, but he invariably looked through her. Amrita got the uneasy feeling that this studied act was a camouflage. She would have loved to discuss her doubts with Rover, but the only communication that they shared, such as it was, was when they were in bed together. Twice, sometimes thrice, a week she would hear Rover's Honda (a gift from Sangita) revving up down the quiet road where she lived and she would drop everything in the rush to meet him downstairs. He refused to come up to the flat and in a way it was a relief for Amrita. Mrs Pinto was bewildered enough.

The night Rover failed to show up after calling her to say he would be there, Amrita panicked. She knew he drove recklessly. It was an integral part of his macho act. She called his place repeatedly and getting no answer, decided to set out in search of him. It was while she was waiting for a cab at the traffic intersection that she felt gloved fingers grip her arm in a pincer-like hold. 'Lover boy isn't going to come for you tonight, baby. Come on, let's go, enough of this rubbish.'

She didn't have to turn around to see who it was. She had already smelt her. 'What have you done to him?' she demanded, her voice rising hysterically.

'Done?' Minx mocked. 'I haven't done a thing. What did you think I'd do? Chop off his balls? I was tempted to, but then I decided that wouldn't have been punishment enough. You want to know where he is? Let's go and find him.' She marched Amrita to the waiting jeep. Wordlessly, they drove a few miles to the Gamdevi police Chowki. 'I had him busted. And then picked up. He's been worked over by my boys. Don't worry. He's still in one piece—though you might have problems recognizing him.'

Amrita felt her hair stand on end as Minx swaggered through the thana, familiarly greeting the policemen on duty. She took Amrita into the inspector's room and introduced her casually, 'Kulkarni, meet my friend, Amrita. You must've seen her on television—Silkscreen shampoo girl. Yes, yes, she's also in the Vishal sari ad. Arrey, very good, very good—you keep your eyes open for pretty girls, I see. OK, we want to check how that animal is doing. Take us to the lock-up.'

Inspector Kulkarni summoned a passing havaldar and directed him to escort the two girls to where Rover was. Amrita took in her breath sharply at the sight of her lover lying in a helpless heap on the stinking floor of a dark cell. He was covered in his own excrement and had been beaten badly. 'Saala, refused to admit anything,' the havaldar said, tapping the tip of his lathi against the palm of his hand. We know how to make these rich fellows talk. It's easy. Generally one or two slaps are enough. But this fellow was tougher. Body-building karta hai. Thought he was a hero when he came here. Wanted tea. Cigarettes.' The havaldar laughed, as Amrita felt herself gagging. Rover was unconscious. She could hear his laboured breathing as he lay in the filth, his clothes torn off his body. Rover's eyes were puffed and swollen and blood had clotted on his forehead.

Amrita turned to Minx and sobbed, 'How could you? You nearly killed him.'

Minx nodded. 'Nearly, is right. But I didn't. It would've been easy. Nobody would've known. Our boys are very good at these things. But I told them not to go that far. He's a bad chap, baby. Doesn't deserve someone like you. You should've listened to me. Now look what you made me do.'

Something gave in Amrita's head, and she launched herself at her tormentor, but Minx needed only one hand to stop the blows. 'Remember where you are and who you are. Well-brought-up girls don't create scenes in public. Let's go somewhere quiet and cool. We need to talk. I think you still haven't understood. You don't know the meaning of real love. You think this joker loves you? No. He fucks you like he fucks hundreds of other Amritas. But you aren't like any of them, you are special. You should have the best. Trust me.'

Amrita did not have the strength to resist as Minx guided her out of the police station. Once outside, she placed her hands on Amrita's shoulders. Amrita shuddered as she forced her to look into her eyes. 'I love you, baby. Accept that. Accept me. What you saw tonight was very ugly. Horrible. I agree, I hated having to watch them pulp him. You should've seen the way he howled. Like a kid, I tell you. I was shocked. I'd expected him to be tougher. More manly. But he howled and howled. They were going to give him the bamboo treatment also. But I stopped them. It wasn't necessary. And he might have died. Of shock. I've seen it happen. Funny, no? They can stand being buggered by gorillas. But one bamboo up their ass and they die!'

Amrita doubled over and threw up near the kerb. She only brought up bile. Minx held her tenderly while she retched again and again. 'Let's go home, darling,' Minx murmured, 'I have a surprise waiting for you there.'

Amrita, too weak to resist, followed her meekly into the car and waited. Minx had some unfinished business to take care of at the thana before she could join her. Amrita laid her head back weakly and watched as Minx reached for her wallet and passed a few crisp notes around. It was going to be a long ride home.

Amrita walked slowly up the steps to her flat. Minx had disappeared ahead of her, and gone straight up to

Strange Obsession

Amrita's room. By now Minx had made herself into such a permanent fixture in Mrs Pinto's home that nobody paid any attention to her. Before Amrita could push open the door of her room, Minx opened it with a flourish. 'Come in, madam, entrez,' she smiled, sweeping the floor before Amrita with one of her dupattas.

Amrita felt a blast of cold air hit her as she walked in. 'What's going on? What's this?' she asked.

This, my darling, is an air-conditioner. I thought you needed one to cool you down. Your mother told me you couldn't sleep without one during the Delhi summers.'

Without a word, Amrita stormed out of the room and went and sat down at the dining-table. It had been a ghastly night. She was furious with Mrs Pinto for allowing all this nonsense. She also knew her landlady would demand more rent claiming her electricity bills had doubled with the installation of the air-conditioner. Minx came out carrying two wine glasses in her hand. 'Let's celebrate,' she said and sat down across Amrita.

'How dare you,' Amrita cried, 'really . . . how bloody dare you?'

Minx looked at her innocently and asked, 'Something wrong? How dare I what? Don't tell me you disapprove of air-conditioners all of a sudden?'

Amrita held her breath for a few seconds before saying evenly, 'OK, Minx. You win. I don't have the energy to fight you. Let's just sit down and talk about this. What's going on here? Forgive me, I am puzzled. But this doesn't look like normal behaviour to me. Maybe there's something wrong with me, not you. Maybe it's the city. I really don't know. Does Bombay do this to people? Does everybody behave like this?'

Minx laughed and pinched her cheek playfully, 'Relax, relax, relax,' she said settling down into a chair. 'Don't ask such philosophical questions. I haven't had my first drink yet.'

Amrita continued, 'No, Minx, this is important to me. I need to clear my head. I really am confused. I have never experienced anything like this in Delhi. Perhaps you people in Bombay are used to such stuff.'

Minx lit up a cigarette and looked thoughtful. 'You're right. I must have come on too strong or something. Can't help it. I'm a Gemini. We do things in extremes. Even love can't be casual. I love you. You don't have to accept that either. I'll just have to keep trying. Keep proving it to you.'

Amrita intervened, 'Oh no! Please don't do that. That's where all the problems begin. You say "I love you" to me as if it's perfectly natural for one woman to say it to another. I think it's abnormal. You are abnormal. I don't know what you're looking for in me. I have already told you I'm not made that way. I don't like women . . . I mean . . . .'

Minx stopped her by placing a finger on her mouth. 'And I have also told you that I don't want you to do anything you don't want to do. I think I should tell you a little about myself. Will that help?'

Amrita nodded. Maybe she should have had this conversation earlier. Maybe she would then have kept Minx at a distance from the beginning.

*

'I had a lousy childhood,' Minx began and Amrita immediately sensed that talking like this was not easy for Minx. Minx looked at her quickly to see whether she was laughing before she continued, 'I know what you're probably thinking—here's another one of those filmi-type sob-stories. But it's true. I was lonely as hell. My father's transfers and my mother's social work left me to amuse myself on my own. Most of my time was spent in the havaldar's kholis playing with their children, eating their food, even talking their language. It's the same old rubbish . . . only child, lonely child, boarding-schools . . . you know . . . .' Minx trailed off. 'I was thrown out of two schools . . . expelled. My mother was so ashamed. She didn't know how to face her friends in the Bridge Club. My father handled me the only way he knew. By belting me.' Minx pushed up the sleeves of her shirt to show an old scar to Amrita, 'See this? The belt buckle got me here. He stopped only after he saw the blood.'

Amrita stared at the jagged scar across Minx's muscular arm. 'I still don't understand how you became like—this,' she said quietly.

'By "like this" do you mean my appearance or my behaviour?' Minx enquired.

'Both. I suppose,' Amrita said.

Minx waved her hand in the air and tipped cigarette ash all over. 'I'll save that for another day. But what I'm going to tell you now, you will never forget. Just as I can never forget it. I don't even know why I'm telling you. Perhaps it's because for the first time in my life I feel like I truly love someone—you.'

Amrita winced. Despite what she had just heard, she could not help feeling repulsed at the sound of those words on Minx's lips 'Stop it,' she said, her hands over her ears. 'I refuse to listen to your love talk. It makes me sick.'

Minx caught hold of her roughly. 'Why? Why does it make you sick? Why should it? Because I belong to the same sex? Is that my only sin? You find it sickening to accept my love . . . but what about that animal Rover's love? That's OK. You enjoy that. How come? And don't tell me "because they are men. And it's normal". Bullshit! There is nothing abnormal about my feelings for you. It is your problem that you have hang-ups. And, like I told you, I don't expect you to return my love, just accept it.' The words came out in a rush and Amrita could see how agitated Minx had become. The conversation wasn't going anywhere and her eyes were beginning to get heavy.

'Please, Minx,' she pleaded. 'I can't handle any more of this. Why can't you understand that I have a life of my own . . . friends of my own . . . a family of my own. I have a right to all that. You cannot force me to accept you . . . or your so-called love.'

Minx stood up abruptly and picked up her pack of Cartiers. 'OK, baby, I get your point. Don't worry. I'm not going to kidnap you or create a scene. But before I leave, I want to tell you my secret. A secret I have kept locked up for all these years. Nobody . . . nobody knows it. When I tell you, you will become a part of it. A part of my life. Forever.'

Amrita got up and started to walk rapidly towards her room, 'I don't want to hear it . . . don't tell me . . . don't tell me,' she pleaded, rushing away from Minx.

'Oh no, you will listen. Right now,' Minx said, catching up with her and blocking her way. 'Look at me . . . look into my eyes when I tell you this. And listen very, very carefully. You will never hear these words again . . . .' She forced Amrita to face her and looked squarely into her eyes. Amrita found herself shaking involuntarily as Minx gripped her hand. 'My father . . . .' she started and suddenly her voice cracked. Amrita stared open-mouthed as Minx underwent a transformation in front of her astonished eyes. For a moment there was just the sound of Minx taking in her breath very quickly, very sharply, as if she had been running hard and her heart was about to burst. Amrita stood rooted to the spot, unable to move even though Minx had released her, the woman whimpering helplessly as she leant against the door frame was not the Minx she knew. This person was speaking in a child's voice, lisping . . . her body crumpling slowly, and folding finally in a curled-up heap at her feet.

Gently, Amrita lifted her up. 'Come and sit down for a while,' she said. Meekly, Minx followed her into the room.

'It's very cold in here,' she said, huddling against the pillows and pulling a quilt up to her chin. Amrita waited. Minx had stopped sobbing, but she was very still and quiet. 'Let's not discuss anything,' Amrita said.

Minx shook her hand firmly. 'No. I have to get it out. And it must be tonight. Listen . . . . My father . . . yes . . . the same man who is so powerful, so respected, so feared . . . is a beast. A beast of the worst kind. He . . . he . . . raped me.' Amrita drew in her breath sharply and put her arms around Minx.

'Yes . . . that's what he did to me. I was thirteen years old. Just thirteen. Can you imagine what it must have been like? No you can't. Nobody can. He wasn't drunk. He doesn't touch the stuff. He was just horny. And frustrated . . . so frustrated. I was too scared to do anything . . . say anything. I didn't ask . . . but he told me . . . he told me about my mother . . . that she refused to have sex with him. That she hated him. "I only have you now," he told me. And I felt I had to make him happy. He looked so miserable. I felt guilty . . . of course I did. He made me feel it was my duty. You understand? My duty. "If your mother doesn't, you have to," he told me. I believed him. I thought that's how it was in other people's homes too. He told me to swear I wouldn't tell anybody. "It is our secret," he said. I was too scared anyway. Who would I have told? But I did . . . five months later I confessed to the havaldar's wife. That was my one big mistake. That was when everything started to go wrong . . . .' Weakly, Minx reached for her cigarettes. 'My father never forgave me for betraying him.'

'How did he know you'd told the woman?' Amrita asked.

Minx looked at her strangely, 'Do you think she kept quiet? Can any woman keep a secret—an explosive one at that? No way. Within a couple of days it reached my mother's ears. At first, she refused to believe it. She called me into her room. She was all dressed up to go to the club. I remember her Pochampalli sari—purple with little yellow elephants. She didn't know how to bring the topic up. But one look at her and I knew she knew. All she asked was "Is it true?" And I nodded my head, too scared to say anything. The look of disgust and hatred in her eyes is something that still haunts me. She turned away and started fixing hairpins into her bun. I didn't know what I was supposed to do. I ran up and tried to hug her. She pushed me away savagely, "Get away you filthy creature," she said. "I always knew you were a pervert. You and that father of yours."'

Minx broke down and Amrita went to fetch her a glass of water. She was calmer when Amrita returned. 'She didn't come back that night,' Minx continued. 'When my father got home he summoned me to ask where she was. I shrugged, but my expression gave me away. He lunged at me, "You told her our secret," he bellowed and started raining blows on my back. I didn't tell her, I didn't, I screamed, with pain. "Liar," he yelled and continued to hit me. The noise attracted the orderlies on duty. Two of them walked in and intervened. He might have killed me that night . . . .' Minx trailed off.

Suddenly she did not look half as ugly as she usually did to Amrita. Her face had softened and the look in her eyes had altered. She was less wary and almost feminine at that moment. Spontaneously, Amrita hugged her. Minx settled into her arms like a grateful child, and Amrita began to rock her gently. 'That feels so good,' Minx said and for a while both of them were silent with just the hum of the brand-new air-conditioner disturbing the night air.

'What happened after that?' Amrita asked gently.

Minx disengaged herself and carried on, 'My father got into his jeep and went to look for her. She was staying at a friend's house. Initially, she refused to return. I don't know what he said to her, but I remember the sound of the jeep returning in the early hours of the morning. I've never spent a more agonized night. I was alone in that huge house, lying on my bed. I hadn't eaten anything for hours. I held myself responsible for what had happened. I thought of hanging myself or taking a fistful of my mother's sleeping pills. I didn't want to live. I didn't want to face them.'

Even though Amrita hadn't met Minx's parents, she could picture them clearly as Minx spoke. The words were not emerging as haltingly now, as Minx was rapidly regaining control of herself. It must have been close to dawn, but neither of them were sleepy. Amrita asked her, 'How did it end?'

Minx shrugged indifferently, 'How do these things end? Both of them met me the next morning at the breakfast table and behaved as if nothing had happened. But I knew that my mother had cut me out of her life forever. As for him, he never referred to this incident again. And he never came back to my bed. Overnight, I went from being the daughter, the only child, to a ghost or a shadow. A stranger. A non-entity. They became cold and impersonal and pretended that I didn't exist. That was the time I took to the streets. I dropped out of school a year later. Made friends with all the local dadas. And here I am . . . trying to make friends with you.'

Amrita regarded her sympathetically. More than anything else, she wanted to reach out, extend her hand and reassure Minx. But she could not. What she had just heard had touched her, but she had felt as if she had just finished watching a deeply moving film. The emotion drained away gradually once she had reached the end of the story. Minx seemed to be pleading with her. Begging for her acceptance. Yet, Amrita could not give it. And she did not want to pretend. Suddenly Minx sighed wistfully, 'God! How very beautiful you are.'

Amrita tried to change the topic. 'I have a busy weekend coming up,' she announced, 'maybe we should both try and get some sleep.'

Minx got up reluctantly and squared her shoulders. 'I get the message, kid,' she said jauntily and Amrita was relieved to note she was back to her usual couldn't-care-less self.

'Good night,' Amrita said softly. Minx leaned over to kiss her. Amrita managed to turn her face just in time, and avoid Minx's lips descending over hers.

'Still holding back?' Minx mocked and without waiting for a response, walked out of the house.

Amrita closed the door and latched it quickly. She had made up her mind. Tomorrow morning she would start seriously looking for a new place to stay.

Ten

Sheila was insistent. 'Don't be silly. What's your problem, Amrita? It will be much easier this way.'

Amrita was not convinced. She rather liked Sheila, especially after they had shared a hotel room on a modelling trip to Calcutta. Sheila was an outgoing, easy-to-live-with person. Unlike most of the other models she was not bitchy or competitive. She had given herself two years to make a success of her career after which she planned to marry her steady boyfriend in New York. The idea of sharing Shiela's Versova flat wasn't bad at all. Sheila had been cribbing that it was getting increasingly expensive to maintain it on her own. Amrita had been there for a couple of post-show and had been charmed by the ambience.

'What about transport?' Amrita asked anxiously. With regular hikes in cab fares, that was going to be a major consideration, for Versova was more than twenty kilometres from South Bombay.

'No problem,' Sheila said cheerfully. 'I have a first-class railway pass. You can get one too. Besides, there are always sweet guys hanging around, only too eager to drop girls like us home.'

Amrita pulled a face. 'Yes, sure. But they don't do it for nothing.'

Sheila pushed her playfully, 'It's an ego thing for them . . . . I've heard Vikram and all boasting they've made it with me. All bull. As long as I know and my boyfriend knows it's rubbish, that's all that matters. Let those idiots fantasize. We get our lifts. That's what matters. It's cool.'

Amrita continued to voice her doubts. 'What if I don't get assignments for a month? How do I pay the rent and share expenses? With Mrs Pinto, it was a fairly flexible arrangement. I don't want to ask my brothers or parents to subsidize me . . . my self-respect is at stake.'

Sheila slapped her on the back and teased, 'Oh my! Such a propah little lady. Don't worry. I'm a real Shylock. I'll get the money out of you. Besides, stop being so bloody modest. You've put us all out of business after getting here. If you don't get assignments, what about the rest of us?'

Amrita laughed. It was true. She had been hogging all the plum jobs and her rates had gone through the roof, upsetting the market. This had led to some hostility and jealousy, but she had been far too busy to bother about it. Some of the girls, like Sheila, had accepted her supremacy with grace and good humour. Others had not been as sporting. But Amrita was smart enough to realize that nobody did anybody a single favour in the cut-throat modelling business. You either delivered, or you were out. And right now Amrita was delivering—ad after sensational ad.

Her last campaign for an upmarket cosmetics house had taken the media by storm. Amrita was being hailed as the 'Supermodel of the Nineties' by news-magazines which featured her in syrupy cover stories. Through it all, Amrita had plodded on conscientiously, turning up on time for assignments, co-operating with stylists and art-directors, minding her own business and conducting herself with absolute professionalism. It had paid off. She was earning good money and steadily at that. Sheila joked with her. 'I think you'll probably buy me out in six months' time at the rate you're going. I believe you've turned down a fabulous movie offer. You're nuts! Ravindra Shah is the biggest—you can't get any bigger. He gives the greatest breaks. And you said no to him! You should've given him my number at least!'

Amrita, fresh-faced, make-up-free, with her hair gathered carelessly in a ponytail, told Sheila that she was not looking for a role in Hindi films.

'Don't knock it till you've tried it,' Sheila advised. 'You'll earn lakhs and lakhs. Two years from now you'll probably want to buy my whole building, forget sharing my flat.'

'No way,' Amrita said, 'two years from now, I'll be married.'

Sheila nudged her conspiratorially, 'Anybody I know?' and then she added, 'but with that crazy woman in your life, how can you think of marriage?'

Amrita sat up with a jerk. 'What do you mean by that?'

Sheila held up her hands, 'Sorry, sorry, sorry. No offence meant. But you know how small this world is. We've all seen her. And heard all about what she did to Rover. Why do you think all the boys have been staying miles away from you? Nobody wants to mess around with that female. Not even Karan. And he was really keen on you.'

Amrita looked at her witheringly, 'So . . . how come you aren't scared?'

Sheila laughed, 'Who me? Forget it. I'm far too bindaas. What can that lunatic do to me? Besides, I have a boyfriend. She knows I could never be interested in you,'

Amrita thought of saying something nasty but changed her mind. Instead, she decided to probe further. It was important to know what people were saying. Sheila was only too glad to chatter on once she found Amrita encouraging her to. 'I don't like to gossip,' Sheila said, 'but people have been talking about the two of you.

Minx is weird, man. We all know she is a lesbo. But what about you? We thought you were straight!'

'I am straight!' Amrita cried out angrily. 'I can't help it if that weirdo has latched on to me.' And then she broke down. Sheila was all sympathy and understanding as Amrita unfolded the story of how Minx was making her life miserable.

'One of the reasons I want to move out is her. In fact, it's the main reason.'

'What makes you think she won't turn up here?' Sheila asked anxiously.

Amrita shook her head, 'Who knows . . . I have a feeling even if I go and hide away in the Himalayas, she'll find me there. But I didn't want to conceal anything from you. Out of all the other girls I've met in Bombay, you've been the only one who has been sweet to me . . . really sweet. I don't want you to be in any trouble because of me.'

Sheila paced around restlessly before saying, 'Look, I'm not afraid. I'm used to goondas, eve-teasers and purse-snatchers—you don't know what Bombay trains are like. People don't fool around with me. I've also attended self-defence classes. I'll teach you a trick or two. Don't get so nervous, yaar. I agree Bombay isn't Delhi. But we Bombaywallis are tough too. Don't be nervous. One well aimed kick in the groin is enough. I've made quite a few loafers thanda that way. You'll learn . . .'

Reassured by her friend's brave words, Amrita decided to move, and fast. It was far too irresistible a proposition to discard lightly.

Eleven

Amrita moved out on a bright and sunny Saturday. She knew that Minx would track her down eventually, but she wasn't going to let that stop her now. Mrs Pinto was relieved to see her go. She had decided she was going to take in only young, male P.G.s henceforth. It worked out better that way. They even provided the feni for her long evenings. And they gave her the much-longed-for company that she so desperately craved. These model-type girls and air-hostesses were all the same—selfish bitches with no morals. Boyfriends and parties, that's what their life revolved around.

Before leaving, Amrita gave Mary a generous tip even though she had been anything but helpful. Sheila had brought over her boyfriend's Maruti Gypsy to load Amrita's stuff. 'Don't be absurd,' she'd advised without really knowing the history behind the air-conditioner, 'take it. It's brand-new. We can always sell it.'

Amrita imagined her thinking that some besotted lover had spent forty thousand rupees to keep her in the cool. She smiled to herself but didn't let Sheila know who had made the gift. There would be time enough for that later.

Mrs Pinto was pretty cross about the gaping hole left by the machine. She deducted five hundred rupees from Amrita's deposit, grumbling, 'I'll have to get a carpenter to repair that. And paint it over. What a bloody nuisance.'

Amrita apologized profusely. 'Auntie' Pinto wasn't a bad sort, she thought. Another landlady would have insisted on the P.G. paying for more than just the carpenter.

Sheila was bubbling over with enthusiasm. 'Versova is a great place, you'll see. Lots of restaurants, lots of boutiques. If you find a boyfriend quickly, we won't even have to cook at home. Vicky travels too much. But when he's here we're out hogging every evening.'

Amrita clung to her seat as Sheila sped down the road, chattering incessantly and barely keeping an eye on the traffic. Amrita had two free days to settle down in Sheila's flat and then it was back to a non-stop schedule.

The festive season was round the corner. This meant dozens of fashion-shows, calendar jobs and new campaigns. She was looking forward to participating in the biggest fashion event of the year—the fancy auction of what had been dubbed 'Art Wear'—high-fashion outfits which bore original doodles and slashes of colour by prominent painters. A British auctioneer had been invited to conduct the proceedings and the city's elite were to be present. A contest to pick the most outstanding model at the show had also been announced. The winner would be given an opportunity to work for a Parisian couturier for a season. Eight of Bombay's top models and two girls from Delhi had been selected for the show.

Amrita's mind was on the show, and she didn't really notice the persistent honking of a car behind them. 'Who the fuck is that?' Sheila cursed as she swung the car to the left.

'Probably some VIP on the way to the airport,' Amrita said absently.

The honking continued and Sheila glanced into the rear-view mirror. 'Some crazy female at the wheel,' she said as she changed gears and the car picked up speed. Amrita was instantly alert. She did not have to look back to know that it was Minx.

'Don't stop!' she told Sheila, 'just keep going. Let's try and lose her.'

Sheila stared at her with surprise, 'Someone you know?'

Amrita nodded. 'It's her. Minx. The same mad woman who keeps following me. She means business.'

Sheila looked into the mirror again and shuddered. 'Ugh! She's really ghastly. I hadn't noticed just how much earlier.'

Amrita said tersely, 'Well . . . she isn't a beauty-contest winner, that's for sure.'

'What does she want from you? Why don't you just give her an autographed picture or something and shoo her away?' suggested Sheila.

Amrita sighed, 'It isn't that simple. I can't seem to get rid of her. She isn't one of those harmless fans. I don't know . . . this one is demented.' They had managed to shake off Minx for a while. She hadn't been able to make the traffic-lights.

'Thank God!' Sheila announced. 'I think she's gone.'

Amrita turned around, 'No such luck. I can see her. Don't worry, she'll catch up.'

Sheila concentrated on the road, 'We'll get Vicky to fix her. She won't be able to try her tricks with us once he's through. You haven't met my boyfriend yet . . . he's quite a man. Tough, tough, tough. One shove . . . no, shout, and she'll vanish.'

Amrita was silent. She did not want to go into elaborate explanations at this stage. Sheila would find out soon enough.

Ten minutes later Minx had caught up with them. Her car was alongside now. Sheila stuck her head out of the window and screamed over the din of the traffic, 'Get lost, bitch!'

Minx pretended she hadn't heard.

They drove along bumper to bumper, with Minx refusing to look in their direction. Amrita stiffened at the sight of her . . . something about her manner sent a chill down her spine. Minx looked maniacal . . . and it was strange that Sheila did not seem to notice.

'Be careful of her,' Amrita warned, as Minx abruptly swung towards them, pushing Sheila to the edge of the road. Sheila jammed on the brakes, just managing to prevent her Gypsy from crashing into the kerb. Amrita's make-up bags fell forward and Amrita herself hit the dashboard with a dull thud, before falling back sharply into her seat.

Sheila jumped out from the driver's seat and strode up to Minx, who continued to sit in her jeep, staring at the road in front to her. Sheila hauled her out roughly, screaming, 'Just who the hell do you think you are, you bloody bitch?'

Minx turned to face her, 'I don't want to waste time with you. Just give her to me,' she said softly. It was then that Amrita noticed the pistol lying on the seat next to Minx.

Amrita came up to Sheila slowly and caught her by the arm. 'Don't get into this,' she told her quietly, 'let me handle it.' As discreetly as she could, she pointed to the gun which Minx was now fondling in her lap. Sheila saw it and was visibly startled but refused to budge. 'I bet it's a toy gun,' she said, laughing shakily.

Without a word, Minx picked it up and blew out one of the Gypsy's tyres. 'Sorry, but it isn't a toy,' she said.

Amrita leaned over and pleaded, 'Listen, leave my friend out of this. Let her go home.'

Minx laughed, 'How? She isn't going to get a cab on the highway. Tell you what. Why don't both of you hop in and I'll take you home. Come on. Let me get your things.'

Minx got out of the jeep and went towards the Gypsy, whistling, 'If I Were a Rich Man'. Sheila was too stunned to say anything. She took Amrita aside and whispered, 'Why are you allowing her to behave this way? Let's yell and scream. I'm sure somebody will stop if we create a scene. And then we can report her to the police.'

Amrita whispered back, 'Forget it. It's a long story. I can't tell you anything just now. Let's do as she says. I'll explain everything later.' Amrita ran up to Minx, caught up with her, and said imploringly, 'Don't be angry. I didn't want to hurt your feelings. But things were getting a bit much at Mrs Pinto's.'

Minx whirled around and snapped, 'Stop lying to me! I'm not that big a fool. You were trying to run away from me—admit it. Well . . . don't try it again. I've told you before . . . I'll find you wherever you are. One more thing—warn this woman—don't bother to explain, I know all about her—that if she comes anywhere close to you, she's finished.'

Amrita nodded dumbly. By now she knew there was no point in upsetting Minx when she was in this state. Silently, the three of them got into the jeep and they drove off at great speed. Minx did not require directions. She screeched to a halt at Sheila's apartment and jumped out, while the other two scrambled out behind her.

As they began unloading their things, Minx walked up to Amrita, leaned over and kissed her tenderly on the cheek, 'Look after yourself. And if there's anything you need—and I mean anything—call me.' She then turned to Sheila and said crisply, 'I'll send over an electrician in half an hour to fix the air-conditioner in Amrita's room . . . and don't worry about your electricity bills, I'll take care of them.'

With that, she was gone, leaving the two staring at the jeep as it zoomed away, trailing clouds of dirty exhaust in its wake.

Twelve

'Forget it, yaar,' Sheila consoled Amrita. They had been sharing Sheila's flat for ten days now and Amrita was inconsolable about an assignment she'd lost to another model. 'How could that bitch do this to me?' she kept saying.

Sheila reasoned philosophically, 'This profession is full of the Lola types. So what if she's stolen your campaign? There will be other, bigger ones.'

Amrita blew her nose noisily into a large handkerchief. 'I thought there was some sort of an unwritten code. I don't go stealing other girls' assignments,' she cribbed.

Sheila went off to to make a fresh cup of tea and continued talking from their small kitchen. 'Everybody isn't you, Amrita. It has become a filthy business these days. New girls are willing to do anything—undersell, undercut, screw around. You heard about Lola and Karan? Quite a story.'

Amrita shook her head. 'Frankly, I don't want to know. I'm so disgusted. Why can't models be more professional? This was my campaign. It meant a lot to me. I would've got my ticket money to Paris and back out of it. Now I won't be able to go.'

Sheila came and sat down by her. 'Look, sweetie, this is a tough business. Nobody believes in fair play. Nobody has scruples. You turn around for a split second and someone comes along to grab your shoot. I know it's a lot of money . . . you'll just have to work harder for the next month or so to make up.'

Amrita sipped her tea in silence before saying, 'It's not the money as much as the attitude. I'm feeling so cheated . . . so betrayed. I swear I wouldn't do this to another model.'

'Lola isn't just any new model on the make. She thinks she is big shit. And she's going to make it to the top. Very quickly at that. She's one of those who'll stop at nothing. It has started with you—she's going to fuck around with a lot of others. All of us had better watch out,' said Sheila.

Amrita conceded reluctantly, 'She does have a great figure. Her hair is all wrong, though. But she manages to frizz it up nicely in photographs.'

'Don't forget she has a sugar daddy. Karan is really pushing her. I don't know what he sees in her, frankly, I mean, after you,' Sheila said laconically.

Amrita tried to change the subject, 'Oh, come on . . . there was nothing between us. You know that. He was sweet to me initially, that's all.'

An urgent ringing of the doorbell interrupted their chat. Sheila looked up from what she was doing, 'Who could it be? I hope it isn't that bloody neighbour constantly borrowing things—dahi one day, tomatoes the next day . . . even sanitary pads, can you imagine?' By then Amrita had reached the door in three long strides and opened it.

'I need to talk to you urgently . . . privately,' Minx said looking pointedly at Sheila.

'Come in,' Amrita said resignedly.

'No . . . you come out. I need ten minutes, that's all,' Minx replied, twirling the jeep keys.

Amrita exchanged glances with Sheila before going into her room to fetch her bag and sandals.

'Don't be long,' Sheila called out after her. 'Lunch in half an hour.'

The minute they were in the car Minx turned to Amrita and burst out, 'I've heard about it . . . what Lola did to you. Don't worry . . . it has been taken care of. Lola won't pose for another photograph or do another show again. I've seen to it.'

Amrita stared at Minx in horror with a sick feeling in the pit of her stomach. There was a wild gleam in Minx's eyes as she sat very still, looking at the road in front of her. 'I did it to make you happy. I did it for you,' she said calmly, tapping the wheel with her fingers. Amrita tried to get out of the car and run back into her building. But Minx caught her. 'Why do you behave like this with me? Don't you understand even now—I'd do anything in the world to make you happy. I thought you'd be pleased. She deserved it after what she did to you.'

Amrita finally found her voice, 'Did you kill her?'

Minx laughed lightly, 'Don't be silly. I didn't have to. Come on . . . I'll show you something . . . .'

'Where are we going?' Amrita asked woodenly.

'Not too far,' Minx replied, ' just by the creek—you know, where all those boulders are.'

Amrita's mouth was dry as Minx hummed and whistled at the wheel. 'It was so easy, I'm still laughing at what a stupid girl that Lola is. Stupid and greedy.'

Amrita asked. 'How did you find out about her getting my assignments?'

Minx turned to her with a broad grin, 'Don't be silly, baby. The whole world knows. All your ad people are talking about the bitch and how she screwed with you. How could I let her get away with it? Your prestige, your reputation, your image, was at stake. No, no, no. She had to be taught a lesson. God! She was so stupid. I'd expected her to be smarter somehow.' And Minx resumed humming the ghazal she had been tonelessly singing. They came to a deserted spot close to the beach.

Minx pointed to a rock almost ten metres away. 'That's where I did it.'

'Did what?' Amrita asked, her voice barely rising above a whisper.

'Fixed her face,' Minx replied easily.

'How? With what?' demanded Amrita.

Minx reached for her pocket and pulled out a vial. 'This,' she replied and chucked it into the sea. Amrita looked puzzled and Minx realized she didn't know what the vial contained. 'Acid, baby, acid. Easy to carry. Easy to throw. No hassles. It does the job thoroughly and cleanly. In seconds. Oof! You should've heard her screams. I thought those kolis from the village would come running.'

Amrita shuddered involuntarily and sat down by the edge of the sea. 'How could you do such a thing? I'm going to report you to the police. Or better still, I'll go and tell your father.'

Minx lit a cigarette. 'Don't bother to waste your time. Nobody is going to believe you . . . nobody knows I did it . . . and nobody can prove it . . . not even Lola.'

'What do you mean . . . she must have seen you,' said Amrita fighting to control her voice.

But Minx was obviously on a high. She strolled to the jeep and came back with a can of imported beer. 'Have a sip—you're looking thirsty,' she said, taking a big swig herself. 'No,' Minx continued, 'she didn't see me. I mean . . . she didn't see me as you are seeing

Strange Obsession

me. I was dressed differently. I had a wig on. And large-framed, tinted glasses. Believe it or not . . . but I wore a sari for the job. The first time in my life . . . and possibly the last . . . I felt so ridiculous in it. But it was important. I had to look my part.'

'And what was that?' Amrita asked.

'Well, I'd told Lola I was a TV serial producer. She came here with me thinking the crew was setting up a situation on the beach for a screen test. I'd taken the trouble to get everything organized, including a script. The test required wind-blown shots of the heroine. She loved the part. I pulled out a camera and told her to pose on those rocks. I told her, "Let's get a few stills . . . the crew is late, must've got held up somewhere." She was most co-operative. One flick of the wrist was all that was needed—just one flick. She fell over backwards against these rocks there. Probably bust her ass on the sharp edges. Bas, it was over in seconds. She lost consciousness. And I did my work quickly. By the way, the serial part wasn't made up. That project is still on. Now you can do it. And get back your campaign too.'

Amrita stared at her disbelievingly and said, 'You're lying! I think you are lying. You are making this up. For some mad reason of your own.'

Minx raised her index finger and said, 'One minute. I knew you'd say this. Of course, you'd have heard about it by tonight or tomorrow morning since Lola has been admitted to a hospital and Karan is there with her . . . but I wanted you to know it from me . . . here, take a look at these.'

Amrita recoiled as Minx chucked a packet of polaroids into her lap. The first one itself was so grotesque that she averted her eyes and suppressed a scream. It was a gruesome close-up of Lola's beautiful face eaten away by acid, one eye was shut and the skin stripped off to reveal the cheekbone. Half her lips had disappeared and the acid had left a corrosive trail down her slender neck. Amrita threw the rest of the photographs at Minx and vomited into the sand. 'You sick bitch!' she cursed, 'I hate you. You won't get away with this. I'm going to phone and tell everybody.'

Minx finished her can of beer and crushed it slowly. 'No, you aren't. If you do, you'll be the one picked up by the police. You are the obvious suspect. Why would I want to harm that pretty little girl? All the other models know how angry and upset you were that she'd stolen your campaign, your ads and your boyfriend. Ha! Ha! Where do I come into the picture?'

Amrita looked at Minx with rage and hate in her eyes, 'No matter how far you go to win me, I'll never like you, never love you—never, never, never.'

Minx suddenly grew agitated. She flicked the half-smoked cigarette into the sea and cried out, 'Why? What more do I have to do to prove myself? Kill? I'll do that too. Just tell me—who? You want me to kill someone? Anyone? I'll do it. I'll kill for you. I will Amrita . . . maybe then you'll love me.'

Amrita turned her face away and said, 'As if you can make someone love you by doing all this. I look at you and feel disgusted. I hate the sight of you. Go and kill whoever you want. It has nothing to do with me. Kill, murder, destroy . . . do it. I'll hate you more . . . you hear that . . . I hate you, despise you, spit on you. Why don't you kill yourself instead, huh?'

Minx looked at Amrita, searching her face for something. Finally she said, 'Will that make you happy? Will that please you? Then I'll do it—just tell me to, and I'll do it. I'll kill myself. I'll give you my life—what more can I give you?'

Amrita got into the jeep. 'You make me sick. Whether you live or you die doesn't matter to me. Now take me home.'

Minx had lost her usual swagger as she climbed slowly into the driver's seat. Wordlessly, she drove Amrita home. As Amrita climbed out of the jeep, she heard Minx calling after her, 'I did it for you . . . only for you.'

When Amrita entered the flat, she heard Sheila speaking on the telephone. 'Oh my God!' she was saying, 'I don't believe it. Who could have done such a horrible thing to her?'

So, she knew. Amrita sat down heavily on the first available chair and in that instant knew that she would have to keep quiet about Minx and Lola.

She waited for Sheila to put down the phone before asking innocently, 'Something wrong?'

She heard out Sheila without twitching a muscle in her face or giving anything away. At the end of her story, Amrita put her hand to her mouth, feigned shock, and exclaimed, 'My God! What a ghastly accident. I wonder who it was?'

Sheila looked at her darkly and said, 'I thought you knew . . . .'

Thirteen

Karan was in the hospital when Amrita got there to see Lola. Seeing her he walked up deliberately. 'Satisfied?'

Amrita looked at him, her eyes full of fear and pain and begged, 'Please, Karan . . . don't say that. I didn't expect you to react like this.'

They were standing outside Lola's room in a long, neon-lit corridor. 'Don't bother to go in there and see her,' Karan warned, 'it might worsen her condition.'

Amrita clutched his hand desperately and cried out. 'Stop it! Why are you blaming me for this? Do you think I'm capable of doing something so terrible to another human being?'

Karan shook his head and looked away. 'I don't know you any more. I don't know what you are or aren't capable of. But all of us in the modelling world hold you responsible for what happened to Lola.'

Amrita asked quietly, 'Were you in love with her?'

The question touched a raw nerve in Karan. He whirled around and said harshly, 'You know the answer to that. No! I wasn't in love with her. But I liked her. I was seeing her . . . .'

Amrita nodded, 'Yes, I know. I came here to say how terribly sorry I am that this happened. And Karan . . . you must believe me when I say I didn't have anything to do with it. Nothing at all. I was as shocked as all of you when I found out.'

Karan's hollow laugh broke the silence. 'It isn't any of my business what you do with your life or who you hang out with. But if I were you, I'd stay miles away from Meenakshi Iyengar.'

Amrita looked down silently and in a quiet voice asked, 'Don't you think I want to? That's why I moved to Versova. But, what has that got to do with this . . . with what happened to Lola?'

Karan's eyes searched Amrita's face. In a voice laden with disappointment he said, 'She has also taught you to lie and act, I notice. What else have you learnt at her feet? Go on, tell me.' Amrita tried to reach out and hold Karan's hand, but he shrugged her off before continuing, 'You and she might get away with this. Maybe the police will oblige the Inspector-General's daughter by suppressing the evidence or fudging records. Both of you can fool the world and pretend you had nothing to do with this. But you can't fool me. Whatever comes out of this investigation, I know that you were behind the crime. You and that lesbian friend of yours. Nobody else could've done it.'

Amrita refused to get provoked. She forced herself to stay calm. 'Why do you think we did it?' she asked after a pause.

'Who else?' Karan countered. 'Lola was getting all your assignments. She'd walked away with your campaign . . . she was a threat to you. I am not justifying her behaviour, or the way in which she went about grabbing your jobs. But it's obvious that the person most affected by her growing success was you. Why don't you admit it, at least to me? I'm not going to report you or anything. But I'd respect you a little more than I do right now if you did.'

A small voice in Amrita's head warned her against confessing that she knew anything about the incident. She stared at Karan dumbly and said, 'I wish I could make it better for you by saying I was involved in this ghastly affair. But as it happens I only heard of it when someone phoned.'

Karan shook his head disbelievingly and said, 'If this is what ambition does to a person, it's better to remain in the slow track. I hardly know you any more. Just a few months ago you were an able, simple, beautiful girl from Delhi. I was amused watching your attempts to be a hip Bombay model. That's what attracted me to you. And now . . . now, you've become a cold-blooded, ruthless—I hate to use the word—bitch. Even worse than the other girls who used to put me off with their lying and scheming minds. Maybe Minx is responsible for doing this to you. But she doesn't control your life or own you. Or does she?'

Stubbornly, Amrita argued, 'I don't know why you are saying such cruel things to me, Karan. I thought we were friends, good friends. I really enjoyed being with you. And, suddenly, you stopped seeing me. You never even bothered to explain why. I could also retaliate and accuse you of half a dozen things, but I won't. I'm sorry you've chosen to adopt such an attitude, that's all.' With that Amrita picked up her bag and walked away.

*

Karan experienced a strange sense of loss on Amrita's departure. He asked himself why he continued to feel the way he did about her. Why he was still interested enough in her to monitor all her moves, follow her career and keep tabs on whom she was seeing. He had heard about the Rover incident, of course. Everybody had. It was devised by Minx as a sign to keep people away from Amrita. And nobody in their right minds wanted to go anywhere near her. It was different for Karan. He would still have risked everything, even after that last run-in with Minx. But it was Amrita herself who had put him off. He did not know what to make of her any more. She kept to herself and seemed single-minded in her ambition to become India's highest-paid, most-sought-after model. He wanted to remind her that she had already achieved that target. And in such a remarkably short time that even her rivals marvelled at her meteoric rise. But obviously Amrita wasn't satisfied with being a spectacular success in her own country. She wanted to make it abroad—in Paris, no less. It was not an impossibility; others had done it before her. And if she had not pushed herself so relentlessly, she would have achieved that ambition as well.

But Amrita had not reckoned with Lola and the sensation she created when she first hit the modelling circuit. Lola was two inches taller than Amrita and stood six feet tall in her stockinged feet. That was her biggest advantage over her rivals. And she had a body so long-limbed and lithe that garments hung on her like fluid sculpture, falling easily, beautifully, over perfectly moulded lines, creating the sort of dream silhouettes couturiers killed for. She moved well on the ramp making the most of her relaxed stride and graceful carriage. Karan compared the two girls and concluded that though Lola was no great beauty, she somehow reflected the 'Nineties Look' better than Amrita, whose chiselled perfection often acted as a barrier, making it difficult for the girl-on-the-street to identify with her.

While Karan was thinking of all this, the police inspector emerged from Lola's room. He had a smirk on his face as he chatted with the hospital RMO. 'The girl is in such bad shape . . . she will pull through, of course, but even her parents won't recognize her now,' he was saying casually.

Karan rushed up to the men and asked anxiously, 'Is she conscious? What did she say?'

The policeman looked at him curiously, 'Are you her brother, father or husband?' he asked snidely.

'Just a friend—a good friend,' Karan answered.

'Then, I suggest, you get out of here. Don't get involved in these lafdas. This is a police case, you understand? Attempt to murder. Tomorrow we'll pick you up and put you in jail. Would you like that?'

Karan stood his ground, 'She has nobody of her own in Bombay. No relatives. Her parents are in Bangalore. As her close friend, I have a right to know,' he said.

The inspector turned to the RMO and said, 'Then you tell him. I have other jobs to attend to. A suicide in Pydhonie. Wife-burning in Nagpada. It's a hard life for us.' He stretched out his hand in Karan's face, 'Boss . . . some chai-paani?'

Karan shoved a ten-rupee note into his open palm and turned to the RMO.

'Tell me, sir, how is she? What really happened?'

Strange Obsession

The RMO was grim-faced as he replied, 'Whoever did this to her, meant business. Did the girl have enemies?'

'Why?' Karan asked.

'Because the person who attacked her was a professional. Maybe a hired hand. It wasn't just an acid attack—the poor girl was carved up nicely. Her insides were minced with a switch-blade shoved through her vagina. Only a sadist would mutilate an innocent young girl like that. Who will marry her now? Her chances are permanently destroyed.' Then after a minute, he looked at Karan curiously, 'Are you her boyfriend by any chance?'

Karan smiled, a twisted smile, 'Does it make any difference? But tell me, doctor, what did she tell the police?'

The RMO invited Karan to walk with him while he took his ward rounds. 'Not too much. She is very weak and doesn't have the strength to talk. She speaks in whispers through one side of her mouth. We had to record her statement today, because there were chances she wouldn't survive the night.'

Karan was shocked to hear him say that. 'But she's going to be fine now, isn't she, doctor?' he demanded.

The RMO shook his head uncertainly. 'She has stabilized somewhat. I've put her on a drip. If her heart holds up, she'll pull through. Can't say till tomorrow morning. Anyway, the police are satisfied. Their job is over.'

Karan persisted, 'What did she tell them. Please, doc, tell me. I know it's probably confidential—but it's important . . . please.'

The RMO said tersely, 'She said it was a woman who did it to her. A young woman. That's all. Sad to think a woman could do such a thing to another woman, isn't it?'

Karan wasn't surprised. At all. It only confirmed what he had suspected all along. He wondered whether he should go to the police and tell them about Amrita's visit to the hospital that morning. Or mention that he was sure Minx was involved. But he decided against it. Like the inspector had told him, it was better to stay out of such lafdas. He thanked the RMO and left the hospital abruptly. He knew where he had to go and whom he had to meet.

*

The bar was crowded as usual. Friday nights at The Watering Hole, were generally busy. But Karan found her in minutes. She was seated at a banquette in a secluded corner sipping a Bloody Mary. As always, she was dressed in black, and was alone. She smiled as she saw him towering over her. 'I thought you'd get here, somehow,' drawled Minx, reaching for her cigarette. 'As a matter of fact, I've even taken the liberty of ordering your favourite drink.' She snapped her fingers and signalled to the bartender. Within seconds a Tom Collins was at their table.

'Cheers!' Minx said happily, raising her glass. Karan stared passively at her. How could she remain this cool, this unperturbed? It was maddening. 'You shouldn't have done it,' he spluttered. 'This time you've gone too far.'

Minx cocked an eyebrow and said, 'Too far? Or not far enough? Listen, Karankins, it's time we become buddy-buddies. Know what I mean?'

Karan couldn't control himself any longer. 'You are a demoness. How could you do such a thing? What will you get out of it, huh? A kiss in gratitude from Amrita? Three extra seconds of her time? What? Tell me?'

Minx studied him coolly. 'Karan,' she purred, 'stop being so hysterical. Let's enjoy the evening—it's not often that I get to have a drink with you. Besides . . . I haven't the foggiest notion what it is you are going on about.'

Karan brought his hand down on the table heavily. 'Stop this bloody nonsense at once. You know very well exactly what I'm talking about. There is a young girl lying on a hospital bed, close to death. And you are sitting here playing games with me. You did it. You and Amrita. You've ruined a beautiful woman's life—you have killed her. She may not be dead. But I wish to God if that was what you'd intended, you'd finished the job. Lola won't be able to stand the shock when she finds out just what it is that the two of you have done to her.'

Minx took large sips of her drink and pulled on her cigarette. 'God!' she drawled. 'Look at you, haven't touched your glass. Come on, sweetheart. It's Friday night. Relax. Enjoy yourself.' Seeing his face, she continued, 'Oh-oh. Have I ordered wrong? Would you have preferred a beer instead?'

Karan picked up his glass and threw the contents in Minx's face. People at adjoining tables stopped chattering and stared. Minx picked up a pink napkin and calmly mopped her forehead.

'I hate waste,' she said to Karan. 'If you didn't want the drink you could've given it to me. Good booze down the drain. Didn't your parents teach you anything?'

Karan couldn't believe Minx's cool. She spoke again. 'We could be—should be—friends, you know, Karan. We have so much in common. We even share a passion. You love her. I love her. Let's face it. It seems silly not to collaborate.'

Fourteen

Amrita had sunk into a deep depression after Lola's 'accident'. She dropped out of two shoots which had immediately been scooped up by a relatively new model. Sheila warned her, 'Snap out of it. If you slop around the house like this, you'll find yourself without fresh assignments. Stop moaning and groaning. Come on, let's go shopping. That should cheer us up.'

Reluctantly, Amrita went off to her room to change out her of old jeans and wear something perkier. These days it was difficult for her to move around anonymously in the city. Each time she stopped at a traffic signal, people from adjoining cars would nudge, wink and occasionally call out her name. She had spent a small fortune getting an enormous pair of Paloma Picasso sunglasses. Not that they helped. She slid into a pink knit mini that an air-hostess friend of Sheila's had brought back from New York. Sheila whistled when she saw her emerge from her room. 'Look at those legs!'

she sighed. 'I'll never be able to wear something like that and get away with it.' She patted her thighs, 'It's time to make my peace with them . . . but ugh! I can't stand the bulge.'

Amrita came over and patted her bottom, 'I may have great legs—but look at this. A perfect derrière—isn't that what the agencies call it?'

Sheila laughed lightly, 'Come on, let's get out of here.'

'Where to?' Sheila asked, as they slid out of the complex and on to the highway.

'Anywhere,' Amrita said moodily. Her mind was on Minx. She had been very quiet since the Lola incident. Amrita figured she was lying low. Possibly ashamed of herself or, at least, of confronting Amrita. No phone calls. No flowers. No cards. It was almost scary.

Sheila broke into her thoughts. 'It's great to be driving around like old times without that pest following us around,' she said after glancing into the rear-view mirror. Amrita nodded. She asked herself whether she was relieved . . . or a little disappointed. Had Minx found someone else? Was she out of town? Sick? Or just plain uninterested? Quickly, she got rid of the thought and concentrated on the road ahead of them. Without a warning she announced, 'My treat. Let's go eat a whopping meal at a fancy restaurant somewhere.'

Sheila's eyebrows shot up. 'With me dressed like this? It's bad enough nobody glances in my direction when we're together—and today, with you in your sexy, hot pink mini, I'll probably be mistaken for your maid.'

Amrita laughed, 'Oh shut up and stop fishing,' she said, 'you know you look gorgeous in anything . . . even in your housecoat. I'm the one who has to wear DK gear to attract attention.'

The restaurant was packed when they entered. They managed to squeeze into a corner table. It was a newly opened Chinese place which specialized in unusual roasts and salads. The crowd that hung around there represented the ad, art and theatre worlds.

Sheila whispered, 'What are we doing in this pseud joint?'

'Being seen,' Amrita whispered back. They ordered two beers and sat back to stare at the other tables.

It was Sheila who spotted Minx first. Without a warning she let out a small shriek and clutched Amrita's hand. 'She's here!' she said.

Without turning around, Amrita knew who it was.

'And he's here too!' Sheila exclaimed.

That's when Amrita got interested enough to ask, 'Who?'

'Karan,' Sheila continued in an excited whisper, 'they're together.'

'What?' Amrita cried, 'Can't be. What the hell could they be doing together? Don't make it obvious . . . just watch for a while and check. Have they seen us yet?'

Sheila shook her head. They're sitting in one of those tiny cabins and seem totally engrossed in conversation.'

'Let's pay for the beers and get out of here,' Amrita said. Suddenly, she had lost interest in the outing.

Sheila was in no mood to budge. 'Rubbish. Just relax. They don't own the place. Why should we spoil our fun?'

'What fun?' Amrita said tiredly, adding, 'maybe I should get away for a few days. Go to Delhi. Meet my parents.'

The waiter was hovering around impatiently. It was peak hour and tables were in great demand. Sheila placed the order before Amrita could change her mind and leave. It was while they were polishing off their plate of spare ribs that Amrita felt the unmistakable touch of Minx's fingers on her bare shoulder. 'Following us around?' she asked, her eyes gleaming behind her lightly-tinted aviator glasses.

Amrita stared up to see Karan watching her silently. Minx linked her arm through his and said, 'Surprised? To see us together, I mean?'

Amrita tried to feign indifference. She fooled around with the chopsticks and picked up a won ton with deliberate delicacy.

Minx reached across and took the chopsticks away from her saying, 'No. No. No. Not good. Not good. Think of your figure, sweetheart.'

Without meaning to, Amrita pushed her hand away sharply, upsetting a bowl full of steaming soup. Sheila immediately got up and busied herself mopping the mess up while the Chinese lady at the counter came up to see what was going on. Karan had not spoken a word till then. Now Amrita saw him speaking softly to the woman, who nodded and bowed, before going back to the counter. Within minutes she was back with the bill. 'Get up,' he said firmly to Amrita, 'we've got to talk.'

Sheila started to protest, 'Hey! I'm not through yet.'

'Yes, you are,' Minx said as Karan and she steered Amrita through the crowded tables and out of the restaurant.

*

The sun blazed down on them outside. Amrita blinked in the bright light as they stood near the jeep with Sheila still complaining about her ruined afternoon. 'Let's go where we won't be disturbed,' Minx suggested smoothly. 'How about your place, Karan?'

He shook his head. Sheila pulled out her car-keys and announced, 'I'm getting out of here. I don't need this weird scene.'

Minx looked at her briefly and said, 'Get lost.'

Karan caught her just as she was about to cross the road. 'Not so fast,' he said, gripping her arm savagely.

'We need you for this. You are a part of our plan. You are involved, whether you like it or not.'

Seeing her puzzled expression, Minx clarified, 'The day you took Amrita into your house, your fate was sealed. I thought you'd understood that.'

Sheila was beginning to look scared.

Karan released her, 'Don't worry, Sheila. Nobody is going to hurt you. All we want to do is talk. That's all.'

Seeing that Minx was busy with the jeep's ignition Amrita turned to Karan. 'Since when have you and she become friends? Don't you know what she did to Lola?'

Karan looked at Amrita and said with a short laugh, 'What she did to Lola? You should be telling me what you did to her. Who are you kidding?'

Amrita was too shocked to say anything. She heard the jeep's engine come to life and saw Minx signalling to them to climb in. Sheila and she exchanged glances before they got in.

'Where are you taking us?' Sheila asked.

'Not too far,' Minx replied as she put the jeep into gear and tore down the road.

Twenty minutes later they were on the tip of South Bombay, in the secluded cantonment area. 'Nobody will disturb us here,' Minx said as she pulled up near a magnificent old church. 'Let's take a walk around the graveyard at the back.'

It was cool and leafy where they were. Amrita could taste the salt spray on her tongue as a light afternoon breeze rustled through the trees surrounding them.

'Beautiful, isn't it?' Karan asked dourly, gazing up at the imposing spires. Slanting rays of sunlight illuminated the enormous stained-glass windows as the four of them entered the cavernous structure.

'Let's take a pew,' Minx suggested, 'and forget the graveyard. It's too morbid.'

Karan nodded his head in agreement, 'Great location for a kinky fashion spread,' he mumbled casting his eyes around the place.

Amrita shivered.

'Cold, sweetheart?' Minx asked, putting her arm around Amrita's shoulder.

She shrugged her off and said, 'Let's finish what we're here for.'

Minx looked at Karan, 'You first,' she said, 'I'll take a stroll outside and smoke a ciggie . . . can't do that in here. Mother Mary is anti-fags—ha! ha!' She took Sheila by the arm saying, 'Come on, girlie, let's go. These two need their privacy.'

Once they were gone, Karan caught hold of Amrita and said urgently, 'You've got to get out of Bombay. Fast!'

Amrita searched his face, 'Whose side are you on, anyway?'

Karan looked deep into her eyes and said fervently, 'Trust me. I'm on your side and your side alone. Not just for now, but for life. Yes, it's true, Amrita, and you have to take my word for it. My conduct over the next few minutes may appear strange to you. But it is for your good. You have to believe that and keep your faith. I can never hurt you. But this woman is dangerous. I'm playing along with her for your sake. I want to protect you. To be there in case she does something crazy, you understand? This way, she thinks I'm an ally. I want her to start depending on me, confiding in me. Something's going to happen. And very soon at that. I'm just on the verge of a breakthrough. It's matter of a few more weeks. And then she'll tell me everything. All her plans. No secrets. No surprises. I want her to think I'm with her in this.'

Amrita could not figure out what Karan was trying to tell her. But there was no time to lose. Minx would be back any minute and it was possible they would not get another chance like this again. 'Karan . . . help me . . . save me from her, 'Amrita pleaded.

'That's exactly what I'm doing, baby, but I can't explain too much. I need Minx to trust me first. If my behaviour seems strange in future, remember this conversation. And also remember that we are in the house of God. I wouldn't lie to you in His presence.'

Amrita was crying softly, as Minx re-entered with Sheila. 'Good God! Karan, have you been torturing the poor thing?' she asked, rushing up to Amrita.

Karan smiled a sardonic smile, 'Not exactly,' he said out of the corner of his mouth, 'just telling her what's good for her, that's all.'

Minx stared at the two of them suspiciously. 'That's good, that's good!' she said, tapping her feet and calculating her next move. 'Right!' she announced, 'now that we've all become friends, let's make it official.' She pulled out a Swiss army knife from her trouser pocket, and with a quick flick of her wrist, cut herself close to her watch-strap. Fascinatedly, the others watched fresh red blood ooze out. When a sufficient amount had dripped down the length of her arm, she placed her thumb over it till it was covered in red. Dramatically, she turned to Amrita and said, 'With this blood, I pledge my life to you in the presence of these two witnesses.'

Before Amrita could react, she smeared her forehead with blood and put some more in the parting of her hair. While Amrita and the others stood motionless, Minx went and prostrated herself in front of the altar. Karan's face was stony when she returned. They walked out of the church like zombies.

Once outside, Minx said to Karan, 'I suppose you told her how the whole thing is a pantomime . . . and how you have been forced to act like you're my friend and confidant. Don't bother to deny it, darling. It's all right. Everything is going according to plan—even your betrayal. The point is: who is double-crossing whom?'

And then she looked sadly at Amrita, who was shaking in fear.

From a distance, they saw the priest making his way to the church. It was time for the evening service. As they got back into the jeep, they heard the bells pealing. Minx crossed herself as they got back into the car and Karan whispered 'Amen' into Amrita's ear.

Fifteen

Two days later, Amrita was talking nervously to Sheila from the Bombay airport departure lounge. 'Remember, don't let on when I left or where I've gone. Promise?'

Sheila kept assuring her that she would not. 'You don't know what Minx is capable of . . . she . . . she . . . might even hurt you to get the info out of you.'

Sheila laughed, 'You relax, yaar. Don't worry. This time she won't be able to try any of her tricks. My boyfriend gets in tonight, You haven't met him yet, but nobody messes with Vicky.'

Amrita heard her flight being announced and rang off. She paid the extra amount to get herself an executive class ticket. What she did not need was co-passengers striking up a conversation with her. After her photographs had appeared on the cover of News Asia, which had hailed her as the decade's supermodel, it had become impossible for her to travel incognito. That, and the interviews she had done for two popular video-magazines.

She did not enjoy flying. And this particular flight at the crack of dawn saw her at her worst. Bleary-eyed and preoccupied, she did not notice the man in the next seat till the stewardess reached across him to offer her a tray full of sweets. 'A glass of water, please,' Amrita said and went back to fussing with her several packages. While accepting the glass, she accidentally tipped it over, and drenched the person beside her. 'Oh my God!' she said with an embarrassed cry, 'I am so terribly sorry.'

Very carefully, the man recapped his black Mont Blanc pen, took off his Cartier reading glasses, reached for a freshly laundered hanky and turned to her, 'Well, Ms Aggarwal, I needn't feel sorry about skipping my shower this morning,' he said in a voice that was deep, resonant and faintly accented.

Still flustered, she grabbed hold of a corner of her chiffon dupatta and began mopping the water off his chest, apologizing profusely. The man held her off with a soft, 'Don't bother, it's only a shirt. It will dry.'

She looked up into a pair of very amused, nut-brown eyes. She noticed the crinkly lines at the corners and the sprinkling of grey in his thick hair. He was probably in his mid-forties, she figured, as she composed herself and wondered whether her eyes were looking puffy. 'You are so much better looking than your photographs,' the stranger carried on, 'they don't do you the slightest justice.' Amrita was used to that line. Somehow, she had hoped he would say something slightly more original. 'Thanks,' she said briefly and began flipping through a film glossy.

'Don't read that trash,' he said, 'take a look at this instead.' He handed her a copy of Weekend, a newly launched news-magazine that had created one controversy after another with sensational scoops designed to embarrass the government.

'I edit it,' he said, holding out his hand. 'My name is Parthasarthy—but my friends call me Partha.'

Amrita had heard of him, but only vaguely. She had no idea at all that he was this attractive or this young. She had thought he would be close to sixty, paunchy, bald and boring. Tempted to tell him that, but nevertheless feeling shy, she said awkwardly, 'I've seen your name in the papers but I don't read your magazine. I don't understand politics . . . and frankly, I'm not terribly interested either.'

'You don't have to explain,' Partha smiled, 'at your age you should be concentrating on looking beautiful and having fun. Except that this particular morning you are looking beautiful all right . . . but oh, so miserable.'

Amrita stared at him coldly. 'Just tired.'

He held up his hands, 'Ouch!' Partha said in mock pain. 'That hurt. It's my turn to apologize. It really isn't any of my business. I guess I was jealous and showed it.'

Amrita asked, 'Jealous? What about?'

He reached for his burgundy coloured Dunhill briefcase and pulled out a copy of News Asia. 'Because my rival beat me to you—that's why,' he said tapping the cover.

Amrita laughed, 'Oh that! OK. Let's make a deal. I'll make it up to you for spilling water on your new shirt—yes, I know it's new, you've forgotten to remove the label.'

While Partha hastily tore off the tiny price tag, Amrita continued, 'I'll do a set of exclusive pictures—maybe a fashion spread—for you. For free. How do you like the idea?'

'You've got it. Deal,' said Partha extending his hand. 'Our head office is in Delhi—and I see that's where you are headed. Here's my card.'

Amrita took it and held out her hand.

'What do you need?' Partha asked.

'A pen . . .to write my Delhi address and phone number. I don't have business cards.'

Partha fished out a smart Cartier pocket note-pad and gave it to her. Amrita scribbled quickly and handed it back to him.

'Good,' Partha said, 'so we're in business, then.'

There was a long pause. Amrita did not plan on having breakfast. She rummaged around in her voluminous handbag and pulled out an eye mask. 'I need some sleep,' she said before dozing off.

When she awoke an hour later, Partha was across the aisle in another seat, deep in conversation with a high-powered industrialist. She watched him groggily with a smile on her lips. Yes, she concluded, this Mr Parthasarthy was definitely one hell of an attractive man.

Sixteen

Amrita's parents had not been informed of her arrival and there was nobody at the airport to receive her. Mr Parthasarthy left the plane as soon as he landed and she watched him striding out briskly, swinging his bag as he walked towards a slim, elegant woman waiting for him. It had been an interesting encounter, Amrita thought to herself as she waited for her luggage.

She hailed a cab outside the airport and gave her address. Already she felt differently about Delhi. The cabbie spoke Punjabi and hearing the language of her childhood brought a smile to her lips. She hadn't spoken it in months herself. She wondered how her parents and brothers would react on seeing her unexpectedly. It was a short ride to Vasant Vihar—perhaps ten minutes from the airport at that hour, no more. She felt her heart thump as she spotted the neat bungalow. She was surprised to see the family lined up near the gate as if they were all waiting for her. As the cab pulled up, her brothers ran towards it excitedly. Before it could stop, they had half opened the door and dragged Amrita out.

'How the hell did you know I was coming?' she asked laughing and crying at the same time. She was caught up in their bear hugs and could see her mother fluttering around while her father paid off the cabbie and took charge of her bags. 'Your friend from Bombay—that nice, young girl who takes recipes from me—called ten minutes ago to say you were on your way. By the time your brothers got through to the airport to check on your flight, the plane had landed . . . we decided to wait for you here . . . .' her mother explained, fussing over her, gazing at her slimmer-than-ever form with a worried frown on her face. Amrita's eyes betrayed her nervousness at the mention of Minx. A look which her father was quick to notice. But she determinedly flung away all thoughts of Minx. It felt wonderful to be back and as Amrita ran towards her old room, she felt she hadn't really been away at all—everything was just the same—the smells and sights she knew and loved. The servants emerged from the kitchen to greet her as the dog circled her, and yelped with excitement. She picked up Poochie and held him hard. She switched on the light in her room and stepped back with a small shock—her bed was covered with roses—heaps and heaps of long-stemmed, blood-red roses. That wasn't her mother's style at all. In any case, she wouldn't have had the time to organize it since Amrita's visit was a surprise. Only one person could be behind this, only one.

Amrita found her brother standing by her side looking at the flowers with a huge grin on his face, 'You must have got a really big chamcha in Bombay, yaar,' he said, shaking his head. 'Just five minutes before your taxi arrived, some fellow drove up in a fancy car. He asked whether you'd arrived and when Mummy said no, he went to the limo and came back with his arms full of these . . . must've cost a bomb. We tried to count and calculate.'

Amrita's expression was grim. Finally, she burst out, 'Didn't you people ask him who he was and all that? Any stranger can walk into this house and leave junk for me, huh?'

Her brother looked hurt and puzzled. 'Hey, hey, hey. Take it easy, kid,' he said. 'What's the matter with you? Any other chick would've been flattered. The man was bringing flowers, not snakes. Besides, Dad spoke to him.'

'Yes? And what did he say . . . go on, tell me, I'm interested,' Amrita went on, her expression steely.

By then Amrish had been joined by Ashish. The two of them exchanged looks, shrugged and went off to summon their mother. She came rushing up to see what the crisis was about. Amrita was sitting on her bed and crying as she threw the flowers off it.

Gently, her mother came and sat down next to her. 'What's the matter, darling?' she asked.

Amrita could not stop the tears. Safe in the haven of her mother's arms she let herself go like she used to when she was a child. She sobbed uncontrollably for several minutes while her mother held her tenderly and stroked her hair.

After regaining her composure Amrita spluttered, 'Mummy, please don't accept flowers or gifts or anything from strangers. You don't even know who sent these—it could've been anyone . . . it could've been someone dangerous.'

Amrita felt her mother stiffen and she knew she had said the wrong thing. She hadn't meant to scare her this way. Immediately, she wiped her tears and smiled, 'I'm sorry, Mummy, it's just that Bombay is such a different place. Nobody trusts anybody there. People are so suspicious of strangers. I suppose I've become a pucca Bombaywalli myself. Forget it.'

Seeing the obvious relief on her face, Amrita pulled her mother close and kissed her. 'Aren't you going to offer me lassi and paranthas? See, I've been away from home for a few months and you've already started neglecting me.'

Her mother shot up and rushed to the kitchen, yelling at the servants for delaying breakfast.

*

Minx woke her up the next morning.

'Call from Bombay,' Amrita heard her brother's voice as he thumped on her bedroom door. Amrita thought she was dreaming. She pulled on her gown and rushed into the living-room. It was past nine o'clock. She had overslept as usual. But what a deep, wonderful sleep she had enjoyed!

'How's my angel? Bombay isn't the same without you, baby,' she heard Minx croon. She was tempted to bang the receiver down but decided against it—she could see her father watching her over the edge of the Hindustan Times. Amrita decided to play it cool. She tried to keep her voice calm and the conversation natural, as Minx chatted away.

'Like the flowers? I'm sorry I couldn't organize chrysanthemums. Delhi has gorgeous blooms at this time of the year but you left at such short notice. Anyway, enjoy yourself, darling. Relax and get back some colour into your pale cheeks. You need the break. Don't worry about things in Bombay. They'll be taken care of. Nobody can grab your assignments. I won't let them. Neither will Karan. Besides, you know very well it's impossible to replace you.'

Amrita listened in stony silence, remembering to keep her face as expressionless as possible. After about five minutes Minx rang off cheerily. Amrita replaced the receiver and faced her father. He was obviously waiting for an explanation.

'She's a friend, Meenakshi, you know . . . from one of the agencies,' Amrita said shortly.

'You mean Meenakshi Iyengar? Was that her on the line? We know her . . . . Charming girl. Just charming. Well-mannered, too. Mummy has her number. Whenever we feel a little worried and can't reach you, we talk to your friend. She knows everything—where you are, when you'll be back and all that. You were lucky to make such a friend in that city. I'd heard nobody has time for anybody there.'

Amrita nodded her head, 'That's true,' she said sardonically, 'but I seem to find people with all the time in the world.'

Her father smiled broadly, 'That's because you are special; people like you. They always have.'

'Sure,' Amrita said and went back into her own room for a bath.

*

Sheila spoke to her three days later. 'The cops were here, Amrita,' she told her.

'What on earth for?' Amrita asked.

'I can't tell you too much over the phone . . . but they were asking questions—funny questions. About you and Lola. She's still bad. But talking. They've got her statement.'

Amrita's mind was racing. 'Tell me briefly what Lola has told them.'

'She said it was a woman who did it. A tall, slim woman in a sari . . . with long hair and large sunglasses.'

Amrita feigned surprise, 'God! Wonder who that could be? Can you think of anyone who fits that description?'

Sheila paused before replying, 'I don't know how to say this, but they seem to think it's you.'

'Rubbish!' Amrita burst out. 'Didn't you tell them it wasn't me, that it couldn't be me? We were together at home when it happened, remember?'

'Yes, I know all that. But I'm scared, Amrita. These guys are funny types. My boyfriend's getting mad at me. He keeps asking, "Why are you getting mixed up in all this?" I don't know what to do.'

Amrita sensed Sheila was trying to tell her something but did not know how to put it. The heat was being turned on, and she realized Sheila did not want to get involved. 'Look,' she told her, 'just tell them to get off your back. Say you have nothing to do with it or me. I'm sorry it's become so messy. But you also know I had nothing to do with Lola's attack. Just tell them that, that's all.'

Sheila hesitated. 'They're getting pretty tough around here. I . . . I . . . don't know how to tell you . . . but maybe you should stick around in Delhi . . . till. . . till. . . you find another place for yourself in Bombay. I'm really sorry, Amrita. But my boyfriend's mad as hell. He wants you out. Actually, Minx came over after I called her. . . .'

Amrita exploded, 'Why the hell did you phone that woman of all people?'

'I didn't know what to do . . . whom to call. My boyfriend told me to remove your things from here. What could I do? I didn't want to just chuck them out on the street. Minx was very helpful. She packed everything carefully. Nothing's missing . . . I'm sorry, darling, but I didn't have a choice.' Sheila disconnected before Amrita could say anything more.

So that was it. There was no place for her go to in Bombay. and no one to turn to—except Minx.

*

Amrita's mother sensed something was terribly amiss with her daughter and asked her gently about it. They were alone, out in the small patch of lawn behind the house. The mali was busy pulling out radishes from the vegetable beds lining the hedge. The boys were away—one with the father, the other at college. It was a time both Amrita and her mother had generally enjoyed in the past—chatting companionably over nimbu-pani, her mother absorbed in her knitting, with Amrita chattering away about nothing in particular. Today, the atmosphere was tense as Amrita stared moodily into the far distance.

'Aren't you feeling well?' her mother asked, not wanting to push her too much. Amrita was reluctant to tell her family about the strange developments in her life. She was certain they would prevent her from going back to Bombay or insist on one of the brothers accompanying her. Amrita did not want them to discover the ugly truth about Minx, Lola or even Sheila. This was something she wanted to sort out on her own. But it was not going to be easy. Karan, the one person she had begun to trust implicitly was beginning to send out mixed signals. Still, Amrita longed to talk to him, if only to ask him what to do about getting back to Bombay and work. All those pending assignments, all the money still to collect. Amrita was not through with Bombay. Her mind raced on, trying to think up some excuse for her present state, something to divert her mother's concern.

Fortunately both of them were spared the ordeal of engaging in a meaningless conversation by the sound of the phone.

'I'll get it,' Amrita said, jumping up. 'Hello?' she said without much enthusiasm.

'Am I speaking to the vision in white on Flight 406 last morning?' the voice asked smoothly. She recognized it as Partha's immediately.

'Oh . . . it's you,' she said with a light laugh.

'Disappointed?' he asked.

'No, just surprised,' Amrita replied.

'OK—business first. We'd like to run a profile on you for our Sunday supplement. It's not really my job to call and fix up these sort of features, but I couldn't resist. Besides, I suggested the story at our edit meet this morning. Game?'

Amrita paused, 'What does it involve?' she asked.

'Well, no money, for starters. But plenty of prestige. You'll see when it appears. I'm certain you'll be able to double your charges.'

'Who's going to do it?' Amrita continued.

'My word, you sure are a toughie,' Partha teased, 'most people jump the moment they hear we're interested in featuring them.'

'I'm not "most people",' Amrita said quietly, adding, 'besides, I don't need the publicity. I already have far too much of it for my own good.'

'Is that right? Well, why don't you tell me all about it over lunch?'

Amrita thought quickly. It was one way of getting away from her mother's questioning. Besides, she did find Partha more than a little attractive.

'One o'clock at Valentino's,' she announced and rang off.

*

He was sitting at a corner table when she walked in. She was wearing a beige linen suit. It was a particularly flattering outfit, tailored by a Bombay designer known for his great cuts. No matter that all he did was take apart imported Rodeo Drive boutique outfits and recreate them in his workshop. Amrita had shelled out close to six thousand rupees for it but had been told it was a good investment. 'Darling, you must dress the part,' Raoul had purred when she went for a fitting. 'You are a supermodel and you must look like one. Younger people think of you as a role model—they want to dress the same way, project the same image. You have a responsibility.' Not entirely convinced, but wildly tempted, Amrita had gone along and settled for the expensive suit.

Seeing the appreciative gleam in Partha's eyes, she knew she had not wasted her money. 'You look fabulous,' he said, rising to greet her. She surveyed his studiedly casual jeans and T-shirt and said dryly, 'Is this how successful editors dress for power lunches?'

Partha struck a comic pose, 'Actually, I'm marking time in this profession. My secret ambition is to join the movies after a sucessful stint as a supermodel. How does that sound to you?'

'Phoney,' Amrita said shortly and sank into her chair.

'You really are disgustingly, obscenely beautiful, and you know it,' Partha said, staring hard at Amrita's freshly-scrubbed face, with just a hint of kohl in the eyes. Her hair was pushed off her face into a carelessly knotted bun through which she had stuck a couple of enamelled chopsticks. Shoulder-length earrings made out of uneven wooden beads formed her only fashion accessories. The handbag was a Tussard knock-off bought in Bombay's Daboo Street (which managed to fool even discerning Italian buyers with its impeccable craftsmanship lavished on copies of designer leatherwear). Accustomed to admiring glances and reactions, Amrita handled the compliment coolly.

Partha spread his large, square hands on the heavy pink damask tablecloth. 'Right, let's get down to business. This is a working lunch after all.'

Amrita regarded him evenly. 'Speak for yourself. I'm here to enjoy the meal,' she said.

Partha's eyebrows shot up. 'Is that meant as the come-on of the year?'

Amrita laughed and shook her head, dislodging one of the chopsticks, 'Far from it. I'd heard so much about the food in this place, I was looking forward to sampling it, that's about all.'

Partha ordered expertly and briskly. It turned out he had been a foreign correspondent for years, with stints in Rome and Paris, and knew a lot about European food. It was obvious he fancied himself a gourmet. While he was discussing the wine with the waiter, Amrita excused herself to go to the ladies' room.

Right outside the entrance of the ladies' room the heel of her shoe broke unexpectedly and she found herself tottering precariously on the polished granite floor with nothing to reach out for but a delicate potted plant. Just as she thought she was going for a toss, she felt a firm hand steadying her. Amrita tensed instinctively at the familiar touch. Her eyes dilated with fear as she heard Minx say, 'Take it easy, kid!'

Amrita turned around, clutching her ankle, which after being suddenly twisted, felt painful. 'My God!' she said, 'can't you leave me alone?' Her eyes were smarting with tears.

Minx was dressed uncharacteristically in a smart khadi salwar kameez. She smiled before saying quietly, 'I'm not following you, darling. I'm in Delhi to settle some business, that's all. Our meeting expectedly like this is generally referred to as a coincidence.'

'Rubbish,' Amrita said, 'nothing you do is a coincidence. You're spying on me . . . making me miserable . . . what do you get out of torturing me like this? Tell me, dammit!'

Minx continued to support Amrita, as the two of them stood around awkwardly. 'Darling, you need a new pair of shoes before you limp back to your date,' Minx whispered, leaning close to her. Amrita tried to push her away and, in the process, lost her balance and sprawled out on the shiny floor. Two people helped her up—Partha and Minx.

He spoke first. 'I was wondering whether you'd got lost in the loo or changed your mind about lunching with me,' he said, hanging on to Amrita's elbow.

Minx moved away a little and watched them silently. Amrita, feeling awfully flustered, attempted an introduction. Partha took care of it smoothly, leaning across to shake hands with Minx. Amrita butted in, 'She's an old friend . . . from Bombay.'

Partha turned to her and said, 'Great! Why don't we get her to join the party in that case?'

Amrita shook her head violently and started to say, 'No, she's busy with something else,' but Minx interjected swiftly, 'Lovely idea! I've always wanted to eat here . . . but somehow my mad schedules in Delhi leave me no time for such indulgences.'

*

Amrita could barely put away a morsel as she listened to Partha and Minx chatting away like they were old college buddies. Suddenly she had become the interloper—the unwelcome guest. She sipped her wine and nibbled on bite-sized onion loaves, while Minx held forth on the corrupt babus of North Block and how difficult it was to move a file from Table 'A' to Table 'B'. Partha was obviously intrigued by Minx. Finally, he asked her, 'This sounds rude, but we journalists aren't known for our refined ways—what exactly is it that you do?'

Minx replied easily, 'Oh! I am a professional fixer. People prefer politer terms like "liaison person", but basically, I get things to happen for my clients—licences, permits, grants—I'm sure you know what I'm talking about. I take them through the whole dirty route as efficiently as possible.'

'I see,' Partha said, an interested gleam in his eyes. They fell into an animated discussion leaving Amrita to play with the pasta on her plate and wonder what she was doing there. At one point she heard Partha asking Minx, 'What if I were to suggest a story—either you write it, or we get someone to do it. I'd be happy to carry a first-person account of how an important document moves in a ministry. I'd like to track it from its origin in Bombay till it gets to the top dog for its final signature. The whole bit, complete with bribes, big and small. Think you could do it?'

Minx lit up a Cartier after offering Partha one and leaned back in her elegant chair. 'It depends,' she said thoughtfully. 'I have done a bit of writing off and on—but these days my focus has shifted.'

Partha pushed a little but not too much. He switched his attention to Amrita abruptly and said, 'And how do you know this divine creature. Isn't she exceptional?'

Minx leaned forward and brushed Amrita's cheek with the back of her fingers. 'She is truly special—one of a kind. We are old friends. Amrita is a kid . . . a baby . . . far too trusting. Bombay is a big, bad city. I'm her guardian angel.'

Partha laughed, 'Really? Well, well. I got the impression this young lady can take pretty good care of herself.'

Minx replied, 'You don't know her. Very few people do. She is like a fragile flower.'

Partha's eyebrows shot up. In a sardonic voice he added 'Fragile flower, did you say? Any particular one?'

'Yes,' Minx continued, 'a rare and precious saffron flower. Have you ever seen one in bloom?'

Partha shook his head.

'I have,' Minx said 'and from the very first moment that I saw Amrita, I knew that's what she reminded me of—a delicate, perfectly formed, saffron flower—valued for the fragrance it releases when its stamin is crushed.'

Partha winced and Amrita blushed deeply. 'Ugh! That's one hell of an analogy,' Partha shuddered, 'but I get the picture.'

They were drinking coffee and Amrita was dying to go home. Partha looked at her cheerfully and said, 'So, saffron flower, are you all set for our shoot?'

Amrita nodded, while Minx mussed her hair affectionately. 'My little baby is looking so tired. Tell you what—I'll drop her off and you go back to your edit meet. I believe you have one coming up in the next fifteen minutes.'

Partha shot her a surprised look. 'Who told you that?'

Minx got up and straightened the creases out of her outfit. 'I'm a fixer, remember? I make it my business to know everything about every one.'

Partha paid with a card and escorted the two women out. He was obviously taken a little off-balance by Minx's last remark. 'I'll be damned,' he muttered under his breath as the three of them waited for their cars.

'By the way,' Minx added, 'while you were at lunch, a Cabinet Minister resigned. Another two are expected to follow suit. Perhaps the government fell while we were on the third course. It's possible a new P.M. was installed over coffee. You'd better rush back before the revolution begins.'

*

Amrita's mother greeted Minx warmly referring to her as 'beti' and giving her an affectionate hug. Amrita went to the kitchen to fetch some water and found her brother there.

'How come Mummy knows my friend from Bombay?' she asked, trying to keep her voice casual.

He looked at her with surprise. 'We all know her. She was here this morning and she's the one who calls and gives us news about you when you don't write for weeks. She's a cool girl. I didn't know speople in that crummy city were so friendly.'

Amrita refrained from speaking out aloud, and Minx joined them a moment later.

'Hi!' she greeted Amrish, 'you're looking good, kid!' she said adjusting his T-shirt. Amrish blushed, looking immensely pleased.

Minx took Amrita by the hand. 'Let's go and relax in your room—there's so much to talk about.'

Pointedly, Amrita said to her, 'I thought you had a couple of appointments this afternoon.'

Minx shrugged, 'No sweat. I can cancel them. They weren't that important.'

She strolled into Amrita's room and stretched out on her bed with her arms behind her head. 'Notice something?' she asked, searching Amrita's face.

Amrita was busy staring moodily at her own reflection in the dressing-table mirror, picking at an imaginary pimple. She could see Minx's prone form clearly from the tiny stool in front of the dresser. 'No,' she replied shortly and went back to the pimple.

'Look again . . . look more closely . . . .' Minx urged, holding her arms out. Amrita turned around and stared, her eyes blank. 'Nothing,' she said stonily. 'I don't notice a thing.'

In one swift move, Minx pulled off her cool khadi kurta, kicking the door to Amrita's room shut before Amrita could reach it and run out. Minx stood against it, feet apart, forcing Amrita to face her. She wasn't wearing a bra. She never did. Amrita had seen her taut nipples through the form-fitting sweat-shirts she frequently wore. Minx raised her arms and put her hands under Amrita's chin. 'Look carefully, darling . . . after all, I did this for you,' she whispered. Amrita kept her eyes averted. She couldn't get herself to look at Minx like this. Gently, Minx picked up Amrita's limp hand, prised open her palm and stretched open her forefinger. Guiding her hand, she traced a line over a jagged scar which began under her breasts and went all the way under the armpit. 'Feel this . . . it's still tender. Do you know what it is?'

Amrita lifted her eyes to look more carefully at what her finger had been over. She took in her breath sharply saying, 'Oh my God! Did someone hurt you?'

Minx laughed softly, 'No, sweetheart. Nobody hurt me. Maybe I hurt myself. I thought it would make you happy.'

Still puzzled, Amrita stared hard at the raw, angry red wound and noticed an identical one under the other breast. 'Still don't know what I've done?' Minx asked. Amrita shook her head. It was horrible sight. Minx led her to the bed and said, 'Sit down. I'll tell you.' And then she explained to her slowly and patiently, 'It's a tits-job. Where do you think I'd gone for a fortnight? Why do you think I wasn't in touch, wasn't around? Well . . . most women go to this plastic surgeon for cosmetic surgery to enhance their breasts—boy! I could give you a few names—but I actually asked him to reduce mine. You know, slice them off. Don't ask me why, but I got the feeling you didn't like them—that their huge size put you off. I didn't like them either. When I was a teenager, I used to try my best to tie them down. But . . . my father . . . yes . . . that pervert . . . he used to fondle them constantly and tell me how beautiful they were . . . I began to really hate my breasts after that. Maybe I blamed them for whatever was happening between me and my father. I used to curse myself and think that had they been smaller this horrible thing would never have happened.'

Amrita had started at the sight of Minx with her shirt off and those uneven red scars on her chest were making her feel sick. But she felt pity too, and perversely, for the first time, a feeling of sympathy for the wretched woman before her. She heard Minx's voice cracking as she carried on, 'And then I met you . . . fell in love. A love so intense I felt my body would burst. I thought I saw revulsion in your eyes when you looked at me, especially when I thought I saw you staring at my ugly enormous breasts. Two weeks ago I decided to chop them off. Believe me, baby, it wasn't easy. I was scared. I could tell no one, consult no one. But each time I was nervous and tense about the step I was going to take, I thought of you and the expression in your eyes. And then I knew I had to do it. And I knew you'd like what I'd done. Like me, also.'

Amrita began to cry, it was all getting to be too much for her.

'Don't cry, my darling . . . please don't. I can't bear to see you unhappy. And don't blame yourself either. It was something I had to do . . .for myself as much as for you.' Minx held Amrita close and they stayed that way for what seemed like hours. It was dark outside when they finally disengaged. Minx switched on the bedside lamp and fell on the bed pulling Amrita down next to her, She kissed her puffy, tear-streaked eyes and stroked her face, soothing her . . . lulling her.

Amrita lay back against the pillows inertly. Her mind switched into a dream-like state. She shut her eyes and ceased to think or feel, surrendering to Minx who was over her, moving her hands tenderly along the length of her body, caressing her face, kissing her softly. She felt Minx's fingers unbuttoning her linen jacket . . . and she did not resist.

Minx removed her clothes one by one and placed them neatly on a chair close to the bed. Amrita was suddenly conscious, very conscious, of Minx's touch as each nerve-ending in her body came alive under her probing fingers and tongue. The crickets outside her window set up a noisy chorus as Amrita struggled not to lose herself entirely to what was happening to her. Minx had taken each one of her toes into her mouth and was massaging them with her tongue, while her hands reached between Amrita's legs and touched her with teasing, rhythmic stabs. She felt her legs open almost voluntarily, as Minx climbed upon her, straddling her slim hips with her own, covering her breasts with her hands, cupping the nipples and circling them repeatedly till they ached with a sweet pain. Amrita had never known anything like this . . . never. She moaned with pleasure as Minx brought her to a peak, again and again, starting where she'd left off each time she felt Amrita's body going slack under her. After what must have been two hours, they finally fell into a light sleep with Amrita's head cradled in the crook of Minx's arm, their legs entangled.

Seventeen

A loud knock on the door asking them if they were eating in, woke Minx and Amrita out of their deep slumber. Hastily, Amrita pulled on a caftan, leaving Minx to rush into the bathroom with her things. They hadn't had the chance to speak to each other.

At the dining-table Amrita's mother scolded them for being late and keeping the family waiting, 'I've asked the cook to make palak-mutton for you and her . . . and there's rabdi later,' she grumbled, busying herself serving all of them.

It was already late and, sensibly, Minx decided to leave right after dinner. Amrita spent the night uneasily, tormented by the new experience. It was not as if she hadn't encountered girls like Minx at school—but that had been different. More playful and innocent. Somehow, somewhere deep down inside her, Amrita knew she was trapped. There was no escaping Minx now. And that was what made her recoil and cringe. No escape.

None at all. Her future was inextricably linked with the other woman's. The whole thing had gone exactly as Minx would've wanted it to.

The next morning, Amrita got ready for the assignment, packing her voluminous handbag with a few accessories. These days models were required to merely bring themselves to the studio—everything else was taken care of. Amrita couldn't imagine a time when the girls did it all themselves—make-up, hair-styles, clothes and jewellery. She heard the doorbell and knew who it was. She could hear her mother greeting Minx warmly and offering her fresh nimbu-pani. Amrita took her time combing her hair. She wanted to postpone the moment for as long as possible. Ten minutes later she was in the living-room with her mother saying, 'Why, baby, you are looking so pale, didn't you sleep last night?'

Their eyes hadn't met so far. Amrita avoided looking at Minx as she gulped down a glass of warm milk and fussed with her things.

'You'll be late,' Minx said, taking her arm and picking up her handbag from where she had flung it carelessly.

Once inside the air-conditioned, hired Contessa, Minx kissed her lightly on the cheek and said, 'Here . . . I've got something to cheer you up, you look miserable.'

Amrita felt the touch of velvet against the palm of her hand. It was a small box and she did not have to open it to know what it contained. 'Not another one,' she groaned, thrusting it back at Minx.

'Open it, darling. It isn't what you're thinking. Just look inside.'

Minx pressed her to open the tiny box nestling in her palm. Reluctantly, Amrita opened it, and gasped. Resting majestically on a crushed silk bed was an eternity band crafted from a string of exquisitely-cut marquises linked by tiny emeralds.

'Are you completely crazy?' Amrita exclaimed. 'I can't accept such an expensive gift.'

Minx slipped it on her ring finger, raised her hand to her lips and kissed it. 'Don't spoil it all by talking about expenses, darling,' she said, 'this is just an expression of what I feel for you and I will feel this way till I die, that's all.'

'That's all!' Amrita nearly screamed, 'how the hell am I going to explain all this nonsense to my parents . . . and . . . and to others. Do you ever think of that?'

Minx looked at the vast avenues ahead of her and said, 'After last night, darling, no explanations are necessary. You belong to me and I belong to you, it's that simple.'

Amrita winced. She knew this was not the time to go into what had transpired between them the previous night. She decided to keep quiet and wait for the right moment, perhaps over a quiet dinner at the Casa Medici that night. Minx had a dreamy, distant look in her eyes as they got out of the car and walked towards Partha's Bahadurshah Zafar Marg office.

Amrita pleaded with her at the entrance. 'I'll be OK, really . . . you don't have to come with me. I can take care of myself.'

Minx laughed, 'Oh, I know that. I trust you. It's the others. That bastard Partha, I can tell he has the hots for you. One chance and he'll jump.'

Amrita was too exasperated to even argue. 'All right,' she said resignedly, 'stick around if you want to . . . but I hate it. Hate being watched and followed. I can't breathe.'

Minx lit a cigarette and said cheerfully, 'Don't worry, you'll get used to it. How do you think couples stay married for years and years living out of each other's pockets?'

They were inside the busy office before Amrita could think up a suitable response.

*

Minx left Amrita's side only once, for less than five minutes, during the four-and-a-half hours she was at Partha's studio. And that was to go to the common loo down a long corridor. Partha had popped by to say hello and was his usual friendly, flamboyant self. He looked interested but not lechy, Amrita concluded. She could recognize the signs: ad agencies were crawling with middle-aged, self-styled Romeos preying on young girls. She knew how to handle those. Partha was not one of them. He had class and style. She would have loved to take a coffee-break with him but obviously that was not the done thing around his office. Eyebrows had shot up when he had peeped in. She had heard whispered comments on how unusual it was to see the boss in the studio. While Minx was in the loo, Amrita had dashed off a short note to Partha on the spur of the moment. Nothing significant. It was basically to say she had enjoyed the session but wished she had seen more of him. Amrita knew very well how it was going to be interpreted. Maybe she wanted it that way.

Minx was relaxed and friendly throughout the session. She had set up an easy, informal equation with the photographer and the crew and even helped with the reflectors and lights. Ripan, the hot-shot lensman, preferred to work at a maniacal pace with heavy metal music throbbing in the background. 'It relaxes models,' he had explained to Amrita, whose ears had been assaulted by the volume. Minx had gone up to him and spoken a few words. Ripan had changed the music to a more soothing Chopin prelude but had done so most unenthusiastically. Amrita had overheard him mutter 'Bitch!' under his breath.

The eternity band was beginning to cut into her finger. The thought of having to deal with Minx later was beginning to unsettle Amrita. She could not concentrate on the pictures and seemed distracted and spaced out to the others. She could feel Minx's eyes on her constantly, ever-watchful and hungry. After the last frame was shot, Amrita reached for a bottle of baby oil and some soft cottonballs in preparation for removing her make-up.

'Here—leave it to me,' Minx said taking everything out of her hands, 'put your head back and relax.'

Amrita did not want to create a scene but she could not keep the grimace off her face as Minx daubed her eyelids with Lancome's eye make-up remover and spread baby oil over the rest of her face gently.

'Weird,' Ripan mumbled to his assistant.

Amrita could hear the sniggers as the crew bustled around packing up the props and other equipment.

Just then Partha strode in briskly and took in the scene with one quick look. 'Amrita,' he said pointedly, 'I'd like a word with you in my office—my subs are having problems with the captions.'

Amrita scrambled to her feet and started after him. 'Not so fast, baby,' Minx whispered. 'I'm going with you, tell him I'm your executive assistant or something and that all copy about you is routed through me.'

Amrita pleaded with her, 'I'll be back in five minutes, please . . . just five minutes.'

'No way, dear heart. I go where you go. That's the way it's going to be from now on,' Minx said firmly and followed her.

Amrita knocked on Partha's rosewood office door. 'Come right in,' he called out. Seeing Minx behind her he came around from behind his huge desk and said politely, 'I need to discuss something confidential with Ms Aggarwal. Would you mind waiting outside, please?'

Minx refused to budge. 'I represent her in everything. There is nothing confidential between us. You are free to discuss whatever you want in my presence.' And then turning to Amrita she added, 'Isn't that right, sweetheart?'

Amrita dared not look at Partha. She hung her head down and nodded miserably.

'In that case, I have nothing further to say to either of you,' Partha announced, dismissing them.

Minx took Amrita's arm and said, 'Let's go, baby. We don't have to stand around being insulted by a rude man.'

Amrita darted a quick look at Partha. To her surprise he winked and signalled for her to phone. A surge of relief swept over Amrita and she tripped out lightly behind Minx.

'I saw that. Don't think I didn't,' Minx snarled once they were outside.

'I don't know what you are talking about,' Amrita countered.

'Oh yes, you do. Don't fuck with me, OK? Play it straight, I don't like anyone messing with me.'

Amrita decided to keep quiet. Her mind was racing ahead. She had to get away from Minx and call Partha. But when and how?

*

'I'm exhausted,' Amrita told Minx. 'I want to stay home with my family and take it easy tonight.'

Minx didn't budge.

'Please . . . please try and understand. I hardly got to sleep last night. And . . . and . . . I'll probably be getting my period tomorrow. I'm feeling drained.'

Minx pretended she had not heard and started flipping through a magazine. Amrita walked up to her holding the small velvet box with the ring, 'Here, I really can't take it. I'll never be able to explain it to my parents.'

Minx studied her coolly, 'Oh, that shouldn't be a problem. Tell them it's fake, the market is full of beautiful stuff—all fake. Nobody can tell the difference.

Amrita shook her head stubbornly, 'It isn't that. I feel uncomfortable about it. I really can't take it.'

Minx closed the fingers of her hand over the box, 'Chuck it into the Yamuna in that case but don't return it,' she said and went back to her magazine.

Hesitantly, Amrita continued, 'Do you mind leaving? I need to lie down and rest.'

Minx shifted her body, 'Here, come and lie down beside me—there's enough room . . . come on.'

Amrita sighed; she was close to tears. She wanted desperately to be alone. Fortunately Ashish wandered into the room and sat himself down on a chair. He was obviously in the mood for a chat. He reeled off her phone messages and mentioned that Karan had called twice from Bombay. Amrita excused herself and went to the telephone. Ashish and Minx, left to themselves in the room, started a desultory conversation. Instead of phoning Karan, Amrita dialled Partha's residence. She hesitated when she heard his wife's voice, but decided to ask for him anyway. He came on the line quickly and asked, 'You were looking like death. Are you all right?'

'Yes . . . I mean. . . no, not really . . . I need to talk to you . . . to anyone . . . I need ten minutes. Can we meet . . . .' She felt Minx's presence right behind her at that very minute, and her hair stood on end. She whirled around, ashen-faced, to face her.

'Is that the SOB?' Minx asked calmly, taking the receiver from her hand. 'If it is really Karan you're talking to he won't be able to get here for quite a while, will he?' she said replacing the receiver. Both of them had not noticed Ashish standing near the door, watching the scene with a strange expression on his face.

'What's going on here?' he asked coming up to Amrita and putting his arm protectively around her.

'Nothing,' Amrita stammered, 'just a small argument. Honestly, it's nothing. I can handle this . . . please . . . go away, it's OK.'

Strange Obsession

Ashish continued to stand around. 'I don't know what the hell the games the two of you play are, but I find them weird. Amrita, if something's wrong, tell me. I'm your brother.'

Minx watched coolly, tapping a cigarette on the pack and waiting for Amrita's reaction. All of them started when the phone rang.

'I'll take it,' Amrita said shrilly. She jumped on the receiver and nearly screamed into it.

'Hey! What's the matter with you. Stop yelling. I'm not deaf,' she heard Partha chuckle.

'I'll call you in the morning . . . no, later . . . no . . . I don't know. I'll call.' Amrita disconnected quickly. Her brother stared at her. 'I've never seen you like this. Are you in some sort of trouble?' he asked and looked questioningly at Minx.

Minx shook her head. 'Your precious sister can never be in trouble as long as she stays with me. The problem is, she wants to do things on her own. I keep telling her, the world is full of lousy people, let me look after you, help you. You explain to her. You know how men are these days.'

Ashish looked at Minx witheringly, 'Amrita is capable of looking after herself. We all know that. When she decided to go to Bombay, nobody tried to stop her because we had full faith in her. What's worrying me is the change I see. Amrita was never like this. I want to know what's going on.'

Amrita tried to compose herself before saying, 'I've had a long and hard day at the shoot. I just need to get some sleep. Why don't you go and drop my friend back? Delhi taxis are so funny. In Bombay, we can just step out of the house and hail a passing cab. None of this phoning business. Go on, reach her to where she's staying and we'll talk in the morning.'

Minx shot her a dark look before picking up her satchel. 'See you in the morning, sweetie,' she said, kissing her on the cheek, as close to the mouth as she could. At the door she turned around and added 'By the way, I've done a small check on this—Partha has a hysterical wife. And a handicapped kid. She isn't crazy about lady-callers. Delhi is full of sad stories about what happens to besotted females chasing the powerful editor. You want the answer? They generally find themselves out in the cold. And do you know why? Mr Parthasarthy's balls are firmly in his father-in-law's hands—the old man owns the paper. One little squeeze and Partha's down on his knees. Just thought the info would interest you. Good night.'

Amrita had never felt so trapped before. She knew her brother would question her closely the next morning. Ashish was the one she was close to. They had shared secrets through their growing up years and she knew it was impossible for her to fool him.

Another fitful night stretched in front of Amrita. She could not explain to herself what drew her to Partha.

Strange Obsession

It was absurd when she thought about it. The man was so much older and obviously as unavailable as he was inaccessible. She knew very little about him. And yet she felt drawn so strongly that she felt tempted to call him at that late hour. She decided to do it. As an editor of a daily, she reasoned, surely he was used to calls at all hours. Besides, if his wife answered, she would disconnect. Nervously, she dialled the number. It rang five times before a woman's voice answered sleepily. Amrita lost her nerve and hung up, bitterly disappointed and slightly angry at herself. Instead, she called Karan and got him on the first ring. 'She's there in Delhi, isn't she?' he asked anxiously. 'I called to warn you.'

In a voice weighed down by fatigue Amrita said, 'It was too late. Your call. She'd got me by then.' Her voice broke suddenly and she began to cry into the phone, 'Karan what am I going to do? I feel so helpless . . . there is no way she is going to leave me.'

Karan was silent for a while. And then he spoke reassuring, soothing words, 'I'll think of something. Leave it to ne. We can't let her do this to you.'

Amrita stopped crying and asked, 'How are things in Bombay?'

Karan's voice changed as he exulted, 'Baby! You've done it. The other reason I called you was to say you've bagged the "Allure" campaign and calendar for next year. Yes, all of it. You know what a feather it is in your cap. Congratulations! All the other babes are chewing their false eyelashes in frustration. We shoot on your return.'

Amrita's excitement vanished when she thought about where she was going to stay in Bombay. 'Karan . . . you know it's off between Sheila and me. I don't have anywhere to live. I can't come back till I find a place.'

Karan laughed, 'Don't be mad, darling girl. Come here and stay with me. Promise . . . no funny business. Or, hey, why don't we get married.'

'Are you nuts? Married? What's with you, anyway?' She giggled and then sobered up. 'And even if you were serious, she wouldn't let me.'

Karan couldn't believe what she was saying. 'What the fuck is that supposed to mean? Won't let you? Are you her slave? Or is there something you aren't telling me?'

Amrita found it difficult to go on, 'Karan, it's much too complicated. I can't explain everything over the phone. Besides, I don't want to get married. I mean, it's absurd to marry someone because of an accommodation problem.'

Karan continued persuasively, 'Tell me you don't love me, I'll accept that and make you change your mind. But if you really want to know, I haven't suddenly decided to become the white knight rescuing the beautiful damsel. I've been thinking about you a lot these past few days, and I realized I love you, Amrita. You know

I love you enough for both of us. You won't regret it, I promise you that. Besides, given the accommodation problem in this beastly city, it's as good a reason as any to marry someone. Thousands of happy couples will tell you that.'

Amrita wiped her tears and said, 'It's so very sweet of you, Karan. Really, I can't tell you how touched I am. But it doesn't work like that for me. I'm much too fond of you to risk your life—you know what Minx is capable of.'

Karan sighed, 'Don't give me all that crap. She may be the top cop's daughlter but I have my sources too. If she tries any thing with me I'll have her behind bars . . . or strung up from the nearest tree. I don't give a shit about her. But I'm worried about you. Tell you what. Forget I proposed since that seems to scare the shit out of you. Just move in, as a friend. Separate beds. Scout's honour. Stay as long as you feel like till you can organize a place for yourself.'

Amrita sniffed, 'Thanks, Karan. I do adore you. Let me sleep over it. I'll call you in a day or two. Look after yourself and keep all the campaigns hot for me.'

Feeling vastly better after speaking to Karan, she switched off the light and turned in for the night.

Eighteen

'Rise and shine,' Amrita heard Minx's voice and thought she was dreaming. She opened her eyes and found her bending over her and shaking her. 'It's ten o'clock . . . my God! You've overslept . . . did you sleep late, darling?' Minx asked as she fussed around the room, putting away crumpled clothes and looking in Amrita's cupboard for fresh towels.

'Come on, the water's ready, let me give you the best bath you've ever had.'

Amrita pulled the sheets up to her chin and stared at Minx wordlessly. As had become her habit of late, she had gone to bed naked. She could see Minx's eyes sweeping over her body admiringly, and it made her feel acutely self-conscious all of a sudden. She shifted uncomfortably under the light, flower-patterned sheet and said, 'Please . . . if you don't mind . . . why don't you wait for me outside. I'll join you in a minute.'

Minx came up and hugged her. 'Hey. . .you don't have to feel shy . . . not after what we've shared . . . not with me . . . we are one. Every fibre of my body vibrates with yours.'

Amrita winced when she heard those words. She had done a great deal of thinking the previous night and realized what a terrible mistake had been committed. There was no way she could undo it now. No way she could reverse what had transpired between Minx and her. Silently she cursed herself for surrendering to Minx's advances. Minx had not forced her and Amrita could not—did not—want to fool herself into believing that she had. But she also knew she would have to live with that one big regret for the rest of her life and pay for the temporary suspension of her senses two nights before, perhaps forever. Amrita had resolved never to succumb again. And here was Minx cajoling her into a situation with just one outcome.

Amrita opened her mouth to try and explain. Minx covered it with her palm and shushed her.

'Don't . . . don't spoil everything by talking about it,' she said. 'Do you know where I went last night? Go on . . . take a guess . . . you'll never succeed!'

Amrita shrank further back on her bed and lapsed into silence. She knew she would not be able to escape Minx that morning. And the resentment had started building up.

Minx began pacing the room, waving her cigarette in the air. 'After many years, my darling, I felt a strange peace coming over me. I felt close to the Almighty. I walked out of here and looked at the stars. I thought I saw a heavenly sign in the skies. Without thinking I went straight to the Kali Mata Mandir. I wanted to be in the presence of the Devi and thank her for giving you to me. My prayers had been answered. Just flowers and coconuts weren't enough. I bought a goat. The pujari had retired for the night. I woke him up and told him, "This sacrifice has to be performed tonight, right now. No waiting. Five hundred rupees," and he would've sacrificed his own child. As the blood flowed—still hot and very sticky—I dipped my hands into it. I rang the temple bells and danced. The pujari thought I was crazy. In a sense, I was—for you.'

Amrita felt sick listening to her. She wanted to rush into the bathroom and throw up. But Minx was not through: 'I have promised a big donation to the temple. But I couldn't wait to build my own personal shrine. So I walked to the nearby village looking for a mason. Everybody was asleep on rickety charpoys and tried to shoo me away, like I was a mad woman. Have you noticed, sweetheart, how a few notes can make a sane person out of a lunatic? That's all I needed to do, flash some money around. Soon, the sarpanch himself got up and helped me. I would've preferred it to be in marble, of course. But this is really a temporary thing.

We got a few large local stones and painted them white with lime. On a rough piece of wood, I wrote something—a couplet in your honour. We erected the small structure within two hours. And then I went home.'

Amrita had not uttered a word. Her eyes were glazed. Her mind blank. Minx continued to pace the room, her eyes shining with excitement, her voice rising and falling. 'One day I'll construct a magnificent marble prayer hall at this same spot. It will be for people who have a lot to thank God for. People who are filled with love . . . like I am. All thanks to you. It will be a temple of love. To love.'

Amrita rose from her bed slowly, making sure the sheet did not slip off.

'Minx,' she said, keeping her voice calm. 'I have something to tell you . . . .'

Minx seemed to be in a trance. Absently, she turned to Amrita and asked, 'Yes . . . what?'

'It was a mistake . . . the whole thing was mistake. And I'm sorry but I don't love you.'

Minx whipped around and tore the sheet off Amrita's body, 'Don't say that. Don't ever say it . . . understand? I never want to hear those terrible words. Lies. They're all lies. You and I know the truth. We found it together. Don't be afraid of it. There was no mistake . . . you hear?' Her voice had risen considerably and Amrita cowered in a corner, covering her ears to shut out the words she did not want to hear.

Minx came and crouched close to her, pulling at her hands, repeating, 'I love you, I love you' over and over again. The floor was cold and dusty. Amrita felt herself shivering as Minx began caressing her fervently, kissing every inch of her naked body. Amrita crossed one arm over her breasts and stuck her hand over her pubis. Minx gripped her wrists and dragged her arms away, exposing her completely. Amrita started to whimper. Minx kissed her eyes saying, 'I worship you . . . you are my goddess . . . my Devi . . . I live for you. I shall die for you.' Minx held her close and buried her face between her breasts repeating, 'My poor darling, my sweet one . . . .'

A little later, she picked Amrita up and walked into the bathroom. The tub was full of water with rose petals floating on top. The air was fragrant with a sweet-smelling attar. Minx lowered Amrita's body into the warm, perfumed bath and undressed herself. Amrita shut her eyes. She did not want to see Minx She did not want to look at her scars. Then Minx lowered herself down and lay by her side, holding her by the shoulders and helping the water lap over her body gently. 'Isn't this beautiful? Aren't you feeling good?' she asked kissing her wet mouth and opening it with her tongue.

Despite herself, Amrita's body, soaked and relaxed, began to respond to Minx's pleasuring. Her thighs spread a little to allow Minx's hands in. She felt her nipples stiffen as Minx's tongue circled them maddeningly. Her eyes remained shut as she blocked out the image of Minx and thought of other lovers, imagining her hands to be theirs, her tongue to be someone else's. Minx was now on the opposite side of the tub, and Amrita could feel her legs playing with her own, her feet over her belly, massaging it, her toes moving down between her legs, teasing the wet grotto there, as her big toe moved rhythmically against the point of maximum pleasure, manipulating it incessantly, till Amrita felt her body shuddering with the intensity of the sensation . . . begging for more and more, as Minx kept up the pleasure and with her other toe tickled her breasts and nipples. A small scream escaped from Amrita's mouth and within seconds Minx had covered it with her own, using her tongue skilfully to seek out Amrita's and draw it out into her eager mouth. They stayed that way for about an hour, in silence and in peace. Minx broke the spell by standing up and reaching for a towel. 'Let me rub you down, beautiful one,' she said, 'the water's cold and you might catch a chill.'

Amrita opened her eyes and looked at Minx, naked above her. The scars looked angrier than she remembered them.

*

Amrita was now more determined to get away from Minx and make contact with Partha. Plus, she had to think seriously about returning to Bombay and all her pending assignments. She was thrilled about the 'Allure' campaign—it was the number-one glamour account every model chased. And it was hers. Maybe she would be able to make enough through it to buy that ticket to Paris—the one that had slipped out of her hands during that nasty business with Lola. Amrita had often wondered how far the police had got with the inquiry but she dared not question Minx about it. In a way, she felt the less she knew about Minx's mysterious activities, the better for her.

Amrita wrapped a towel around herself and came into her room to dress. Minx was lovingly laying out her clothes for her, picking everything with care. She looked at the shell-pink, flowing, malmal salwar kameez and smiled a small smile. It was the one she'd worn on a date with Rover. It had a small tear near the buttons, where he'd ripped it in his hurry to strip her. Minx was holding it to her nose and inhaling deeply, smelling the remnants of Amrita's favourite perfume, Estee Lauder's Private Collection. 'Oh . . . I really love that smell,' Minx said, letting out her breath, 'I can get high just sniffing it. I prefer smelling it on your body, of course, but when you aren't there, it's like oxygen to me.'

Amrita stepped into her flowered bikini panties and wore her eyelet bra. She caught sight of her reflection in the mirror and stared critically at her upper thighs—was she imagining it, or did they appear slightly thicker?

Minx came up behind her and put her arms around her waist. They stood there looking at themselves silently. 'How terrific we look together,' Minx said happily, 'don't you think so too?'

Amrita tried to change the subject. Minx continued to hold her in a close embrace. 'Just look at us, darling, everything is right. You fit so well in my arms.' Minx kissed her shoulders and her hands started to wander over Amrita.

'Stop it!' Amrita shouted, pushing her away.

Startled by her response, Minx asked her, 'Why? Don't you like what I do to you? Doesn't it make your body feel good?

'That's not the point,' Amrita protested heatedly. 'It's wrong. I hate myself for it.'

Minx held her face in her hands and asked, 'Why? Because of some stupid guilt-complex? Why should it be all right for you to get screwed by scum like Rover . . . but not loved completely, totally and thoroughly by me? Just because God made me a woman instead of a man?'

'Yes, yes, yes, dammit. That's reason enough,' Amrita cried, covering her face, 'I feel such shame. Please . . . I beg of you, get out of my life. Leave me alone.'

Minx's voice was dripping scorn when she said, 'So, that's it huh? That's what you hold against me—that I am not a man? OK, I'll become a man, just to satisfy you. Is that what you want? I've been thinking about it myself. I've met a couple of surgeons too . . . the ones who reshaped my breasts. They're willing to do it. I was the one who was hesitant. But not any longer. Now I've heard it from you.'

Amrita's eyes widened in horror as she caught hold of Minx and yelled, 'Will you stop this nonsense at once? What are you talking about?'

Minx had a wild look in her eyes as she said, 'Want me to spell it out for you, baby? OK, hear this then . . . I'm planning to undergo a sex-change operation. Yes, darling. I'll do it for you. You want a prick to enter you—I'll go out and get one. Money can buy you anything, I've always said. Even a bloody dick.'

Amrita, her eyes blazing, shouted back, 'Maybe that's how it works for you and your kinky world. Not for me. You want me to tell you what I think of your crazy plan? I think it stinks. You may be able to get some quack to stitch on a plastic dick. But will that make me pregnant? Will you be able to fill my womb with a child? Answer me.'

Without another word, Minx picked up her cigarettes and stormed out of the room. Amrita sat down heavily on her bed and clutched her knees. This morning's love-making was crazy, crazy, crazy. Never again, she promised herself. But at least she'd managed to get rid of her for now. She knew, however, that it would not be for long. But she desperately needed some time to herself to plan her next move. She rushed out of the room and went straight to the phone. If she didn't get Partha now, she never would. Minx was not going to be away for more than an hour. Amrita was certain about that. She dialled the number with trembling fingers and got him on the direct line. 'I have to see you. Right now. It's urgent. It's . . . it's more than urgent, it's desperate. I need your help.'

'Meet me at the Machan in fifteen minutes,' he said and rang off. Amrita rushed to the kitchen to tell her mother she was off. She found her father there, helping himself to a glass of water.

She hoped fervently that he had not overheard her phone conversation. To her relief he did not appear worried. 'Have to rush,' she said.

And she was gone, leaving Mr Aggarwal staring at a blur of pink disappearing down the garden path.

Nineteen

Partha was at one of the small tables by the huge French windows overlooking the swimming pool. He was totally absorbed in a thick book and smoking a pipe. Amrita saw him from a distance and smiled to herself. He looked so solid and dependable in his neat office clothes, his hair slicked back and a pair of gold reading glasses halfway down his nose. He rose to his feet when she got to the table. 'You look like a freshly plucked carnation this morning,' he said appreciatively.

'Thanks,' Amrita replied shortly and sat down across him. Without ceremony she started. 'I need your help. Say you'll give it.'

Partha pulled off his glasses and held up his hands. 'Whoa girl! Take it easy. What's all this about? Let's take it slowly all right? Start at the beginning. What's your problem?'

'It's her. The girl you met—Minx—Meenakshi.'

'What about her?'

'Everything about her.'

'Big help that is.'

'She's dangerous, and I'm scared of her.'

'In what way is she dangerous?'

'She's . . . she's a maniac.'

'So? there are hundreds of maniacs roaming around in this world. For all you know, I might be one.'

Amrita sighed exasperatedly before continuing, 'I don't know how to put it—she can do anything. Even kill someone. She must be stopped.'

Partha was looking more aroused than concerned. 'This is sounding like a cheap movie script. Please . . . specifics. Let's talk turkey. If she's a psychopath on the loose, as you insist, go to the police. Why me?'

Amrita leaned forward and spoke earnestly. 'It's no use going to the cops. Her daddy is a big man. Besides, how can I prove anything? Nobody will believe me.'

Partha took both her hands in his and asked gently, 'Has she harmed you in any way?'

Amrita shook her head, 'I'm not worried about me, it's the other people around me. Does that make any sense to you?'

'None whatsoever,' Partha laughed lightly. 'If it's other people you're worried about, forget it. They can take care if themselves. My interest in what you're saying begins and ends with you. I can't play knight-in-shining-armour to the world.'

Amrita's eyes were scanning the crowd restlessly. 'You don't know this female. She'll go to any lengths.'

'Any lengths to do what?'

Slowly, the words emerged, 'To keep me for herself. Now do you understand?'

For the first time Partha's eyes showed a flicker of interest. 'I get it—she's one of the those. I won't call her a lesbo. The correct term these days for them is, I believe, people who practise alternative sexuality. My dear girl, surely you are accustomed to such attention, a smashing woman like you?'

Amrita tried to explain the relationship a little but she could sense she'd lost Partha. He said casually, 'You should get her to see a competent psychiatrist. And while you're at it you might consider seeing a therapist yourself. The ugly things can be worked out. What I'm baffled about is that, of all people, you chose me, a-man-on-the-next-seat-in-an-aeroplane, to reveal your secret to. Why me?'

Amrita looked him straight in the eyes and said fiercely, 'Because I can trust you. Because I think you are powerful and influential. Because I think you like me.'

Partha chuckled delightedy, 'Well done! You are a girl after my own heart. I give you full marks for what you just said. Put that way, how can I refuse. Amrita, I'm at your service. Shoot.'

She smiled with relief and he noticed her eyes glistening. 'It has been so terrible for me ever since she came into my life and took it over,' she began and then went on to narrate the sequence of events leading up to the last night. But even in her candour, Amrita could not get herself to tell him about her two sexual encounters. Not even when he asked her a direct question. 'Have you slept with her?'

Amrita lied, 'No,' and waited for him to switch subjects.

He seemed sceptical about some of the incidents, questioning her closely, as if trying to find loopholes in her story. But Amrita guessed that that was a part of his training as a journalist. How could he take whatever she was saying at face value? Finally, after narrating her peculiar tale, Amrita asked him simply, 'Will you help me now?'

Partha held out his hand, 'Deal. But give me a little time. I need to put on my thinking cap. This is new territory for me. I still haven't figured out what I can do to extricate you from her clutches. Maybe I'll set up a meeting with an analyst friend of mine for tonight. He lives down the road. Shouldn't be a problem. Let's take it from there. Meanwhile—you are a bit too attractive for your own good. I don't like the effect you have on me at all. And don't look at me that way . . . .'

Amrita blushed. Partha was staring so hard at her, she was sure people around them would notice. He was a well-known figure around Delhi and she could see him being recognized along with her. Abruptly, she asked him the one question she had been longing to from the time they had met on the aeroplane: 'Are you in love with your wife?'

Clearly thrown by the unexpectedness of the question, Partha cleared his throat and started fiddling with his pipe paraphernalia. 'That's a pretty direct question to ask,' he said evasively, packing fresh tobacco into the bowl of his pipe.

'Well, you ask people direct questions as a journalist. Why can't you answer them then?'

'All right,' Partha said, drawing deeply on his pipe, 'the answer is no. Does that satisfy your inquisitive mind?'

Amrita was beaming. 'I'm so glad,' she said guilelessly, adding, 'but in that case, why are you still married to her?'

'Ah, that's another story, let's talk about it when we have to. It's complicated and adult and . . . and . . . I don't know. Maybe I'll tell you someday, but not right now.'

Amrita put on her sunglasses and picked up her bag. 'Silly of me to have said what I did. I should have been more sophisticated about it and pretended I was sorry to hear that, eh? That's not how mature women are supposed to behave.'

Partha got up with her, 'And I love you for it. Damn! Why the hell are you so young and so bloody beautiful?'

Amrita leaned over and kissed him warmly. 'Don't hold it against me. I have a crush on you and I'm enjoying it. I'm hoping you'll have one on me too. See you soon.' With that she sauntered out of the restaurant pausing at the exit to turn around and blow him a kiss.

Partha followed Amrita with his eyes through the lobby and out. He hadn't felt this exhilarated, this buoyant, this young, in years. He decided to take the rest of the afternoon off and go to his farmhouse—an hour's drive out of Delhi. He wanted to be alone to think about this disturbingly, devastatingly, beautiful woman who had walked into his life and turned it on its head. And he wanted to devise a plan to help her before it was too late.

*

Minx was chatting with her mother in the kitchen when Amrita got back. 'Hey, you're looking great,' Minx said to her, 'exactly like a freshly-plucked pink carnation.'

Amrita took her breath in sharply and looked flustered, 'Where did you hear that?'

Minx feigned innocence, 'Did I say something wrong? Jesus! You are jumpy this morning, aren't you? I was only paying you a compliment.' Then she turned to Mrs Aggarwal and said, 'God knows what happens to your daughter when she steps out of the house to meet strange people. Suddenly she starts behaving in a funny manner. You heard what I said—did I say something odd?'

Mrs Aggarwal looked fondly across at Amrita. 'It must be the heat outside. Poor child, she hasn't been eating well. She looks so tired all the time. I worry about her life in Bombay. Now that I know she will be staying with you, I'm feeling much better. Otherwise all this P.G. business was making all of us very nervous. Especially after you told us all those stories about Bombay. You see, Amrita will never write or talk about these things. She thinks if we know, we won't allow her to return there.'

Amrita took a bite out of the stuffed parantha her mother had made and asked, 'What's all this about where I'll be staying in Bombay?'

Her mother said, 'Darling, it is all sorted out now—your accommodation problem. Your father and I are feeling so relieved. Meenakshi has promised to take good care of you. I know you'll be well looked after by her. She has spent so much time taking down all your favourite recipes.'

Minx looked at Amrita challengingly, almost triumphantly. Amrita told her mother, 'I haven't made up my mind about exactly what I plan to do or when I have to go back to Bombay.'

Mrs Aggarwal seemed genuinely puzzled, 'Really? But Minx just showed me your tickets for the day after tomorrow. She said you have urgent work there which might go to someone else.'

Amrita glared at Minx but kept quiet. Minx went to her mother and helped her with the paranthas saying, 'It's all right, Auntie. She must be a little tired and confused. She has been working much too hard. I keep telling her to relax. I'd planned a surprise for her on our return to Bombay but I might as well share it

Strange Obsession

with you right now—I'd planned to take Amrita for a short holiday.'

Mrs Aggarwal beamed, 'What a wonderful idea. We'd suggested it too but she'd refused—probably finds it too boring to go anywhere with her old parents now. But if she has agreed to travel with you, nothing like it—it will bring some much-needed colour to her cheeks.'

Minx put an arm around Amrita's shoulder affectionately. 'She is in the best hands with me. I know exactly what she needs even before she herself does. She's going to be fine, just fine in the future. That's my promise to you,' and then she bent low to touch Mrs Aggarwal's feet. 'Auntie, give me your blessings. After all, you are like my mother. What's the difference between Amrita and me?'

Mrs Aggarwal had tears in her eyes as she mussed Minx's hair and bent down to lift her up. 'Why don't you girls go and relax in Amrita's room? I'll send you up some sherbet,' she said.

Amrita stalked off with Minx at her heels. As soon as the bedroom door shut on them, Minx grabbed and tried to kiss her. Amrita struggled out of her embrace fiercely, protesting, 'Stop it! Don't come anywhere near me . . . how dare you deceive my poor mother?'

Minx raised her eyebrows. 'Deceive? Where is the deception? Was I lying about anything? Aren't you taking chances with your career by staying away?

Don't you need a safe home to stay in? And aren't you in need of a holiday?'

Amrita sat on the edge of her bed, glaring at Minx, 'You are a manipulative bitch and I hate you. I really do. But you can't get away with this for long . . . wait and see!'

Minx lit a cigarette, blew smoke in her direction, and asked casually, 'Really? Why? Is that pansy journalist friend of yours going to protect you? Forget it, baby . . . he just wants to get into your pants, that's all. Besides, he won't dare take me on—not after he finally finds out I have the dope on him and his dealings.'

Amrita shot to her feet and rushed towards Minx with her fists raised. 'Bitch! You can't blackmail him! He is too powerful for you and your father. Your loafers in Bombay may be able to threaten people there but this is Delhi and Partha is somebody here—a big somebody.'

Minx smiled a slow, sly smile, 'Sure he is. But big somebodies are the ones who have the most to hide—surely you know that. I've been asking around—digging up stuff. Believe me, sweetheart, there are things from his past he won't enjoy confronting now.'

'Like what?' Amrita challenged.

Minx laughed a hollow laugh. 'Like nothing—nothing I want to tell you, baby. But trust me—that guy is poison. And on several payrolls. I can get his sponsors to squeal—anytime. And then I'll see how his powerful connections help him. You can drink any number of coffees at Machan with loverboy . . . but remember, one false move and the man is dead. I'll carve up his balls and present them to you on a platter.'

Amrita was pacing her room in rage. Minx came up behind her and placed her hands on her shoulders, 'Don't fight me darling. It really isn't any use—haven't you found that out by now? I am good for you. You will bless me for saving you from these vultures.'

Amrita pushed her away and spat out the words, 'I'm not going to spend the rest of my life being controlled by a pervert. And forget it—I won't come back to Bombay with you. Neither will I stay in your home—what nerve! Don't worry about my mother—sooner or later she'll see through you. She isn't such a fool. I'd rather die than live with you.'

Minx continued to smoke thoughtfully. 'We'll see about that, sweetheart. Don't speak too soon. But if I were you I wouldn't go gabbing to strangers with shady pasts. And if I were you, again, I'd stay miles away from men with possessive wives. Nirmala—yes that's her name—can be a tigress. I've heard funny stories about voodoo and tantrics. She is on a permanent pilgrimage. And there isn't a single swami in India she doesn't know.' With that Minx left the room and the house.

Amrita watched Minx walk down the path to her car—a lonely figure in black, kicking at occasional stones and muttering to herself. In spite of everything that had happened, Amrita felt sorry for Minx as she saw her disappear into the distance, a haunted, miserable woman.

*

Karan was shooting a motorbike commercial with four teenagers when he heard the news of Amrita's return. He learnt about it from the stylist on the shoot. 'The maharani is back . . . with the bitch in tow,' Vicki said as he fixed a scarf in a model's hair.

Karan couldn't help feeling deeply disappointed that Amrita had not informed him of her arrival. Keeping his voice studiedly casual, he asked, 'Know where she's hanging out?'

'Where else? In that creature's apartment, of course. God! They might as well get married, the way they're carrying on,' giggled Vicki some more.

The models joined in the laughter and discussed the campaigns Amrita was likely to lose when word got out that she would have Minx hanging around all the time on assignments. 'But I thought she really liked guys . . . I mean, all the guys liked her,' the girl in sequinned jeans commented.

Vicki got busy putting out-sized hoops through her pierced earlobes, 'Yeah, she's straight, that's for sure. But that weirdo with her scares everybody off. Who needs a security guard like that hanging around a studio?'

Karan was silently fixing his lights all the time, thinking of how he could get through to her without Minx finding out. He did not have to worry for long. The phone rang and his heart soared as he heard Amrita's slightly husky, lowered voice, speaking with a strange urgency, 'Karan . . . I'm back and at her place in Colaba. You know, just off Cuffe Parade, overlooking the sea. She has gone down to pick up her mail, so I made this call. I really don't know what's going on—but in case anything happens, you know where I am. Got to go now . . . she's back. I heard the key turn in the lock.' And she was gone.

Karan stared at the receiver in his hand, wondering what to do next. He'd lost interest in the shoot completely. The giggly models surrounding him were getting on his nerves and Vicki with his non-stop bitching was asking to be slugged. Karan wanted to drop everything and pull Amrita out from the hell-hole she had landed herself in. He made up his mind to do just that after the session.

*

'Spoke to him?' Minx asked, her voice light and friendly.

Amrita's stricken expression gave her the answer.

'Let's get a few things straight, sweetheart,' Minx said, going to the fridge for a can of imported beer.

'No hanky-panky, get it? No sneaking around behind my back. These are the house rules. You want to talk to someone, talk. Up front. In my presence. I hate all this shady business.'

Amrita sat on a bean bag, hugging her knees. Minx had a functional, comfortable, fourteenth-floor two-bedroom apartment in a high-rise. The living-room overlooked the vast expanse of sea with the silhouette of Malabar Hill in the distance. It was a pleasant enough flat but entirely impersonal. A person walking in would have easily mistaken it for a company transit flat or a bachelor's home. Minx had furnished it in stark black and white with no-nonsense modern pieces and futuristic lighting. When Amrita first stepped in, she thought she was in a hospital lounge. The white hurt the eyes, especially when the early evening sun beat down on it. There were no curtains in the place, just black blinds. Moulded black lampshades and track lighting on the ceiling cast long shadows at night. The white marble flooring only added to the over-all coldness. The bedrooms too were antiseptic-looking, with black bedcovers and white everything else.

When they had first arrived Minx escorted her into the smaller of the two bedrooms saying, 'Darling . . . I do respect your need for privacy. Look! This is your room—yours exclusively. You can put a "Do not enter" sign on the door if you wish. I promise not to come in without your wanting me to. And here's your own mini-fridge. And an electric kettle with tea-bags. You don't have to go to the kitchen if you don't feel like it in the mornings.'

She opened a well-stocked cabinet brimming over with Pepperidge Farm cookies, Kraft cheese, little nibbly things, nuts, chocolates and a jar of olives.

'It's like a hotel room,' Amrita commented disconcertedly.

Minx picked Amrita up and twirled her around, 'It's home, baby, home. Our home. Yours and mine. Besides, now that you are here, we can change everything—really! Do what you like with the place—repaint, refurnish, anything. It's yours—throw out what you don't like immediately. Get your own kind of stuff—music, paintings, anything!'

'Who pays for all this?' Amrita had asked looking at the CD player, the Bose speakers and the large screen laser video.

Minx had grinned wickedly, 'God, Amrita, you are so naïve. There are dozens of people who owe me . . . or my father. They like to show their appreciation in small ways.'

'Small ways!' Amrita had exclaimed. 'You call this small?'

Minx continued airily, 'What we do for them in return is so much bigger, baby . . . this is chickenshit, petty cash.'

'This place must've cost a bomb—seventy, eighty lakhs, at least,' Amrita had calculated, walking around, taking in the granite in the kitchen and fancy fittings all over.

'Thereabouts at today's market rates . . . but not when I got it. It was a gift, baby, a gift. Guess what my father paid for it fifteen years ago? Just guess? Four fucking lakhs. Big money then . . . not his own, of course. But that is what I call smart thinking and good planning. You agree?'

Amrita had raised her eyebrows and sunk into a black leather armchair. 'I can't stay here permanently . . . you know that,' she had said.

Minx came up and covered her mouth with her hand. 'Sssh . . . there's another ground rule I haven't told you about so far . . . no discussing the future. Who knows where I'll be . . . or you . . . ten years from now? Why waste time speculating?'

Amrita had shaken herself free and said, 'I wasn't talking about ten or five or even one year. I want to move out as soon as I get my own place . . . it might take a week or two. But that's what I'm talking about.'

Minx had sat at her feet on a Tibetan black and white rug. 'Such an obstinate little thing—aren't you?' she had smiled sweetly. 'How long are you going to resist me? Fight me? All your life? Give up, baby. You are home safe with me here. How can you want to go back to grubbing away in some dingy hole? Besides, do you know the going rate for a room in this area? Anything between ten and twenty thousand a month. I know you're doing all the big campaigns, but I also know how the money trickles in. How will you pay your rent? And organize food, travel, clothes? Forget it. Tell you what—stay here till you are on your feet. I mean really and properly. I'm good with money. Let me take charge of yours. I'll invest for you—double it in three years. And then you'll be able to buy something decent and live like a princess.'

Amrita had got up and gone to the large glass windows. Very quietly, she had said, 'I hate it here. I feel suffocated. And spied on. I feel like a prisoner, I can't breathe. I need my independence. Is that so difficult to understand?'

Minx had joined her and had tried to draw her into an embrace. Amrita had stiffened and struggled out. 'Another thing—I can't bear to be touched constantly. I have a thing about it. Don't keep pawing me, OK?'

Mink had held up her hands, 'OK, OK, relax. I was just being friendly. Yes, I can see how you feel. I am human, you know. But did I say anything about denying your independence? All I'm saying is don't do things behind my back. That hurts. It really hurts. Go where you want to go—but let me drop you there. I worry about you. Tell me where you are and with whom—that's all. I won't stop you.'

Amrita had grimaced, 'That's worse than being in my parents' home. I can't be answerable to you. And I definitely don't want you following me around. You've ruined enough of my relationships.'

'Really?' Minx had asked, her voice dry and sarcastic. 'And who are these wonderful friends who so readily ditched you when you needed them, huh? That bitch, Sheila, who used you for your contacts in the ad world? Or Rover, who fucked and chucked you? Or Karan who is too much of a sissy to risk anything even for himself? Tell me who? Name one.'

Amrita had winced at the harshness of her words, especially as they were partially true. She didn't really have any friends in this city. The modelling world was selfish and insecure. She thought of Partha in Delhi and wondered whether even he would come to her aid if she ever needed it. Looking at the unending expanse of sea through the glass windows, she had suppressed a sob. She was stuck—at least for the time being. The sensible thing to do was to put up with Minx for now. And wait for the right opportunity. It would come. It had to.

Amrita had turned to Minx with a soft smile playing on her lips and put her arms around her neck, 'You're right,' she had said. 'I only have you.'

Minx had pulled her close and kissed her, opening her clenched teeth with her fingers and finding her tongue. Amrita had felt her hands reaching under her silk blouse and unsnapping her bra. 'No,' she had said. And, then she had added, 'Later, OK.'

*

Amrita read the small, front-page report about Partha with a sinking feeling. It was terse and to the point. He had been injured in a road accident while driving to his farmhouse on the outskirts of Delhi. Doctors attached to the intensive care unit of the Medical Institute, where he was rushed, had stated that his condition was stable. The Gypsy that he'd been driving was mangled beyond redemption. The accident was described as a 'lucky escape' for the editor.

Amrita could hear Minx humming happily in the kitchen as she scrambled eggs for breakfast. The lone servant in her flat was a part-time bai, a young widow who'd arrive with a kid on her hip and clean up the house efficiently. After a tea and snack break she'd attack the dirty pots and pans, wash the clothes and disappear. Amrita was surprised to discover that Minx did all her own cooking and seemed to enjoy it. With a flourish, Minx brought out two octagonal black plates heaped with fluffy eggs and bacon done to a crisp. 'Breakfast, beautiful,' she announced and went back into the kitchen to fetch coffee.

'Have you read the papers yet?' Amrita asked.

'No, anything interesting?' Minx asked.

Wordlessly, Amrita folded the paper and stuck the item under her nose. Minx read it swiftly and tutted, 'Poor man . . . silly of him to speed around in an unstable car like that,' she said and helped herself to a fork heaped with egg. Amrita searched her face closely. It was impassive and relaxed.

'Have some,' she said pushing a plate towards Amrita.

'I can't . . . I feel like I'm choking,' Amrita replied, pushing it away.

'Don't tell me you are feeling that bad,' Minx said reaching out and holding her hand, 'the man is alive. Cheer up!'

Amrita took a deep breath and asked, 'Do you have anything to do with this . . . "accident"?'

Minx bit into a lavishly buttered toast and said, 'Don't be ridiculous. Me? I've been here . . . with you . . . you know that.'

'Sure I know that. But you don't have to be there to organize it . . . .'

Minx laughed, 'Silly girl . . . you've a wild imagination. Do you really think I'm that powerful—that enterprising?'

'Yes, there is nothing I'd put past you. Nothing at all. You are capable of anything and everything.'

'I'm flattered, darling. But you are being perfectly absurd. In any case, if it was a hit, someone botched it up badly. I hate clumsy messed-up jobs.' With that Minx rose and whisked away Amrita's plate. 'No breakfast? Too bad. But I hate waste. I guess you'll have to be taught basic discipline. You've been spoilt in your parents' home. A child who skips one meal doesn't get the next—it's as simple as that. So, sorry, sweetheart. No lunch for you today.'

Amrita was shocked to hear the tone of her voice. She started to say something, but Minx cut her off. 'Save it. And stay home. I have some stuff to attend to for an hour or so. No monkey business in my absence. Got it?'

Amrita stared blankly at a spot on the wall. Minx picked up her car-keys and walked out. Amrita rushed to the window to confirm that she had left and then she charged towards the telephone. There was a lock on it. She ran to the front door and was not surprised to find even that bolted from the outside. Minx's flat overlooked not only neighbouring homes but the sea on three sides. There was no way she could attract anybody's attention. She went to the bedroom to lie down and think. There wasn't much time—perhaps another forty-five minutes. Her mind was a blank, plus she was ravenously hungry. She went towards the neatly organized kitchen for a snack—Minx had locked the door to it as well.

Amrita stepped into the other room—Minx's room—for the first time since her arrival. It had a familiar smell—one that had started to make her skin crawl. She looked around at the black walls and black fittings. Minx had reversed the colour scheme here by keeping the rest of it white. Nothing was out of place—not one carelessly flung T-shirt or piece of paper. The bed was narrow and hard with a wooden Chinese pillow and a white blanket. Minx never switched off the air-conditioner in her room, and Amrita found herself shivering as she poked around. The cupboards were locked. They were enormous—wall to wall, and up to the ceiling. Amrita wondered what on earth was stuffed inside them considering Minx had such few belongings. Couldn't have been her clothes, she seemed to live in those black jeans and a set of sweat shirts, mostly black, which Amrita found in a neat stack on a chair. There was no mirror or dressing-table in the room. The bedside table had open drawers and Amrita squatted to look through the few things there. Bills, memos, a leather-bound phone book, a copy of the Bhagvad Gita and piles of telex messages. Quickly, she scanned the first few but soon gave up. They were coded. Amrita picked up Minx's worry beads and rubbed them. She'd noticed that Minx rarely left the house without stuffing them into her pocket first. How come she'd forgotten them today? She lifted the heavy, white bedcover and peeped under the bed—nothing but cartons of Cartier along with six bottles of Royal Salute.

Amrita went into the bathroom, which was enormous. There was no mirror here either. She opened the cabinet above the basin and found the usual stuff—throwaway razors, deo, cakes of imported soap, body lotions, shampoos and bath salts. A disappointingly normal bathroom if one ignored a strange looking contraption in one corner. Amrita took a closer look—perhaps it was one of those new-fangled exercise machines, she mused, staring at the levers. A quick look at her watch showed that Minx would be back any minute. The bathroom was lined with locked cupboards too, besides a mini-library of books nestling in a bookshelf. No magazines. No newspapers. The books themselves were on strange subjects. Amrita found at least a dozen devoted to butterflies. She wasn't surprised to note the absence of novels. Close to the sunken bathtub, Amrita spotted a small television screen—a Japanese one. Hidden away in a niche in the black-tiled wall was a VCR. Amrita opened a black-painted wicker basket expecting to find soiled clothes. Instead it was packed with video cassettes—no labels, no titles, nothing to indicate what was on them. She'd never noticed Minx displaying the slightest interest in films. Her own room had a brand-new Sony television set with an Akai VCR. Minx had told her to give her a list of films she wanted to watch. Or music she wished to hear.

'Snooping?' She heard the voice and dropped a cassette from her trembling hands. Minx hadn't made a sound while entering the flat and now here she was, a mere six feet away, staring coolly at her, arms akimbo.

Amrita began to stutter foolishly, 'I was bored.'

Minx came up and put her arms around her, 'Don't be scared, it's all right. This is your home. Come on . . . stop shaking. I'm not going to hurt you. I am here to love you.'

Amrita allowed herself to rest her head against Minx's chest while she rocked her back and forth. Minx led her out to the dining-table and said 'Voila!' It was full of fruits and flowers, arranged artistically around a silver tray with a green-eyed black cat on it. 'A companion for you. I thought you'd like her,' Minx said coming up from behind and hugging Amrita.

The cat was absolutely beautiful. And Amrita couldn't resist reaching for her. Cradling her in her arms, she went and sat on the bean bag while Minx unlocked the kitchen and put something into the mixer. Neither of them heard the phone ringing over the noisy whirr of the machine. It was when Minx switched if off that the persistent sound attracted their attention.

'I'll take it,' Minx said, grabbing the receiver. Amrita continued to stroke the cat while Minx spoke in a low, muffled voice into the receiver. She was talking in Hindi—goonda Hindi, full of slang. There was a payment to be made and Minx was arguing about the amount. 'No way,' she heard her say, 'it was goofed up badly. That was not our agreement. I don't care. This is going to get messy. Who will take the brunt?' She heard her slam the phone down and come back into the room holding two tall cocktail glasses aloft. 'To the new addition,' she said giving Amrita a frozen strawberry daiquiri with a hibiscus decorating the rim. Amrita grabbed her drink and drank greedily. Her stomach had been growling with hunger for a while. The cat purred contentedly in her lap. Minx looked preoccupied as she sipped her own drink and toyed with the flower. Abruptly, she put down her glass and went into her bedroom to speak to someone over the extension there. Her voice was far too soft for Amrita to make out anything. She stroked the sleek creature and cradled her warm furry body against her cheek. Minx came back looking more relaxed. 'It' s all settled—thank God,' she said lighting a cigarette with obvious relief.

Amrita had nearly drained her glass and her head was beginning to feel light and giddy. 'What did you put into this?' she asked Minx.

The kitten jumped off her lap and went to bask in a square of mild sunlight coming in through the blinds.

Minx strode up to Amrita and hauled her up from the bean bag. 'Come on, let's enjoy the moment,' she commanded leading her to the dining-table. With one swift move she removed Amrita's Singapore caftan. Amrita stood there unsteadily, not knowing what to expect next. Minx pushed her back on to the dining-table crushing all the fresh flowers under her body.

'What are you doing?' Amrita protested.

'Worshipping you, beautiful,' Minx said gathering up a few flowers and strewing them across her naked limbs. 'How absolutely stunning you look this way,' Minx exclaimed, arranging Amrita's lush hair around her face. 'Hold it right there,' she said, rushing into her own bedroom.

Amrita's head was swimming. She lay back on the blooms, wondering weakly what Minx was planning next. Minx was back in seconds, holding a nifty video camera in her hands. 'I love these modern gadgets, don't you?' she asked as she switched on the red button and began filming Amrita.

When she realized what Minx was doing, Amrita awkwardly tried to sit up, clutching her hands over her pubis and breasts.

'Stop that, you silly girl,' Minx said harshly. 'You are spoiling everything. Now I'll have to repeat it all over again. Lie back the way you were and play with yourself—use the flowers and fruits. Go on—don't you have any imagination? Do it . . . .'

Amrita was too woozy by now to do anything. What had Minx put into the drink? She lay back looking up at the ceiling, hoping that Minx's little game would end. But for Minx the fun had just about begun. She walked around the table filming Amrita from every angle, issuing instructions that she refused to follow. Just as abruptly, Minx stopped and put the camera down on a chair. 'Fine you don't want to play. Not right now. It's OK. We'll do it some other time.'

Amrita rose and sat up on the table. The kitten joined her gracefully. Amrita's head was spinning. Minx stared intensely. 'What a sight the two of you make,' she said, 'I'd love to capture you like this—the way the world will never see you.'

Amrita blushed and tried to walk towards her room. But Minx pushed her back on the table roughly. 'Stay where you are. Don't move till I tell you.' Amrita felt her knee stinging where Minx had slapped it smartly. She folded her legs under her and sat back, fondling the kitten. 'If only Karan and all the rest of those wolves could see you like this—click you like this!' Minx breathed heavily. 'But they never will . . . this image will remain exclusively mine forever.'

Amrita shifted uncomfortably and said, 'I want to pee . . . please . . . let me go.'

'No way,' Minx hissed. 'You will move when I command you to. Right now, you are my slave, let me feast my eyes on you.' She came up to Amrita and began caressing her body with a rose, taking deep breaths along every inch of skin. The kitten kept up a persistent, pathetic mewing.

'I think the poor thing is hungry. Let me give her some milk and I'll come back here,' Amrita pleaded.

'Shut up and stay still,' Minx said pushing the kitten off the table with a sweep of her hand. She was looming over Amrita now, forcing her to arch her back and contort her body. Once more, she grabbed the camera and starting shooting her in startling close ups, focusing on a few square inches at a time. 'I want to remember every bit of you—every pore, every mole, each little hair,' she said as the camera panned over her body recording each detail.

Hunger, the work and the oppressive heat combined to make Amrita feel faint. She could barely keep her eyes open as she heard Minx muttering entreaties, zooming in and out, arranging and rearranging her limbs and the flowers over them, parting her legs and focusing on the separated petals . . . moaning with obvious pleasure at the sight. After what seemed like an hour, but was probably just a few short minutes, Amrita saw her leap off and rush into her bathroom. When she did not return for a few minutes, Amrita plucked up sufficient courage to climb off the table. On the way to her room, she saw Minx's bathroom door ajar and went up hesitantly to see what she was up to. Amrita found her in the bathtub, steeped in sudsy water, watching the just-shot tape on the small screen—replaying certain portions over and over again—and shutting it off periodically to lie back with her eyes shut, trapped in a fantasy of her own, her hands moving rhythmically between her legs and her mouth repeating Amrita's name.

Twenty

Six months later, as Amrita sat on the bean bag filing her nails, waiting for Minx to return, she thought to herself how easily she had fallen into a pattern. Nothing seemed strange to her, not even Minx's wild swings in mood, or her pathological need to possess her. Amrita's career was on the upswing after a slight slump. The ad people did not really care whether Minx and she were an item, as long as their appointments were kept. Most of them had developed an uneasy relationship with Minx who accompanied Amrita everywhere. They had found out soon enough that she was not too tough to handle provided they kept on her right side and stayed away from Amrita.

It was an unwritten rule that Amrita would not shoot for Karan. In any case both of them were booked right through till the end of the year and the rumour was that Karan had found a new girl—another

'Face of the Nineties', who had bagged three of the biggest campaigns for the following year.

Minx was a big asset as far as Amrita's contracts and schedules were concerned. She handled both with enviable efficiency, making sure to squeeze the best terms from notoriously tight-fisted clients. She handled Amrita's earnings well, investing shrewdly in shares that were bound to appreciate over the next five years. She had also put down upfront money for a property on the outskirts of Pune, referring to it longingly as 'our retirement home'. Initially, Amrita had been wary and suspicious, insisting on sitting through all negotiations and scrutinizing each contract thoroughly till one day Minx had told her, 'Look, beautiful. You can trust me. I don't need your money. I have heaps of my own. I just want to make sure your interests are protected. Also, it gives me a personal thrill to see you become the highest-paid model in India. I want to ensure that you remain there. And you will—if you leave it to me. I'll make you a rich woman.'

Amrita left it all to Minx after that. In any case, she didn't really have a head for money and it was a relief to have someone handle hers.

*

Each month, Amrita would receive ten thousand rupees as 'pocket money' which Minx would hand over with

Strange Obsession

a smile and a kiss. 'If you're a good girl I'll hike it to fifteen,' she would say, while Amrita grabbed the envelope gleefully. The first time Minx handed over the cash to her she had said, 'This is yours—use it carefully. Don't blow it on junk. I won't ask you what you do with it. But if it's anything that might make me angry I'd advise you to think a million times.'

Minx didn't have to spell things out. By now Amrita knew what was taboo. The thrill of getting the money was childish and Amrita knew it. There was nothing, really, that she could do with it. Minx took care of everything—clothes, toiletries, travel and food. Even jewellery. The first major piece of 'serious' jewellery she received alarmed her. It was an incredibly beautiful Art Deco bracelet set with rubies and diamonds. 'I know a little about this stuff,' Minx boasted, watching Amrita's expression. 'I got this from a broke maharani. There's more where that came from, by the way.'

Amrita gazed at it for a long time before slipping it on to her slim wrist. 'But where on earth would I wear something like this?' she asked Minx.

'You don't. These are called investment jewels. You never wear them. You keep them in a vault. Come on, let me show you a safe place.' She caught her hand and led her to her bedroom. There, behind a large, stylized black and white canvas was a safe. 'Keep it here. I don't trust bank lockers,' she instructed. Expertly she turned the knob till the right combination appeared. She swung open the heavy steel door and Amrita gasped. It was like Alladin's cave, filled with rare pieces, almost all of them from Minx's favourite Art Deco period. While she examined a diamond and emerald brooch, Minx pulled out a large leather box and opened it. There were several velvet-lined trays in layers, each one containing an array of antique watches. Men's watches mainly, but also a few exquisite women's watches.

'What are these?' asked Amrita looking at them closely.

Minx laughed a satisfied laugh. 'A few years ago, I met a strange Belgian man in one of those shady Colaba cafés—my regular beat then. He was an international dealer in antique watches. We became friends. I got him some contacts. That's how I was hooked. I started to read about time-pieces and watches . . . I discovered there was big money to be made abroad if you knew the right people. I became his scout and supplier for a while. And then I was on my own.' After a pause she added, 'I trade in them, I keep my favourites but the rest, I flog. Not here, naturally, though there are a few connoisseurs willing to pay those kind of prices. My beauties go abroad. It's a good side business to have. They're small enough to travel in a handbag. Nobody suspects a thing. Most of our dumb customs officers think they are junk. It's easy, easy, easy.'

Amrita tried on a couple but she noticed how nervous it made Minx. 'The balance is most delicate,' she said. 'And repairs cost the earth. Treat them well and they behave beautifully. One wrong move, and it's gone.'

Amrita handed the watches back to her. There were still things about Minx that continued to surprise her. Just when she thought she knew everything, Minx would spring something new—like her watch trove. It was easy to like Minx when she was like this—enthusiastic, preening and childishly smug. It was the other Minx who scared her. That Minx made only an occasional appearance these days. Amrita had learnt to predict down to the minute when the switch would occur—it was generally after a long photography session during the course of which Minx would withdraw after watching Amrita interact with the others, laughing, smiling, even flirting lightly. The rage would begin to build on location itself. Amrita would watch for the signals from the corners of her eyes—the chain-smoking, pacing, nervous fidgeting and finally a terse command, 'Come on, let's get out of here.'

The tantrum would begin the moment they were out of earshot. Minx would fly at her, eyes ablaze with rage, 'Bitch! Whore! When will you change? When will you learn?' The first few times Amrita had shrunk back into the seat of the car and sobbed into her dupatta. Gradually, she had conditioned herself to switch off and concentrate on the road. At home the tantrum would continue for a couple of hours, with Minx rushing around the place, punching pillows and sometimes the wall. She had struck Amrita a couple of times—stinging blows across her face—and then collapsed at her feet begging forgiveness, kissing her toes and wetting them with her tears. These scenes invariably ended up with a contrite Minx making love to Amrita, followed by giant-sized bouquets and an expensive gift. Amrita had learned to accept the love-making as part of the strange, twilit life she led now. It took a few hours, but it was worth the price.

Amrita lived for her shoots and shows—the only time she got to meet people; 'normal' people, as she reminded Minx sometimes. They did go out to discos and even parties but were treated like a steady couple. Nobody dared ask Amrita to dance, and other invitees spoke to them only as a duo with no individual conversation. Occasionally, Karan would be around, but he was careful to keep his distance. Just once Amrita had run into him unexpectedly in her host's guest-room when she had emerged from the loo and found him waiting to go in. Thrown by the unexpectedness of the situation, she had grabbed his hand and pleaded, 'Karan, save me, get me out of here.'

He had pushed her away roughly with a brusque, 'Forget it, kid. I value my life.'

Amrita had whirled around sensing a presence. It was Minx standing by the door, smoking calmly and watching her—watching them.

'Sad! Sad!' she had said to Amrita running a finger down her cheek. 'No saviour for you. Too bad, all your boyfriends are minus balls. No knights in shining armour. What a pity. You seem doomed to spend your life trapped with a witch.'

Amrita had tears streaming down her cheeks which Minx wiped away carefully. 'It's not so bad, darling,' she had soothed, 'life could be a lot worse. Think of it, instead of me it could be one of those hijras,' Minx had said mockingly, pointing to the trendily-dressed crowd thronging the tiny apartment.

Twenty-one

Partha had not had the time to think seriously of Amrita. He had been far too busy capitalizing on his hit-and-run story. The CBI had been assigned the task of unravelling the mystery but had come up with nothing—no leads, no clues, no theories. It was assumed the file would be closed after a couple of years of pretended digging around. Meanwhile, Partha had given a series of interviews to video news-magazines (from his hospital bed) and assorted publications, some of which had run him on the cover, heavily bandaged and almost unrecognizable. There were speculations galore and a few malicious rumours ('his wife must've arranged it') but Partha had chosen to politicize the incident, claiming it was a terrorist group from down south that was after his blood for having launched an ongoing campaign against their activities in Tamil Nadu. The government had rushed to provide him with 'adequate protection'. Partha was now entitled to a police escort of his own—a social perk he valued greatly.

Amrita had flipped through a few of the magazines carrying his story and winced at the gory pictures. Minx had refused to comment just as conveniently as she had blithely ignored the Lola incident. While Amrita whiled away her time between shows and assignments watching Hindi films on the video, Minx would lock herself into her room with its newly-installed fax and telex machines. All day, and sometimes late in the night, Amrita would hear the beeps and pings of the machines and wonder what business Minx was transacting and with whom. 'Stocks' was Minx's standard reply when Amrita asked. The few messages she had intercepted made no sense to her and Minx was not at all forthcoming with her explanations. But Amrita was not overly interested either. Between the two of them they were clearing enough to lead a more than comfortable existence.

*

Amrita had taken to sending some of her earnings to her mother in Delhi. These were invested for her in the form of jewellery. She knew her parents had been pleasantly surprised by her success and the money she was making. But behind the pleasure, lurked a certain anxiety—an anxiety her mother expressed during their frequent phone conversations. 'Baby, you don't sound like yourself at all. What's wrong?' she would ask repeatedly. Amrita evaded her questions with excuses,

'I have a migraine today,' 'Late night yesterday,' 'I've got my period,' but she didn't entirely convince Mrs Aggarwal.

Mrs Aggarwal had confessed to her husband that she was worried about their only daughter, 'We should be looking out for a groom for her,' she had taken to saying at the breakfast-table each morning. The brothers used to exchange knowing looks and say, 'How do you know that she hasn't found someone in Bombay? That city is such a fast place and she mixes around so much.' But Mrs Aggarwal would defend Amrita staunchly, 'Not my girl, she's a good child. She'll marry the man Papa and I find for her.'

'Ha! Ha!' the response was always swift and mocking. Deep down Mrs Aggarwal knew her sons were right but that didn't prevent her from discussing the matter.

The burden of finding a suitable husband for Amrita must have been weighing so heavily on her mind that the moment she saw Rakesh Bhatia walking in with her husband she knew he was the man. She pulled her husband into the bedroom to ask who he'd brought home with him.

'A young businessman—NRI. He's looking for investment opportunities in India. Mr Ganju—you know that exporter friend of mine—put him on to me.' He recognized the look in his wife's eyes immediately. 'No . . . you aren't thinking of approaching him, I hope. We know nothing about him. Please control yourself.'

But Mrs Aggarwal's mind was racing. He was the son-in-law of her dreams—tall, fair, sharp-featured, neatly-dressed and well-mannered. He had even touched her feet when they were introduced! Imagine that! In today's day and age, a young man, a foreign-returned young man, who had not forgotten tradition. She liked him even more for that. He called her 'Ma-ji' not 'Aunty-ji' and that was another mark in his favour. Spontaneously, she asked him to stay for dinner. When he hesitated, her husband frowned in her direction and looked embarrassed. But it only took him a second to agree. Mrs Aggarwal rushed off to the kitchen to instruct the cook to prepare kheer. And methi paranthas. And pakoras. She was sure he'd been starving himself in America and would relish wholesome, home-made food.

Rakesh, she discovered, had lived in America for the past ten years, visiting India three times annually. Mrs Aggarwal didn't let up on the questioning, even when his mouth was full. She found out his family history within the first five minutes and established a common link through his grandmother. Other enquiries followed, including questions on his type of business (electronic components) and in a not so round-about way, his financial status. Rakesh was frank and open, answering her with an amused tolerance but never mocking her curiosity or snubbing her. Mrs Aggarwal appreciated that. Finally, unable to resist the temptation, she rushed into her bedroom and came back with a fat album. Mr Aggarwal knew perfectly well what she was up to. He excused himself from the room and on some pretext, called out to her. When Mrs Aggarwal came out she saw her husband outraged: 'What are you doing? Aren't you ashamed of yourself? He is a total stranger.'

Mrs Aggarwal tried to calm him down. 'Trust me in this,' she said, 'my instincts are rarely wrong. He is the man. Even my God agrees. While I was praying, a flower fell. That was the sign I was waiting for.'

Her husband shook his head exasperatedly. It was no use; when his wife was like this it was best to withdraw. He went back to join Rakesh, while she stayed behind for a moment to have another quick word with her God.

'Your daughter?' Rakesh asked as they flipped through the album.

'Yes,' Mrs Aggarwal replied excitedly. 'She lives in Bombay . . . she is a very famous model in India.'

Rakesh pointed to another picture and said, 'She is very beautiful, if I may say so.'

'Oh yes, isn't she? She could easily have won the Miss India title but she didn't want to take part. Now, she is getting film offers daily . . . daily. But she's not interested. It is not a good line for girls from good families,' Mrs Aggarwal chattered on, as she went back for more photographs, magazine clippings, calendars and posters.

Rakesh took his time scrutinizing the pictures. 'You must be very proud of her,' he said glancing through another pile of glossy prints.

Mrs Aggarwal beamed, 'Yes, indeed we are,' and then she blurted out, 'you should meet her.'

Rakesh looked up, 'I'd love to but when and where?'

Mrs Aggarwal looked nervously at her husband before suggesting, 'Let me phone her right now. She could come to Delhi. Or maybe your business will take you to Bombay soon?'

Rakesh tugged at his left earlobe thoughtfully, 'I was planning a trip to Bombay sometime next month . . . maybe I could bring the date forward and go next week.'

Mrs Aggarwal all but jumped up with excitement, 'You're going to get along. The two of you . . . forgive me for being so frank . . . but I felt it as soon as I met you.'

Rakesh smiled at her warmly, 'You don't have to be so embarrassed, Ma-ji,' he said, 'I have two sisters myself . . . and a mother who is always looking out for . . . for . . . friends . . . for them.'

Mr Aggarwal shifted uncomfortably in the sofa. Rakesh looked at the time and got up. 'I'll phone and give you my schedule,' he said to Amrita's mother.

Mrs Aggarwal stopped herself from winking conspiratorially at him. 'I'll be speaking to my daughter tomorrow,' she added, 'I'll tell her to expect you next week.'

*

Minx was in a foul mood that Friday. 'The deal's off,' Amrita heard her saying over the telephone. Idly, she wondered which deal and then went back to polishing her toenails. The phone rang again. 'You take it,' Minx said grumpily and went off to wash her hair.

The excitement in Mrs Aggarwal's voice came through loud and clear as she told Amrita, 'Darling, I've found a boy for you . . . don't say anything till you've met him.'

Amrita looked over her shoulder furtively to check where Minx was. She heard her call out, 'Who is it?'

'No one—Mummy,' Amrita answered shortly.

Mrs Aggarwal was chattering away, 'You'll like him too. I'm sure of it. I think you'll get along . . . he's handsome, well-to-do . . . .'

Amrita cut her short, 'Mummy, I'm not looking for a husband. When did I tell you I wanted to get married?'

Hurt by the sharp tone of her voice, Mrs Aggarwal stopped abruptly. Amrita apologized quickly and said, 'I'm sorry, Mummy. But right now I'm very busy . . . I have so many jobs on hand. I really love my work.'

'I know all that baby . . . but at some point you'll have to think of your future.'

Bitterly, Amrita thought to herself, 'My future has already been decided for me,' but to her mother she said, 'It's sweet of you, Mummy, but I don't think I'm ready for marriage yet.'

'All young people say that these days—look at your brothers. I'm not that old-fashioned, my dear. All I want you to do is see him when he comes to Bombay.'

Amrita wanted the conversation to end before Minx got back to the room. 'Tell me his name . . . and . . . don't give him this number. You call me and let me have the Bombay address and I'll phone him.'

Mrs Aggarwal seemed puzzled, 'Why, darling? Is there some problem with your phone?'

Hastily Amrita assured her, 'Nothing at all but since we don't have a full-time servant and since both of us are so busy, I don't get any messages.'

Mrs Aggarwal understood that and rang off after repeating his name twice. 'Don't forget, baby, the name is Rakesh.'

It was only later as Amrita lay on her bed after a tense dinner and a desultory attempt at love-making that something occurred to her. Suddenly, she was wide awake and sitting bolt upright in bed (Minx had retired for the night to her room). This was the opportunity she'd been waiting for, dreaming about. Rakesh was the one who was going to help her escape! Amrita felt a tingling sensation down her spine at the prospect. She did not care who he was, what he did or how he looked. All she was interested in was getting out. She recalled the most significant part of her mother's brief conversation, 'He lives in America, in New York.' That was the key and the magic word was America. Amrita smiled to herself. Sure, Minx could always follow her there, but it would be a different story. Minx's tricks would not work with the police in New York. She would report her to them. They would pick her up—lock her away. Deport her. Anything at all. And finally she would be free. After that Rakesh would not matter. She would divorce him. Find herself a job. Start another life. A life without Minx. Her eyes were shining brightly in the dark, as she hugged herself and thought about the future.

The lights outside her room seemed to glow brightly that night. And for the first time in months Amrita fell into a deep, deep sleep, a smile on her lips.

*

Amrita met Rakesh at the Rangoli. She had picked the restaurant with care. It was the unlikeliest place for her to go to and the last one Minx would think of. It had been surprisingly easy for her to set it all up. She had told Minx she was off to the Oberoi Towers' Shopping Arcade for a couple of hours. Absently Minx had said, 'Don't be naughty and don't spend too much.' Amrita was relieved she had not been subjected to the usual grilling. She figured it was because of Minx's intense preoccupation with her mysterious business. In any case, their relationship had settled into a placid groove and Minx seemed far more relaxed about it. She even joked, 'We've become a dull old married couple,' much to Amrita's embarrassment. For her part, Amrita had slipped into a stoical, resigned frame of mind. There were times she bitterly resented her situation but at other times she told herself life could have been a lot worse. Minx could still be tiresome but now that she was less and less suspicious, Amrita was able to cope with her far better. The old rages and accusations were limited to stray post-party scenes and Amrita had taught herself to laugh those off. She no longer reacted with hurt and she did not bother to defend herself. She knew it took just a small gesture on her part for Minx's anger to vanish. And, cleverly, Amrita learned to wait for the right moment before making it.

Meeting Rakesh had assumed an importance she was not prepared for. Everything hinged on how it would go. Amrita dressed carefully that morning. She did not want to scare him off by overwhelming him with her presence and yet she wanted to make an impression—a big impression. She chose a pastel coloured salwar kameez with delicate badla-kam. She looked like a Mughal miniature. The make-up was kept to a minimum and she wore her hair swept into a top-knot into which she had stuck a couple of tortoise-shell pins. She had stopped wearing junk jewellery since Minx didn't approve of it. She chose a pair of flawless solitaires for her ears and a rope-like gold chain around the neck. From her collection of rings, she picked five filigreed ones. Some set with tiny diamonds and some without. Amrita also did not want to draw too much attention to herself since she knew Minx would subject her to close scrutiny before she left the house.

But all she said was, 'Very pretty. Don't forget your sunglasses.' Then, as an afterthought Minx added, 'Aren't you wearing far too much jewellery just to go shopping?'

Amrita stared guiltily at her fingers and began removing a couple of rings. Minx came up and hugged her. 'I was only teasing. Run along and come back soon. Pick up a croissant for me if you can.'

Amrita rushed out before Minx could stop her and hailed a cab. Minx did not like her to do that at all. She looked up at the window and found her staring. She waved casually and was relieved when Minx waved back. It meant she was not hostile.

Amrita tried to visualize Rakesh. She had liked his voice and approach over the phone. And she trusted her mother's assessment. Mrs Aggarwal was known to be even more finicky and critical about people than she was.

The cab took a sharp left and stopped before the handsome stone entrance of the restaurant. Amrita paid off the cabbie and tripped lightly up the stairs. The interior was dark and it took her a while to look around. Most of the tables were empty, as she had hoped they would be. Oh God! Maybe he'd stood her up. She was about to leave when she spotted a young man walking in. He could not see her but she could see him clearly. She liked what she saw. He was dressed casually in well-worn jeans combined with a sports shirt. She liked his windblown hair and the lightness of his step as he took the stairs two at a time. He probably played tennis or some other energetic game, she figured, as he came through the door and ran his fingers through his hair.

'Hi!' she said walking up to him, 'I'm the one you're looking for.'

Rakesh smiled a warm, friendly smile and took both her hands in his. It was such a spontaneous gesture that she liked him immediately.

'Your mother was right,' he said, 'you are the most beautiful girl in India.'

Amrita acknowledged the compliment with a small bow.

He couldn't take his eyes off her. They sat at a table for two and he ordered tea; then he changed his mind and asked for vodka-tonic. Seeing her expression, he said, 'I need it to face someone like you and not pass out.'

Amrita laughed, ordering a capuccino for herself. 'Are you always this nervous . . . or should I make that flirtatious?' she asked.

Rakesh took a large sip and said, 'Always.'

There was a slight pause and then both of them started to speak simultaneously, 'You first,' Rakesh said gallantly.

'No, no . . . you,' Amrita smiled, sitting back to watch him.

'OK,' Rakesh said, 'I guess you know what all this is about.'

'Tell me.'

'Your mother,' Rakesh said, 'whom I've fallen madly in love with, has manoeuvred us both into this wonderful situation with what is described as "matrimony" in view.'

Amrita blushed and looked away.

Rakesh placed his hand over hers and said, 'Look, don't feel all awkward and shy. She meant well and I'm not such a bad chap. I mean well too. In fact, I mean so well, I want to take up her suggestion and marry you. Absurd, insane, crazy, whatever . . . but I feel it right here,' and he tapped his heart. 'I know this is for me. But only you know whether it is the same for you. I like what I see very, very much. This has never happened to me before. I like your family, and as far as I'm concerned, this is it. What do you say?'

Amrita fiddled with her cup of coffee and then said, 'Mind if I smoke? I suddenly feel like a ciggie.'

Rakesh summoned a waiter saying, 'Actually I do mind. I think it's a foul habit. But I guess you've earned it. You deserve a cigarette break—but—just this one. OK?'

Amrita shook her head gratefully. Smoking was a habit she abhorred too, but now with Minx's constant puffing, she had taken to smoking an occasional cigarette herself.

Amrita reached for her bag and pulled out a pack of Cartiers. Rakesh raised an eyebrow and asked for an ashtray. 'What are well brought up Punjabi kuddis coming to these days?' he teased watching her fingers shake as she nervously tried to light up. 'Here let me do that,' he said, taking the cigarette from her lips.

'I thought you were anti-smoking?' she demanded.

'I am,' he replied. 'Most reformed chain-smokers get that way.'

She tried to pull the cigarette out of his mouth agitatedly. 'I don't want to be held responsible for starting you off again,' she cried.

'I have nerves of steel. Don't worry,' Rakesh said taking a deep drag before giving the cigarette back to her.

It was more then two hours later that Amrita remembered to look at her watch. She let out a small scream. 'I have to go,' she said worriedly.

Rakesh didn't ask any questions, he called for the check and got up. She gathered her things and nearly ran out of the restaurant. There was a strong sea breeze outside and as they stood near his car, her top-knot came undone, and cascades of russet coloured hair flew around her face as she bid him a flustered goodbye. He looked amused, watching quietly as she fussed with her handbag, hair and sunglasses all at the same time.

'Do you have transport?' he asked, looking around at the empty car lot.

'No, I'll take a cab,' she answered quickly.

He shrugged, 'I could always drop you off, you live right round the corner, don't you?'

Amrita immediately became flushed and tense. She snapped at him, 'Yes, I do. But I prefer to find my own way home.'

Rakesh raised an eyebrow quizzically, 'Jealous boyfriend lurking around?'

She stared at him angrily, 'You have no right to talk to me like this. We don't know each other. You're a stranger. I think it's awfully rude of you to make such personal remarks.'

He put his arm around her and said, 'You frightened little girl. Take it easy. I was only kidding. But whoever it is who's making you this nervous—I envy him.'

She turned to go. He stopped her. 'I'm here for another two days. Will we meet again?'

'I don't think so. I don't know,' Amrita said.

He refused to let go of her arm. 'I know you more than you think I do. Don't run away from me like this. I'm not going to push you into anything but I meant what I said earlier. I'll be good for you. And I know you'll be great for me. Trust your mother. You won't regret it.'

Amrita could barely concentrate on his words. He slipped her his business card saying, 'Call me. I'm staying here,' he pointed to the Oberoi Towers across the road. And that was when Amrita remembered the

Strange Obsession

croissant. 'Oh God!' she exclaimed. 'I've forgotten the croissant!'

Rakesh continued to stare at her. 'Croissant?' he asked.

'Yes, oh help! I have to come to your hotel.'

'Be my guest,' he said happily.

*

Amrita was paying for the croissant at the cafeteria counter and Rakesh was slurping away at a strawberry float when she heard Minx call out to her. The package with the croissant in it fell out of her hand as she whirled around to face Minx.

'Where have you been, darling?' Minx said, holding her hand and kissing her forehead. 'I was so worried when you didn't return. I decided to come here and check you out.' She stopped talking and held Amrita's clammy hand. 'Hey! What's the matter? Where are your shopping bags? Something wrong? Your hands are so cold.'

Amrita was shaking. Suddenly, she felt another hand on her shoulder—a heavier, firmer hand. Rakesh's voice was saying, 'It's all right. She'll be OK. Just leave her to me.'

He leaned close to Amrita's ear and whispered, 'You don't have to be scared. I know about her.'

Amrita stared at him with startled, wild eyes. He nodded, 'I do my homework—something my father taught me.'

Minx pushed him away roughly and reprimanded Amrita sharply, 'Behave yourself. You are in a public place. People are staring.'

Amrita appealed to Rakesh with her eyes. He stepped in between the two women and caught Amrita's hand, 'Come with me,' he said to her, urgency in his voice. 'Don't think. Trust me.'

Amrita made a move towards Rakesh. Suddenly, she felt something cold and hard jabbing her ribs. Minx was talking rapidly to Rakesh, 'Take a look at what's in my hand, loverboy. Try any funny stuff and she's dead. You too.'

Rakesh looked down at the snub-nosed pistol held in her hands and looked up into Amrita's stricken eyes. 'What's it to be?' he asked quietly.

'Please go away, leave me alone. I'll be OK.' Amrita said, her voice barely audible.

Minx nudged her forward with the barrel of the gun and the three of them walked swiftly out of the arcade.

*

Once home, Amrita threw herself down on her bed and wept uncontrollably, her body shaking with sobs that refused to subside. Minx pretended to busy herself with some telex messages that had come in during her absence. They had not spoken a word to each other on the drive back home. After an hour or so, Amrita rose unsteadily to her feet and went towards the bathroom to wash her face. Minx was waiting for her on her bed when she got back. Amrita recoiled at the set expression in her eyes. And then her eyes wandered down to her hands, the memory of the gun still uppermost in her mind. Instead, she spotted a box of matches. Minx was playing with the matchsticks, lighting them one by one and waiting for the flame to reach her fingers. 'Take off your clothes and lie down,' she commanded.

Amrita trembled at the tone of her voice. She folded her hands and entreated her, 'Please, I beg of you. I'm sorry for what I did. Forgive me . . . . Please forgive me.'

Minx stared at her coldly, 'There is nothing to forgive. All bitches in heat are the same . . . sniffing around constantly. Unfaithful, foolish, ungrateful. Why should you be different? The mistake was mine. I thought you'd changed. I started to trust you ... a little. You took advantage of me. I don't like that. I shall have to punish you. I don't like that either. But it has to be done.'

Amrita fell to her knees and crawled to where Minx was. She held her feet and pleaded, 'I'll never do it again. I promise you. Never, ever. Please don't hurt me.'

Minx bent down and lashed at her, savagely ripping open her pretty pink kurta. 'Shut your mouth. Whore! Slut! I've given you everything—a comfortable life, money, jewels, everything. What more do you want? A cock to fill you up? You'll get that too.' Minx kept tearing at Amrita's clothes till her kurta was in shreds.

Amrita tried to cover herself with her hands. Minx pulled her towards the bed and threw her down. Amrita shut her eyes and lay back limply. She knew she could not fight Minx. It was always easier to submit.

For a long and agonizing minute, she could not hear anything and wondered where Minx had gone. But she did not dare open her eyes. She stiffened when she heard the soft sound of a match being struck and Mink's breath on her face.

'A bitch in heat,' Minx laughed, bringing the match close to her eyes and singeing the tips of her lashes.

Amrita tried to move her head, but Minx had pinned her down. The room soon filled with the acrid smell of burnt hair. She heard her strike another match. Minx was moving lower down her body. She was muttering something Amrita could barely hear. 'This should make you hot,' Minx cackled and moved a lit match over Amrita's pubic hair which crackled and curled when the flame touched it. She drew up her knees and cried out in the pain. Minx struck her across the face. 'Be quiet. This is what you were looking for with that stud, weren't you? Some body heat. Now you are going to get it. I've just begun. There are lots of surprises in store for you, baby.'

Amrita grabbed a pillow and tried to defend herself by clutching it to her. Minx lunged at her, pushing her off the bed. Without a warning she forced her legs apart with her knees and Amrita experienced a sharp, searing pain as something hard and long was shoved into her. 'Enjoy, enjoy, enjoy,' Minx laughed pushing the object in and out. 'Think of him. That's how it would have felt, come on, show me how much you like it, I got it specially for you . . . . '

The last thing Amrita recalled before passing out was Minx on top of her, head thrown back and laughing manically. When she sensed the approaching blackness she welcomed it: 'I want to die,' she sighed before closing her eyes.

*

There was a white haze is front of her when she came to. Disoriented and scared Amrita asked thickly, 'Where is she?' Her words sounded slurred to her own ears and she could not focus.

'Madam has gone out for an hour. But I'm here,' a female voice informed her.

'Who are you?' Amrita asked groggily.

'I'm your day nurse—Miss Rekha,' the woman replied.

'Whats wrong with me?' Amrita asked.

'Ask madam. Or the doctor. I'm only here to watch you,' the woman replied.

Amrita looked around the room and saw flowers on the dressing-table. 'How long has it been?'

'Three days,' the nurse said. 'You are very weak. Madam said not to allow you to speak.'

Amrita nodded and looked listlessly around. She could not move her arms as she was hooked to an intravenous drip. Her body felt sore and stiff. 'Take this off,' she told the nurse impatiently.

'No, no, no. Please don't do that. Madam will get very angry with me. I'll get you some fruit juice from the fridge.'

The nurse scuttled away.

Amrita couldn't get up from her bed and when she tried to lift her head, it fell back heavily. All her energy had been drained from her. She felt sapped and defeated.

When the nurse came back with the orange juice, the doorbell rang. She didn't make any move to answer it. Amrita told her weakly, 'Please open the door.'

The nurse shook her head, 'Madam has told me not to. Strict instructions. She will be back soon. I can't open the door. Sorry.'

Amrita mustered up all the strength remaining in her body and sat up in bed, upsetting all the tubes and knocking down the stand from which the I.V. drip was dangling. Alarmed by the expression in her eyes the nurse scampered to the door and opened it.

'Mummy,' Amrita cried out at the sight of Mrs Aggarwal walking uncertainly into the living-room, 'I'm here . . . help me,' Amrita wailed.

Her mother was by her side in minutes, 'My darling, my baby . . . what has she done to you?'

Amrita fell into her arms, crying uncontrollably, while the nurse stood there staring. Amrita whirled around and said, 'Get out of here.'

Strange Obsession

The woman refused to budge.

Amrita told her mother, 'Pay her and throw her out immediately. I don't want to speak in her presence.'

Mrs Aggarwal opened her bag and handed over three hundred rupees to the woman. She still didn't move. After a pause, she said, 'Give me a hundred more and I'll go.' Seconds later she was out of the house.

Before Mrs Aggarwal could say anything Amrita told her, 'Mummy, let's not wait in this hell. I'll tell you everything once we get out of here but let's hurry.'

Mrs Aggarwal held her daughter close to her heart and her eyes filled with tears. 'You silly, foolish girl, why didn't you tell me what was happening? Why did I have to hear it from Rakesh?'

Amrita hugged her back saying, 'I'll explain everything, but first, help me pack. I'll take what fits into one suitcase. That's all. Let her keep everything else. I don't really care. I want to get out, that's all.'

They hurried to her room and started packing swiftly. Amrita had taken the precaution of locking the door. She knew if Minx got back, she wouldn't hesitate to break down the door—this way atleast they'd have some warning.

'Phone Karan—here's the number,' Amrita instructed her mother. 'Tell him to get here as fast as possible. Ask him to bring a friend with him—someone tough. He'll understand.' She threw her clothes hastily into the largest suitcase she could find. She emptied out her dresser and cupboard. She ran into Minx's room to find papers, files, share certificates. Everything was locked away. She came back into her room for a final look-around and realized she wanted nothing.

Her mother was waiting for her, looking calm but intensely sad. Amrita took her hand in hers. 'Is he coming?'

Her mother nodded.

The two of them dragged the heavy suitcase across the room. The doorbell rang noisily and they stood still, not daring to breathe. It rang again and Amrita placed a finger on her lips indicating to her mother to remain silent. They heard someone pounding at the door viciously and then there was no sound. Amrita went to the door and put her ear to it. Turning to her mother, she said, 'It can't be her. She wouldn't have left so easily.' Slowly, she removed the chain and opened the door. The landing was deserted. The two women pushed the bag out and waited for the elevator. They heard the sound of a jeep—it was either Karan or Minx.

Amrita prayed harder than she ever had in her life. Her mother's face was ashen. The elevator was held up on some floor. Finally, they heard the ping of the indicator. It had stopped on their floor. Amrita braced herself, she felt stronger, braver, with her mother by her side. The doors slid open and Karan walked out with Billoo, his assistant.

'Let's go,' he said efficiently, taking the heavy suitcase and grabbing Amrita's hand.

'This is my mother.'

Karan nodded in Mrs Aggarwal's direction. Two minutes later they were speeding away.

'Where to?' Karan asked.

'The airport,' Amrita answered shortly.

Her mother looked anxiously at her, 'Darling, are you sure you can make it? You're looking very weak.'

Amrita stared at the road ahead with a determined look in her eyes, 'I can make it, you'll see.'

Karan was quiet as he negotiated the jeep though the traffic, while his assistant kept a look-out for anybody following them.

'Do you have money for the tickets—we'll have to get them from touts,' Karan said.

Amrita nodded, 'I got paid for that boutique campaign last week. It's all here with me,' she patted her satchel.

'You'll just about make the flight,' Karan said looking at this watch.

'We have to make it, we just have to,' Amrita said, her knuckles white against the dark tan of her handbag.

*

Amrita and her mother were safely airborne when Karan met a crazed Minx running blindly out of the parking lot.

'She's gone,' he told her as he walked towards his jeep.

'No! You fucking liar—you bloody son-of-a-bitch. She can't leave me. Where is she? Where are you hiding her?'

Billoo stepped in between them just as Minx lunged at Karan, a small silver blade glistening in her hand. He caught her wrist and pushed her away as Karan continued to walk towards his car. Minx let out a banshee-like scream and collapsed on the asphalt, flailing at the ground with her fists, till her blood stained the rough road and a couple of traffic assistants strolled up to see what was going on. She caught one of them, 'Take me to the control room,' she screamed. 'That flight has to come back. There's a bomb on it.' They looked at each other wondering what to do as she continued to scream, 'Bring the flight back. Call the police. Do you know whose daughter I am? Tell the Chief Minister! Ring up Delhi! I'm telling you—there's a bomb on it, a bomb.'

Karan called out to the men, 'Don't worry about her—she is crazy. Ignore her. The woman is mad.'

Minx spat in his direction and hurled a stream of abuses at him. 'Arrest that man. He is a criminal. Catch him. He kidnapped my woman. He helped her escape. She is gone . . . my woman is gone. I will kill him. I will kill myself.'

Karan started the jeep. They could hear Minx ranting above the roar of take-offs and landings. Karan turned around for a last look. More than twenty people had gathered around her. Their laughter and blatant curiosity mocked her anguished screams.

'Amrita's safe, but what about us?' Billoo asked.

'At least we've saved one life . . . how many people do even that?' shrugged Karan.

Twenty-two

'Why didn't you tell me what was going on all this time?' Mrs Aggarwal looked more pained than angry. 'Why did I have to hear it from a stranger?'

Amrita smiled wanly, 'I didn't know Rakesh was a "stranger" . . . I thought he is your future son-in-law.'

'Do you mean that, baby? Do you? Don't fool me . . . not after what we've been through,' said Mrs Aggarwal, her eyes lighting up.

Amrita lay back on her bed and looked dreamily up at the ceiling, 'Of course I mean it. Now, we'll have to ask him whether he's still interested.'

'Leave that to me,' Mrs Aggarwal said happily, busying herself with Amrita's clothes. 'He phoned this morning before you were up, but I hadn't spoken to you, I didn't know your mind.' Then, as an afterthought she added, 'That other man, Partha, had also phoned. God knows how he learnt you were home.'

Amrita sat up in bed, 'I know how he knows. One of his assistant editors was on the same flight—that woman with the big bindi and white Kanjeevaram sari. She must've told him.' She noticed her mother frown as she pulled out her old clothes from her cupboard. 'Don't worry, Mummy. He's a friend, that's all.'

Mrs Aggarwal replied tersely, 'I don't understand this friend business. A man and woman can never be just friends. Besides, isn't he married?'

'So what?' Amrita laughed. 'I'm not going to have an affair with him or anything.'

Mrs Aggarwal sat down on her bed. 'Look, darling, the ordeal you've been through has been bad—something your father and I could never have imagined possible. Don't complicate matters further. Rakesh is a wonderful boy. Marry him and forget the horrible past—go away as far as you can.'

Amrita shook her head firmly. 'No, Mummy. I don't want to run. I can never deny my past. Whoever marries me has to accept what happened. I will not lie about it.'

The phone rang and a servant came in to say it was for Amrita. She picked up the extension lazily. It was Karan calling from Bombay. 'Amrita . . . something horrible happened last night. Minx tried to kill herself.'

Mrs Aggarwal noticed Amrita's face drain of colour. 'Give that to me,' she said, grabbing the receiver roughly. She heard the details from Karan quietly, spoke a few words, and put the phone down. Turning to Amrita, she said, 'I'd expected this. Anyway . . . she's alive . . . recovering. Jaslok Hospital.'

Amrita gulped, 'How did she do it? A gun?'

Her mother shook her head, 'No . . . she slit her wrists in the bath tub.'

'I wish for her sake she'd died,' said Amrita.

'There's a suicide note. The police—and her father—have it. It's a long love-letter to you. Karan thinks the press will get hold of it.'

Amrita stared gloomily around her, 'I'm sure that's going to happen.'

'That would scare away not just Rakesh, but any other man,' her mother said, more to herself than to her daughter.

'Maybe it's written in my destiny,' Amrita sighed deeply as the phone rang again. It was Partha. 'We've got the story,' he said calmly, 'and I'm not going to run it in my paper.'

'Thanks,' Amrita whispered, 'but not every editor is you.'

Partha told her to expect the worst. 'It's a good story, Amrita. It's got everything. You're going to be hounded to give your side of it. What is it you plan to do?'

Amrita played with a strand of her hair moodily. 'I don't know. I hadn't thought about it. I certainly don't want publicity. God knows I've had more than enough.'

Partha told her briskly what to say to reporters when they called: 'Better still—get out of town. The scandal will die in due course . . . they all do, even the biggest ones,' Partha advised.

Amrita squared her shoulders and said, 'Why should I be such a coward? I haven't committed a crime.'

Partha fell silent for a while. 'It's really your decision. You could brazen it out if you want to but I wouldn't recommend it at all. Think of your family. Is it fair on them?' They spoke some more before Amrita disconnected, promising to phone back if there were any further developments. Partha's last words stuck in her mind as she bathed. Till then she'd only been preoccupied with herself; when the story broke, they were all going to be equally affected—her brothers, her father and her mother. She decided to hold a family conference and discuss the matter.

'We are behind you one hundred per cent,' said Ashish, while his brother nodded in agreement.

Amrita's father looked concerned as he counselled his wife quietly. Finally, he broke the silence to say, 'This is something we shall have to face whatever the consequences. We don't yet know how or why Amrita brought all this upon herself . . . but she has gone though hell . . . if more is to follow it is our duty to support her.'

Mrs Aggarwal and Amrita had tears in their eyes as Amrita went up and hugged her father.

*

On Partha's advice, Amrita refused all interviews issuing a terse 'no comments' when pushed to say something.

The calls from Bombay didn't cease as Amrita stayed home trying to sort out her thoughts. Rakesh was away in New York and had called once to ask whether she was all right. The sound of his voice—calm and cheerful—had reassured her and she'd told her mother, 'He still wants to talk to me.' She spoke to Partha daily and on his recommendation asked for police protection, certain that Minx would show up in Delhi sooner or later. It had not been easy to convince the police that her life was in danger. Plus, the protection offered was for a limited duration only. Amrita knew she would not have got even that had it not been for the pressure Partha had kept up with his contacts in the police.

Two weeks later, Amrita was restless and bored. She told her mother, 'I can't sit around all my life waiting for that maniac to turn up. I have to do something—anything.'

Her mother looked at her thoughtfully; she knew her wilful daughter only too well. 'Why don't you work with you father? That way you'll get a hang of this business in case . . . in case . . .' and she trailed off.

Amrita completed the sentence for her. 'In case Rakesh comes back and wants to marry someone else, right?'

Her mother looked away uneasily. 'I wonder why he hasn't called again. He'd told Papa-ji he'd be in Delhi within a week. We don't know where to reach him either.'

Amrita shrugged indifferently. 'Really, Mummy. Please don't treat me like some hard-up woman nobody will look at. Why is everybody so desperate? All this is behind me now. I want to work. Make my life again.'

'No more modelling?' her mother wanted to know.

'I don't want to go back to Bombay. I used to write quite well in school and college. Why don't I ask Partha for a job? I don't mind starting as a trainee. I'll learn, I'll try hard. At least I won't get bored.'

She ignored her mother's sceptical look and decided to phone Partha that day itself.

But two hours later, Rakesh was on their doorstep, looking relaxed and triumphant. Mrs Aggarwal rushed out to greet him and guilelessly asked, 'Where were you? We were waiting for your call.'

Rakesh smiled a slow smile. 'There's a lot to discuss. I'd gone abroad on a secret mission.'

Amrita stared quietly at him. Suddenly she felt almost shy in his presence. He had greeted her formally by shaking her hand. He was like a complete stranger—a maddeningly attractive one.

Rakesh's eyes twinkled as he said, 'I'd gone to meet my parents and get their official permission to marry Amrita, that is, if she still wants to marry me. I'm an old-fashioned man in that respect—I wanted my parents to give me their blessings.'

Amrita turned her face away to hide the rising colour. Her mother was laughing with relief and calling out to the servants to bring some sweets. 'Let us celebrate,' she said, holding out her arms to both of them. Amrita glanced across the room and caught Rakesh's eye. He winked and mouthed the words, 'Say Yes'.

*

Two ugly stories about the Minx-Amrita affair appeared in the press on the day her engagement to Rakesh was announced. It was to be a small intimate ceremony for the two families and a few close friends. Nobody referred to the articles in the paper. Partha had been invited along with his wife, but she had chosen to stay away. Amrita had never looked more beautiful than she did as they exchanged rings, clad in a shocking pink and gold gharara. Rakesh was dressed simply in a khadi-silk kurta-pyjama, his hair slicked into place neatly, his eyes dancing naughtily at the stiffness of the occasion.

Amrita had warmed to his parents at their very first meeting and had been struck by their understanding of the situation confronting her. She was, after all, the most-gossiped-about celebrity of the decade, with something or the other appearing about her in the glossies and weekend papers nearly every day. Most of the write-ups had concentrated on the 'strangeness' of her relationship without actually calling her a lesbian. This could not have been easy to stomach for quiet, moderately conservative people like the Bhatias who had been living a suburban existence outside New York for the past ten years. But they'd handled it with remarkable equanimity and refrained from making even a slanted reference to it. Rakesh too had laughed it off urging Amrita to do the same, 'Hell! What are we disguising here? Forget it . . . it's not important . . . and it doesn't change a thing. It was your mother I fell in love with first, when she so sweetly produced all your photographs. And then you . . . when you sneaked out of that prison to meet me and forgot to buy a croissant. Really! Couldn't you have thought of a better alibi! To be done in by a croissant!'

Amrita, however, had not been able to overcome her shame and guilt quite as easily. She still spent several sleepless nights agonizing over the events of the past year, wondering how she had allowed herself to fall into such an obvious trap. There were days she wondered whether she was doing the right thing by marrying Rakesh. And now there was nobody to air her uncertainties to. Though she did not keep anything from Rakesh, she sensed that he didn't wish to discuss her past. What a pity she'd never really had any close girlfriends. The one thought that nagged her constantly involved Rakesh's safety. Minx had been unusually quiet. Amrita knew she was back home and recovering rapidly. Karan kept tabs on her. It seemed strange and more than a little ominous that she'd stayed away from Amrita and made no attempt to see or contact her. Amrita knew just how her mind worked and it scared her to think that Minx was in all probability hatching a plot. A plot that would affect Rakesh—not her.

She had raised the subject with him on the morning of the engagement before the few guests arrived. 'Don't be surprised if she turns up,' she had warned as they talked in her bedroom while a maid fixed fresh flowers in her hair. Rakesh waved his hand dismissively, 'Let her show up, we'll pick her up like a stray rat and chuck her into the dustbin. Don't worry and don't let that spoil the day—our day.' Rakesh had kissed the top of her head gently before going out to greet the guests.

Amrita had continued to stare at her image in the mirror for a long time. She had lain awake the previous night asking herself whether this was really what she wanted. Was she using Rakesh to escape from Minx? Did she love him? Would it work? Was she being fair to herself? Even then, as the maid had fussed with her embroidered dupatta and her mother had bustled in and out of her room, Amrita couldn't stop the flood of doubts. Rakesh was attractive, prosperous, generous, amusing, attentive. They hadn't gone to bed so far—he'd wanted it that way and she'd been thankful. This was another thing that had worried her. Would they be physically compatible? Had Minx spoiled her for everyone else—particularly men? Would she ever feel the same way again with another person—a less adoring, less worshipful, less awestruck partner?

Amrita got her answers sooner than she had anticipated. Rakesh had laughingly told her that she would have to wait till their wedding day, two months later, to find out his 'GIB' (Good In Bed) quotient. Amrita had pulled a face on hearing that but had secretly been relieved. The trauma of what she had experienced— the guilt that refused to go away—had instilled a new fear in her mind. She was certain she had gone off sex permanently. When Rakesh hadn't pushed, she'd felt grateful. In her few private moments she had asked herself whether she needed to consult a therapist but quickly dismissed the thought. 'It will work itself out,' she had assured herself. It was, after all, a question of time and new adjustments.

*

It finally happened the day after Rakesh's birthday. He was leaving for New York at an ungodly time and they were to spend his last few hours in India in his new, well-appointed flat in South Extension.

'We'll open a bottle of wine,' he suggested gaily. Amrita hadn't touched anything even mildly alcoholic since her break with Minx—she could not trust herself not to lose control which she did quite easily and alarmingly soon. Hesitantly she agreed. Rakesh had been so warm and understanding during the preceding weeks, that she had begun to look forward to their nightly outings. He did not seem to have any friends in Delhi but that was understandable given his business commitments. They spent all their time trying out different restaurants and taking long walks in the colony park.

When Rakesh brought her to his flat, she was surprised to see the changes—it looked like some new and startlingly different apartment. 'Like it?' Rakesh asked searching her face. 'I had it redone in a jiffy—three frantic days actually. Earlier it resembled a careless bachelor's dump. I asked a friend to make it more lived-in looking, more cheerful.'

Amrita surveyed the place appreciatively. 'It's wonderful, yes, I love it,' she added taking in the well-picked objects: the muted curtains, the expensive carpets and the tons of old silver everywhere.

'This is the first of my surprises for my bride,' Rakesh said coming up behind her and holding her close. 'Besides, this is really a makeshift arrangement—we'll be moving into an old bungalow I've booked—slightly out of the way—but beautiful. I know you'll flip for it.'

Amrita turned around and offered him her mouth—the first time she'd done that. He kissed her tenderly once, and then again with increasing passion as he found her yielding to his embrace. They stood against the living-room wall, their arms wrapped around each other, while their mouths discovered little secrets—a crooked tooth, a soft crevice, an eager tongue. Rakesh picked her up and started towards the bedroom. But such was the urgency of his desire that they collapsed on a thick carpet a few feet away. He held her tight, while she clung on to him whispering, whimpering, crying and moaning, uncertain of her body's responses to what was to follow, but overcome with longing nevertheless.

'Amrita . . . Amrita . . . Amrita,' Rakesh repeated her name throatily as his fingers undid her buttons and clasps impatiently. Finally, when she lay back naked, he stopped to look at her, his eyes expressing the admiration his words were still groping for. Amrita shut her eyes and tried to blank her mind of Minx and the pattern their love-making had fallen into. She told herself not to expect smooth hands caressing her breasts, or a soft face nestling between her legs.

Rakesh took his time to get his fill. And then, he forced her to open her eyes while he undressed, 'Look at me, Amrita, look a t me,' he commanded as he climbed out of his clothes. It was difficult for her not to avert her eyes as he stood above her, his manhood erect, his eyes steady, his body glistening under the soft light of the moon streaming in through the windows. He bent down and half raised her, holding her face very close to his. 'It is you and me from now on—just us,' he said, and kissed her forehead. 'I want you to remember this moment, this night, for the rest of your life.' And his mouth moved on to cover every inch of her body.

Amrita was conscious of the bristles on his face scraping her tender skin as he devoured her body hungrily, kissing the inside of her elbows, the back of her knees, caressing her all over with long strokes of his artistic fingers. His tongue followed his hands everywhere, arousing her in a new, exquisitely pleasurable way. She had wanted him inside her desperately and begged him to enter. But Rakesh shushed her like one would a child. 'Not tonight, darling,' he had said, as he took a nipple into his moist, warm mouth. 'I will make you happy,' he promised, 'but in my way.' And he did. She felt herself reach one orgasm after another, just by his touch, as his fingers probed her body, stimulating it like she'd never experienced before. Each time she pleaded with him to stop, he'd resume his expert manipulation till her body would feel the fire blazing and her mind would shift to another plane.

'What about your pleasure?' she asked at the end of two hours.

'Mine?' Rakesh laughed, 'Mine is to ensure yours . . . at least for this one night. After that, I'll be selfish.'

Amrita protested, and before Rakesh knew it, had got him on his back and was over him, her mouth eagerly taking him in. Rakesh felt as if his entire being was transported to some other dimension where nothing else existed beyond the warmth and wetness of a ravenous mouth driving him relentlessly to newer, keener, heightened pleasures. After close to an hour, both of them lay in an exhausted, entangled heap, panting with the effort, blissfully fatigued. 'I love you very, very, much, my darling,' Rakesh murmured, stroking Amrita's hair as she rested her head on his chest.

'I love you too . . . but I am scared . . . I can't tell you how much. Every waking moment, and even in my sleep, I keep thinking of her . . . imagining she's there, somewhere, looking at me . . . waiting for a chance again.'

Rakesh held her close. 'The nightmare is over, darling. She won't be able to touch a hair on your head as long as I am alive. This is a promise I'm making to you.'

They fell into a short, deep sleep—the first Amrita had really enjoyed in over a month. It had also been the first time that Amrita felt unconditionally confident about the step she was going to take shortly. Rakesh would make a wonderful husband, she thought to herself happily.

Twenty-three

It was late in the night. Karan was suddenly woken up by the persistent ringing of his doorbell. He checked his bedside clock. It was close to 3 a.m. He cursed as he got into a kurta. Damn! Another one of these drugged-out models looking for a place to sleep, he figured, as he walked towards the door. His eyes were not focused . . . in any case he could barely see in the dark. He tripped over a tripod he had forgotten to pick up the previous night. Shit! He had stubbed his big toe. He stumbled towards the front door and opened it. He spotted a hazy figure—a woman. Minx. 'Let me in,' she said, her voice hoarse, her tone abrupt.

Karan opened the door reluctantly and switched on the light. He took in his breath sharply at the sight. Minx resembled a ghost: her hair dishevelled, her clothes grubby and torn, her expression ravaged, her words crazed. She'd lost not less than ten kilos and her slim figure looked wasted, skeletal. 'I can't live without her,' she said simply and collapsed on his doorstep.

Karan dragged her in more roughly than he'd intended. He lived in a quiet complex and didn't want to attract undue attention at that hour. Minx was not unconscious. It seemed more like nervous exhaustion to him. He sprinkled some ice water on her face adding a generous splash to his own. 'Coffee?' he asked her, after she'd come to and lay still and silent on a beige settee.

Minx shook her head. 'It's true, Karan,' she said. 'I've tried to get her out of my system. You must believe me. I've stopped at nothing—hypnosis, psycho-analysis shock-therapy, tranquillizers, even a witch doctor. Nothing works. I want her so badly, I'm in physical pain.' He looked away awkwardly. Minx continued, 'I know you love her too, in your own way—we can both save her. I need you for that.'

Karan looked at her sharply. 'Save her from what? Forget it. I don't want to get involved in some crazy plan of yours. As soon as you feel better you can leave, and don't come here again, please. I can't help you. Yes, I do love her. But it's a normal kind of love.'

'And what's abnormal about mine? Just because I am a woman does it mean my love is inferior to yours? Or to any man's?'

Karan got up and began pacing the room restlessly. 'I don't want to have a philosophical discussion on the subject. Let me make it clear, Amrita is just a friend, nothing more. And I believe she has a right to live her life on her own. She's already been through enough hell because of you.'

'Hell? Tell me which man would've done for her as much as I did? Would you? I've cared for her more than I did for my own life. I would've died for her. I'm ready to do that even now. That's the extent of my feeling,' said Minx bitterly.

Twenty-four

'I want our honeymoon to be different . . . not the usual going-to-phoren rubbish,' Amrita said to Rakesh as she lay with her head in his lap. He had just come back from New York and they had plenty of plans to finalize.

Rakesh played with her hair and ringed her tawny eyes with the tip of his forefinger. 'It's going to be the best, darling,' he said gently.

Rakesh and Amrita had decided to take charge of their own wedding celebrations and not leave it to their parents and relatives. Firmly, Rakesh had explained their position at a family meeting. 'We want this to be the most memorable day of our lives. Not a circus for everybody else. There is going to be no waste and no extravagance. We've planned a simple ceremony for all of us. And a party to follow.'

Seeing the disappointed faces all around both of them had reluctantly agreed to a modest reception.

Later, they'd giggled over the reactions. 'Did you see Mummy's expression when I said, "No jewellery except a ring and mangal sutra?"' Amrita laughed.

Rakesh added, 'I thought Papa-ji would have a coronary when I broke it to them that we won't book a five-star hotel for the reception.'

Amrita played with Rakesh's fingers, 'I suppose this is the first wedding in the family. They must have dreamed of making a production out of it. Poor parents.'

'I'd rather spend all that on our new home,' Rakesh said thoughtfully, while Amrita added, 'You've forgotten the honeymoon.'

'Honeymoon? I thought we'd already had ours,' Rakesh laughed, kissing her mouth casually, and running his hands familiarly over her body. She jumped out of his arms and ran toward a full-length mirror. 'Tell me honestly,' she demanded, 'have I put on weight?'

Rakesh shook his head saying, 'You are looking delicious. Ripe and ready.'

Amrita surveyed herself critically, 'I agree. But have I put on weight or not?'

Rakesh came up behind her and went over the splendid outlines of her body with his palms. 'Sleek and sexy—just the way I like you to be,' he murmured into her ear.

Amrita struggled out of his embrace, sensing the amorous mood to follow. 'We seem to do little else these days,' she said crassly.

'Nothing else is worth doing,' Rakesh teased.

Amrita sat down on a straight-backed chair and banged the nearest table. 'Business first. Where are we going?'

Rakesh smiled a slow smile. 'It's going to be a surprise. Don't spoil it by asking too many questions. I've planned everything with my travel agent. You just have to lie back and enjoy it.'

Amrita glared at him. 'But what about my clothes? I have to know what to take with me.'

Rakesh laughed, 'Darling, you aren't going to need any where we are headed.'

Amrita refused to join in his laughter. 'Forget it. Let's stay home in that case. Besides, wherever it is that you've thought of surely I can't travel to the airport or station in my birthday suit. You'll have to tell me about our getaway plans at least.'

'Those are taken care of as well. And I'll be quite happy to have a naked woman, my gorgeous wife, in my car next to me. Does that answer your question?'

Amrita crumpled up a paper impatiently and threw it at him. 'Sex maniac,' she screamed as he grabbed her and pinned her arm behind her back.

There were less than two weeks left for their wedding. And even though both of them insisted it was going to be simplicity itself, they knew there were dozens of details still to be taken care of. 'Later,' Rakesh said, nibbling her ear hungrily. 'Later,' Amrita thought as she shut her eyes and surrendered to the ticklish sensation of his sharp teeth on her delicate earlobes.

*

The night before the wedding, Amrita spent hours chatting with her mother, reliving childhood memories and laughing over vivid recollections of the time when all of them used to visit Nainital during the summer vacations. Well past midnight her mother had forcibly got her to go to bed insisting she needed the sleep to look beautiful for her wedding day. Amrita switched off the lights dutifully, but remained awake in bed for some time longer. For days preceding the wedding, she had been feeling uneasy. She knew her fears were linked with Minx. Her silence scared her more than her presence. Once or twice she had been tempted to phone Karan and ask about her. But she had resisted, knowing the call would stir up emotions best left undisturbed. But tonight she had to confront herself—she couldn't put it off longer. Minx had become a part of her consciousness. Much as she tried, she couldn't obliterate her from her mind and there had been times—too many of them—when she'd had to force herself to push Minx out of her thoughts while Rakesh was making love to her. Minx haunted her dreams as well—strange dreams without beginning or end. Sometimes Minx appeared as a benevolent figure, at other times, a psychotic despot. The dreams were invariably intense, complex, confusing and disturbing. Even in her waking hours, Amrita was not free of Minx. There was nobody she could discuss Minx with, certainly not Rakesh. It was a taboo subject between them ever since that tormented evening when she'd felt the urge to tell him much of it and he'd listened unhappily. Amrita wanted desperately to talk her out of her system. To relive everything: the horror and yes, the pleasure. To come to terms with her experience. She felt instinctively that only then would Minx melt into the past and remain there, never to intrude on her present or future. But till such time, Amrita was forced to live with a ghost and keep wondering when it would appear to haunt and torment her again.

*

As the flames from the sacred fire rose higher and smoke swirled around the decorated mandap Amrita looked up, squinting her eyes to keep them from watering. And there through the haze stood Karan at the edge of the small crowd, his eyes fixed on her face. Amrita was so glad to see him. She nearly raised her bejewelled hand to wave. She stopped herself in time and assumed the coy, eyes-downcast stance that was expected from every bride. She hadn't expected him to show up. Their last encounter at the airport had been absurdly incomplete. And yet, she was so delighted by his presence. Something told her Rakesh wouldn't mind . . . wouldn't feel jealous or threatened. She couldn't wait to introduce the two of them to each other. She turned her face to stare at her husband-of-a-few-minutes. How dashing he looked with his flowing turban and impeccably tailored achkan.

A soft and familiar 'click' made her look up again—it was Karan framing the happy couple for posterity. Click! Click! Click! He must have shot dozens of rolls. Later, after the ceremony when the three of them stood chatting comfortably, Karan told Rakesh, 'I never shoot wedding photographs. But this was one marriage I had to cover . . . for myself. . . and for both of you. Wait till you see the results. Sorry if I sound like I'm showing off but I know they're going to be great. You have the most beautiful girl in the world for a wife . . . and the two of you make a great-looking couple.'

Amrita couldn't hold back her tears as she reached over to squeeze Karan's hand. She turned to Rakesh, 'He is my best friend. He saved my life in more ways than one.'

Rakesh smiled and put his arm around Amrita, 'You don't have to tell me . . . I know. I hope he is going to be our friend now.'

Karan shook his head vehemently. 'No, brother, I'm not a masochist. These pictures are going to be a double gift to you—a wedding present and a goodbye.

I loved Amrita once. I still do. It won't be fair to any of us . . . .'

Rakesh held out his hand and Karan took it, 'May I kiss your wife the last time?' Karan asked.

Rakesh said, 'Go ahead . . . that is, if she doesn't mind.'

Amrita stood on her toes and put her arms around Karan's neck tenderly, not caring that they were being stared at. She kissed him on both cheeks and looked into his eyes, 'Thank you,' she whispered, 'thank you, again and again.' She felt Karan's hands on her back begin to tighten their hold. Amrita thought he was going to hug her close and stay that way. But, just as abruptly, he broke free and held her away, 'Look after yourself, kid, and stay away from Minx.' With that he strode away . . . out of the wedding-hall—and out of their lives.

The ceremony was beautiful—everybody said so. For a change the priest didn't chant mechanically and they were spared the indignities of sitting on gilt-painted thrones. Amrita, dressed in traditional red and gold, looked ravishingly beautiful while Rakesh in an ivory-coloured kurta-pyjama with a bright pink turban was princely rather than cartoonish. As they exchanged specially-ordered garlands woven from sweet-smelling jasmine and roses, there were quite a few pairs of moist eyes around the artistic wedding mandap. From the corner of her eyes, Amrita spotted Partha standing unobtrusively next to one of her brothers. Rakesh had refused to come astride a mare for the ceremony, disappointing his parents. But Amrita's brothers had made up for the lack of boisterousness mandatory at most weddings by breaking into an impromptu bhangra on his arrival by car.

The reception was not extravagant and close relatives commented on the low-key nature of the celebration. 'Only son and only daughter—yet look at how simple the whole thing is,' an aunt said to a neighbour. While the guests whispered among themselves, Amrita and Rakesh exchanged conspiratorial looks and secret smiles. They had succeeded in having their way after all.

Amrita still didn't know where they were headed the next morning. All she knew was that the wedding night was to be spent in the bridal suite of the Oberoi hotel. That had been her father's idea—a gift to them. It had not really appealed to either of them, but they did not want to hurt his feelings. As the reception wore on, Amrita began to tire. Her small frame was weighed down with heavy jewellery—her mother's and the sets given by Rakesh's family. Rakesh in a well-tailored sherwani had refused to don another pugri or wear pearl necklaces around his neck. An American friend who had flown down for the wedding expressed his disappointment at the bridegroom's obstinacy, complaining, 'You don't make great pictures bareheaded. The folks back home will be disappointed.'

Amrita was aglow in primrose yellow—a colour that brought out the green flecks in her golden eyes.

While her mother fussed and her aunts criticized, she had undone the elaborate hair-do created by a much-in-demand hair-dresser. Once the pins sticking into her scalp were out, she'd felt better, as she brushed out her heavy curtain of shoulder-length hair, allowing it to fall naturally around her face. She knew she had done the right thing when she saw the appreciative look in Rakesh's eyes as she appeared in the shamiana with two very proud brothers escorting her. Pinky, a neighbour's daughter she had grown up with, winked and made some joke about the wedding night. A brother's friend asked about their honeymoon plans. Rakesh smiled wickedly saying, 'That's a secret. Nobody knows where I'm taking this beautiful woman—not even the beautiful woman herself. I'm planning to kidnap her.'

'Not for ransom, I hope,' someone quipped.

'Why not?' Rakesh shot back. 'It's a good chance to take, considering nobody in the world would be able to pay what I'd demand for such booty.'

Amrita joined in their laughter happily, confident she'd done the right thing with the right man by marrying Rakesh.

Twenty-five

The Oberoi hotel suite was appropriately dressed up for the occasion. Amrita giggled at the sight of the flower-bedecked double bed. 'Just like in Hindi films. I suppose I shall have to sing a song while you stare moonily at me.'

Rakesh threw himself down on the petals and held out his arms: 'Come here, bride, this night is our night. Let's enjoy it.'

She kicked off her golden slippers and fell over him. 'Ouch! Your bangles hurt. Get rid of everything,' he instructed, as he unbuttoned his sherwani. Amrita continued to sit by his side, staring dreamily at the ceiling.

'What are you waiting for?' he asked, leaning over to hold her hand. He stared at the mehendi on her palm and pulled a face. 'It looks like a skin disease. And it smells awful,' he complained.

'Rubbish, this is a work of art. Besides, it cost me six hundred bucks and nearly four hours of sitting around waiting for my palms to dry.' Gradually, she removed her bangles and earrings.

'Leave the necklace on but take off all your clothes,' Rakesh said. 'Remember Liz Taylor as Cleopatra when she goes to bed with Richard Burton for the first time? Wow! What a scene. She's naked except for this incredible choker around her neck.'

Amrita laughed, 'Too bad for you I'm not her.'

Rakesh pulled her down over him and kissed her nose, 'I love you very, very much, you spoilt and silly girl,' he said nuzzling her neck. She cuddled up to him, her arms trustingly round his neck. Within minutes, they were fast asleep, with Rakesh snoring against her hair.

*

It was around four a.m. that they heard someone knocking on the door of their suite. Initially, Amrita thought she was dreaming and tried to go back to sleep. The knocking persisted. Soft and regular but no more than a light tap. Soon Rakesh was roused out of his deep sleep. He nudged Amrita awake and asked groggily, 'Is someone at the door?' She nodded, her body tensing with fear. Rakesh rolled over and drew the covers over both of them. 'Must be some mistake, a breakfast order that's got mixed up.'

Amrita looked puzzled as she stared at the bedside clock. 'Breakfast? At this hour?'

Rakesh reasoned, 'Airline crew. They have weird timings. Go to sleep, darling.'

But Amrita was wide awake by now. 'Let me take a look,' she suggested getting out of the bed and climbing into a bathrobe.

Rakesh opened one eye and mumbled, 'Keep the latch on. . . and ask who it is.' With that, he pulled a pillow over his head and fell promptly asleep.

Amrita took her time to reach the door. She was hoping the person would give up and go away. It occurred to her that it could be the air from a faulty air-conditioning vent or a loose latch. But in her heart of hearts she knew. Amrita knew.

She approached the door and suddenly the tapping stopped. Amrita's heart lurched and she jumped back with a small start. She stood there in the dark with just a dim night light illuminating her slim figure. After a minute or so she began to walk back to the bed. And that is when she heard her name being called in a hoarse whisper. It was more like a chant. She stood absolutely still, unable to move. It was her. Amrita did not have to open the door to know that Minx was outside.

Her hands were clammy as she held on to the latch, uncertain what to do next. She could hear Minx moaning on the other side, repeating her name over and over. In her confusion, Amrita wondered whether to let her in. There was a longing within her, an inexplicable surge of suppressed emotions. She looked back at the sleeping figure of Rakesh, her brand-new husband, and that one glance gave her the answer she was seeking. Amrita turned around and went to the bedside phone. She called up the lobby manager, trying to keep her voice as low as possible so as not to awaken Rakesh. But he was up and listening. 'Please inform your security personnel that there is an intruder outside our door. Someone is trying to break in. Report the matter to the police immediately, or my husband and I will be forced to take action on our own.' She put down the instrument and turned to face Rakesh. 'It's her. She's found us,' she said tonelessly.

Rakesh held his wife tightly in his arms, 'Don't worry, darling, let them take care of her, you are here—with me . . . forever, safe and secure. That's all that matters.' Amrita couldn't hold back her tears any longer. Tears of love, regret and relief.

Both of them sat quietly on the bed, alert to the sounds outside. They heard a small scuffle and shrieks of protest as security guards removed Minx by hoisting her up and taking her down to the duty officer's office. 'Poor Minx. Poor, poor Minx,' Amrita said, while Rakesh continued to hold her, kiss her, rock her.

It was daybreak when their tired eyelids shut again, but neither of them could sleep for long. They were jolted out of their light sleep by the deafening jangle of the fire alarm. It was the sound that shook them awake. The smell registered later. Within seconds they were out of their beds and running towards the door leading to the balcony outside the suite. Rakesh pushed open the heavy doors and dragged Amrita outside. From the relative safety of a broad ledge, they watched acrid smoke snaking into their room from under the main door. Amrita covered her mouth and nose while Rakesh went back into the bathroom to get some wet towels.

It took some minutes for the fire brigade men to break open their door and come in with all the equipment. Meanwhile the sprinkler overhead had doused the flames that had touched the carpet, filling the place with thick smoke as the synthetic fibres curled up and crackled, leaving blackened bald patches all over.

Rakesh and Amrita clung together on the ledge while firemen efficiently put out the flames that had now reached the mattress of their bed. A little later their room was filled with anxious hotel employees including the general manager. 'Most unfortunate, sir, please allow us to shift your bags. We'll make up for this. The stay is on the house for a week—if you want it.'

Rakesh stopped him short with just two words. 'What happened?' he asked. Amrita waited for the reply though she had already guessed by then.

'One of our guests, sir, in the adjoining room to yours, an accident. You know how it is, sir, someone has a nightcap, then falls asleep with a lit cigarette in the hand, most unfortunate, sir. Really sorry for the inconvenience.'

Amrita asked slowly. 'What was her name?'

'Whose name?' the manager asked, maintaining the sangfroid a five-star manager is trained in.

'The guest—next door,' Amrita said.

'If I may ask, ma'am—how did you know it was a lady?'

Amrita smiled sadly, 'It was just a guess.'

Rakesh came up to her, 'Don't be stupid and say something foolish. We don't want to get involved in some long-drawn-out police case.' He turned to the manager briskly, 'If that's all, we'd like to be left alone . . . it's all right. What does it matter who it was? We aren't concerned. Please ready another suite and have our things moved. We'll be checking out at noon.'

The manager fluttered around unnecessarily, trying to persuade them to stay on for at least one more day. 'Please give us the opportunity to make up for this, sir,' he said, but Rakesh very firmly told him to get on with the shifting. 'We have other plans which cannot be changed,' he added, putting a protective arm around Amrita.

Later, when they were comfortably installed in a magnificent penthouse suite, Amrita filled the tub with bubbles. Rakesh strolled in, carrying two glasses of freshly-squeezed orange juice. 'Come on—get in,' she urged, testing the water with her toes. He stripped off his towelling robe and got into the deliciously warm water, pulling her in with him. 'Get ready to be devoured,' he growled playfully, 'your husband is a ravenously hungry man this bright and beautiful morning.'

Amrita threw back her head and the laughter gurgled in her throat. She had consciously tried to push the thought of Minx out of her mind. Was she hurt in the fire? Had they removed her to a hospital? Or a police station? She shut her eyes and surrendered to Rakesh's caresses as he soaped her breasts lovingly before moving his slippery hands lower, between her legs.

'Bliss,' he said. 'This is bliss,' he repeated, as their bodies, light and eager, floated gracefully in the sparkling water, joined together, moving together, responding together, till the unbearably sweet stabbing pain made them forget that they were two and their beings blended, melted, exploded in a rapturous moment neither was to ever forget.

Twenty-six

The drive up to Nainital was cool and relaxed as Amrita and Rakesh chatted companionably. He had refused to drive and had hired a chauffeured limousine. Amrita had organized a wonderful picnic hamper with choice cold cuts from the delicatessen. Rakesh had tapped a friendly diplomatic source and managed to get a case of excellent Bordeaux. He had opened the first bottle twenty minutes out of Delhi, producing glasses, crusty bread and goat cheese. Amrita had pulled out a juicy apple and they had toasted each other happily while the driver strained to keep his eyes on the road.

'I still don't know where we are going,' Amrita pouted as the car sped along nearly deserted stretches of the highway.

'You'll find out,' Rakesh said, 'besides, stop playing dumb . . . you know this much for sure—we aren't going to Kanya Kumari.'

With three glasses of champagne inside her, Amrita was feeling far too mellow to retaliate. She lay back happily on the seat, while Rakesh slyly unbuttoned her silk shirt and pulled it out of the tight jeans into which she had tucked it.

'Stop it, darling,' Amrita protested, giggling uncontrollably.

Rakesh feigned great shock and surprise as he said, 'Why? Is a crime being committed?' She indicated the driver in the front seat, and Rakesh waved her objections aside. 'Forget him—I made sure the car company gave us a eunuch.'

Amrita sipped some more wine, spilling some down her throat. Rakesh promptly licked it off her neck, making so much noise in the process, that Amrita had to nudge him in the ribs. He continued to strip her as she kept up her mock protests. Pushing his hands under her hips, he raised them so as to unzip her jeans. 'How the hell do you get into these bloody things without fracturing yourself?' he grunted, pushing them down from her slim waist.

'Here, let me make it easier,' Amrita said, raising one long leg and then the next. 'Finally . . .' he said with a satisfied grin, triumphantly getting them off her ankles.

'Now all we need is a road block,' Amrita laughed, lying half naked on the back seat of a hired car.

'Keep your panties on,' Rakesh said, 'that way we won't get arrested for indecent exposure. Or, better still, let me enter you and stay there.'

With one graceful move, she shrugged out of her salmon-coloured shirt. Rakesh looked admiringly at her flat stomach and tanned limbs. 'The sun has done wonders,' he commented running his fingers along her belly.

Amrita was wearing skin-coloured silk lingerie trimmed with delicate lace. 'Where do you manage to get all these sexy things?' Rakesh asked slipping a hand into her bra and cupping a breast.

'Contacts,' Amrita answered smugly.

'I prefer the present contact,' he replied, taking a taut nipple between his thumb and index finger.

Amrita felt her body loosening up under his expert touches. 'Enjoy, baby,' he said gruffly as he kneeled on the floor of the car. There was no resistance left in her as his hands gently pushed open her willing thighs. She felt his mouth tugging at her panties. She felt his breath through the fine silk. She felt his mouth as it probed into her, through the fabric. It felt better than having him explore her naked womanhood. Maintaining a maddening rhythm with his mouth and fingers, Rakesh induced Amrita to come—again and again, starting all over just when she was begging him to release her. The movement of the car speeding along helped Rakesh when he finally entered her smoothly and stayed inside for what must have been an hour. It was the bright headlights of an approaching car reflected in the mirror that broke the spell. Before they realized it, night had fallen outside. The driver slowed down as they separated reluctantly. Without turning around, he asked discreetly whether they could take a short break. Amrita buttoned up hastily as Rakesh zipped his fly. 'Yes,' he told the man in the front seat, 'we all need some fresh air.' Amrita was certain she saw the hill fellow smirk. But she did not care . . . not that night. Not when her body was so languorous and limp, she felt like it would have floated up to the stars had Rakesh not been there to hold it down. She turned to him lazily and kissed him long and hard. 'My husband,' she said touching his thick hair, 'my sexy, sexy husband.'

Rakesh stuck his tongue inside her ear naughtily and asked, 'Want a repeat performance?'

*

By the time they reached the isolated wooden, colonial bungalow on a distant hill, it was close to ten at night. The Garhwali watchman, no older than sixteen, came scampering out to greet them, followed by an old mali. A log fire was burning inside the three-bedroom house and all the lights were on, casting a warm glow on the fringes of the dense forests surrounding it.

Amrita put her arm around Rakesh's waist and walked in to survey the place. 'It's gorgeous,' she exclaimed, 'how on earth did you find it?'

Rakesh looked around critically, 'Not bad, huh? The old bugger was right when he told me we'd flip for it.'

Strange Obsession

As the driver and watchman took their bags in to the master bedroom, Amrita and Rakesh warmed themselves by the fire. Winter had yet to set in but the air was cold and crisp in the hills already. 'You still haven't told me,' Amrita reminded Rakesh.

'An old army contact of my father's,' he explained briefly, 'a retired brigadier. He leases the place out when he isn't using it.'

Amrita snuggled up to Rakesh, 'I'm ravenous—for food, I mean.'

Rakesh called out to the Garhwali boy, 'Is dinner organized?'

He came in grinning from ear to ear and assured them there was a warm meal waiting. 'Chicken curry, rice, chapati, subzi,' he rattled off in one breath.

'Great,' Rakesh said asking him to get on with it.

'Drink, saab?' the boy asked.

Rakesh exchanged glances with Amrita. 'Why not? We could do with some rum.'

The boy led them to a wooden bar and handed them the key. 'Everything inside,' he said in broken English.

Rakesh swooped down on a bottle of twelve-year-old rum. 'Is it on the house?' Amrita asked.

'Nothing is on the house, darling,' Rakesh told her, 'I'll sign vouchers for everything.' Then he stared at her anxiously, 'You don't mind living here do you? I mean, we could've stayed in one of those five-star hotels . . . I thought that this would be more romantic.

We'd have our privacy and we'd get to explore the forests around as well.'

Amrita hugged him, 'This is perfect, darling. I hate hotels, I'm sick of living in antiseptic suites, besides our last experience in a five-star joint wasn't all that terrific, was it?'

Rakesh laughed, 'Forget it, sweetheart. It was an accident. These things happen.'

Amrita looked pensive as she said, 'Do they? I'm not so sure.' But by then Rakesh was busy pouring them two stiff shots. And Ram Swarup, the Garhwali monkey, was hopping around chattering ceaselessly about dinner.

*

They awoke to a chorus of birds on the window-sill. It was a glorious dawn, still misty, with dew on the grass outside. Amrita shivered as Rakesh pulled open the cheerful curtains and stretched himself. 'Want to stay in bed . . . or get out for a bit?' he asked. She pulled up the covers and shut her eyes. 'I get the message, baby,' he said, adding, 'I think I'll go commune with nature for a change.' He got dressed briskly, kissed her and left the room. She heard him ordering a two-egg omelette breakfast from Ram Swarup. 'Lots of toast,' he shouted out as he strode down a narrow pathway cut into the forest. Amrita heard dry twigs getting crunched under his heavy boots. She considered joining him and then gave up the idea. She loved her early morning sleep—the time she fell into a dream-like state in which myriad images overlapped.

Amrita woke an hour-and-a-half later. The sun was higher in the sky by now and streaming in through the latticed windows of the room. She switched off the electric heater, checked the time and got out of bed. She expected Rakesh to be back any minute and wanted to greet him squeaky clean and fresh. Hastily she brushed her teeth, splashed cold water on her face, put on a flannel dressing-gown and went out to look for Ram Swarup. He was missing. She called for the mali. He came running from the far corner of the garden where he had been tending a patch of hollyhocks. She asked if he had seen Ram Swarup and the mali informed her that he had gone in search of saab.

'Why?' she asked the mali.

'Well. . . it's nearly two hours since he left the house. He'd told us he'd be back in fifteen minutes. Ram Swarup thought he might have missed the intersection and lost his way. It happens to first-time visitors.'

'Is it safe around here? Any thieves, or daakus?'

The old man laughed, 'No, no, memsaab, all that goes on in the cities, we people are honest and god-fearing. No, it is not a human who can hurt you in these areas, but who can say anything about wild animals?'

'Wild animals? Are there any tigers here?' asked Amrita taking in her breath sharply.

The old man flashed her a toothless smile, 'Not tigers—not at this time or this close to the house. But we do get hyenas and bears.'

Amrita told him firmly, 'I'm going to look for my husband. I'll be back in a minute. Do you want to come with me?'

The mali agreed readily. She ran in to change into a pair of jeans. She pulled a thick sweater over her head, put on warm socks and a sturdy pair of shoes. 'Come on,' she gestured, 'let's get going.'

They met Ram Swarup half a mile down the forest path.

'Did you find him?' Amrita shouted out.

'No, not yet. I don't know why he went so far into the jungle. It's not at all safe . . . even we don't do it,' he said, shaking his head.

Amrita checked which direction he had taken and asked whether he had called out his name. 'I couldn't,' the boy said sullenly, 'I didn't know it.'

'Damn!' Amrita cursed and started to run blindly into the woods yelling, 'Rakesh, Rakesh,' as loudly as she could. There was an eerie echo, nothing more, and the sound of birds fluttering away noisily.

It was the mali who spotted something flapping in the underbrush. He sent Ram Swarup to investigate. Amrita let out a small scream. It was Rakesh's scarf, the one his mother had knitted for him. 'He must be somewhere close by,' she said, 'maybe he fell down . . . he could be hurt. . . let's keep looking.'

They forked out in different directions, Amrita calling his name and the two men separating and looking through the thick undergrowth for clues. It was a shout from the old mali that brought Amrita running to the spot he was standing at. 'Blood,' he said shortly, 'fresh blood.'

With a sickening feeling in the pit of her stomach, Amrita stared horrorstruck at a small pool of blood on a large stone. Next to it was another, more pointed stone, also covered with blood. 'Oh my God! My God!' Amrita whispered.

The Garhwali boy ran up huffing and puffing and joined them. 'Could it be an animal that did this? A bhalu or a wolf?' Amrita asked.

The two men shook their heads and continued to stare glumly at the blood at their feet, 'No, this is the work of a murderer,' the mali said in a low voice.

Amrita caught her throat with her hands, 'Is he . . . could he be dead?'

Ram Swarup said, 'We don't know, we will have to go back and inform the police quickly, before the criminals get too far. It's no use our wasting time looking for saab here . . . it can be dangerous.'

Amrita sat down heavily and started to cry. The mali helped her up gently, 'Let us not lose hope,' he said, 'let us pray . . . maybe this is not saab's blood at all. It could be some ritual sacrifice of a chicken or a lamb . . . these forests are full of tribals. They have strange customs.'

Amrita bent down to examine the blood more closely. 'Here . . . why don't you take a better look . . . I'm sure you can make out whether it belongs to a man or an animal,' she said pushing Ram Swarup down.

He stuck a finger into the blood and tested its thickness after which he smelt it and hung his head down miserably. 'Human,' he declared and began to cry.

The mali took charge of the situation and led them away from the spot. 'We'll phone the police chowki,' he muttered as the small group half-walked, half-ran back to the bungalow.

*

It was only after two hours that three overfed policemen showed up at the bungalow. By then Amrita was close to collapsing with anxiety and hunger—she had refused every attempt by Ram Swarup to get her to eat or drink anything. The Delhi telephone lines were down and she had been unable to call her parents.

But once the police arrived her spirits lifted slightly as she accompanied them to the spot where they had found the scarf and then the bloodstained stones. Amrita described Rakesh in detail and recreated the early morning scene when he had wandered off into the forest leaving her sound asleep in bed. The police took notes and asked the servants questions in the local dialect. Nobody seemed particularly worried, nobody except Amrita. She asked to speak to their superior but was curtly told that they were perfectly competent to handle such a 'simple case'. She demanded an explanation and they said casually, 'Hunting accident . . . happens all the time.' On further probing, Ram Swarup gave her instances of tourists who'd been wounded by mistake by local poachers mistaking them for deer.

'But where is he in that case? Why didn't the hunters bring him back to the house or leave him there?'

The police gave her some garbled story about poachers being afraid in case they were reported to the police and arrested. 'They've probably taken your husband to their village. After bandaging him they'll drop him back at night in the darkness, that is how they usually do it.'

Amrita was not convinced, 'We are wasting precious time . . . I think we should search for him in the villages. And inform check posts to look out for him, in case . . . in case . . . he has been kidnapped or something. They should stop all cars and trucks.'

The police chaps laughed in her face. 'Madam, we know how the villagers behave here. They are simple hill people. Honest. They won't hurt or rob him. It was a mistake, a hunter with either poor aim or poor eyesight or both, that's all.'

'Why can't we search the villages while it is still light?' said Amrita and was once again put off by all four men insisting it would be a waste of time.

'Their villages are up in the hills. Very difficult to climb there,' one of the policemen said.

'We can't just sit around waiting and waiting,' she cried, as the men trooped outside to smoke their beedis, leaving her alone to brood and despair.

By nightfall, Amrita was desperate. The police had wandered away after writing a cursory report. Ram Swarup fetched her some milk and forced her to swallow half a cup. The silence was oppressive with only the sound of night birds and insects to break it. Amrita sat by the phone, her knees drawn to her chest. She was wearing Rakesh's thick pullover. The police theory seemed perfectly ridiculous to her and yet there was nothing she could do in this strange place where she knew nobody. She could smell a woodfire outside where Ram Swarup and the mali sat huddled around it, smoking hookahs. It was close to ten o'clock when they heard a car driving up. Amrita jumped up and ran towards the sound of a powerful engine. Her shapely figure was caught in the strong headlights of the approaching vehicle. It was the district superintendent of police, a frown on his face.

'Bad news?' Amrita asked hoarsely. 'If it is, tell me right now. Just don't lie to me. That's all,' she pleaded.

The man cleared his throat, introduced himself, and said, 'Well, madam, we aren't sure what it is, but we believe it is not as simple as it appears.'

'What do you mean?' Amrita asked.

'It seems to be a professional job,' the officer said.

'Is he dead? Has he been killed?' Amrita asked her voice rising.

'That too is unknown,' he answered.

'What the hell do you know in that case?' Amrita all but screamed.

'It is possible your husband has been abducted.'

'By whom?'

'Maybe a terrorist gang. Or a hired kidnapper.'

'Ransom?'

'Perhaps. But since you have not received a phone call or a note, we cannot say for sure. By now the person or persons would've definitely got in touch, either with you or with us. That is the usual modus operandi.'

'But is my husband alive?' Amrita asked, her voice breaking.

'Good chances, madam. But we cannot commit.'

'Well, thanks a lot, you've been a big help. Now what?' Amrita said despondently.

'Now we wait . . . but, madam, let me assure you, we are doing our best. The villagers have been alerted to report any suspicious movements. We've called the main control room also. There will be car-checks. That is the maximum we can do at this point.'

Amrita nodded, trying hard to keep her temper as the officer prepared to drive off after saluting her smartly.

'No, wait,' Amrita said, 'I need protection. I cannot stay here alone.' The man turned to his assistants and decided which one of them could stay back. 'Very well, madam. But only till morning.'

'Thanks awfully,' Amrita said, her voice filled with sarcasm. She was alone in a strange place with strange men for the first time in her life. And yet she was not afraid. Her thoughts were racing, flying ahead, as she tried to unravel the mystery of her missing husband. In her heart, Amrita already knew the answer—the one that was eluding the police. The one they would never guess. Now all she had to do was wait for the next move. A move she was certain would be made not that night, but in the early hours of dawn. The time of day preferred by her tormentor. One and only one person could have thought of such a plan. And Amrita knew that to win this round she had to be smarter than her adversary and keep her cool. One false move and Rakesh would be dead. Amrita vowed to herself that she wouldn't allow that to happen . . . even if it meant losing her own life.

She fetched a blanket from the bedroom and settled herself into a comfortable armchair for the night. She had a long wait ahead of her and she wanted to be fully prepared for it. Amrita dozed fitfully, conscious of the sound of the mali's cough coming from the far corner of the garden, as he warmed himself by the now slowly-dying-out fire.

*

Nothing happened till daybreak—when Amrita was startled out of her light sleep by Ram Swarup tapping her gently on the shoulder. He was holding a package and mumbling something incoherent. Amrita was wide awake in a second and tore the paper off, expecting to find—she didn't exactly know what. Her heart was thumping loudly. It was a firm, small object, no bigger than the palm of her hand. Feverishly she unwrapped layers and layers of newspaper, questioning Ram Swarup at the same time. 'Who gave you this?' she asked, ripping off the paper.

'A hill-boy from the neighbouring village,' he replied.

'What did he say?'

'Nothing. He said, "Give it to the memsaab inside the house."'

'Damn!' Amrita cursed. 'Who sent this?'

'He didn't say.'

Amrita glared at him. 'Did you ask?'

Ram Swarup shook his head stupidly.

She flared up on hearing that. 'You idiot! How could you not have asked such an obvious question? Why didn't you bring the boy to me?'

'But you were asleep,' he said, hanging his head miserably.

She flew at him like a deranged woman. 'You can tell that to the police when they come later, they'll arrest you—take you away.'

With one final tug the paper was off and something rolled out. It fell to the floor with a sharp, metallic sound. Amrita was on all fours looking for it. She found Rakesh's ring under a cane sofa. She put it on her middle finger and started to cry. It was far too big for her anyway. She went and picked up the remains of the packet and found a cassette inside. No label. No indication of what was in it. But she could guess. He had been kidnapped for ransom after all. Wearily she turned to Ram Swarup and asked him whether there was a cassette-player in the house. He shook his head. A minute later, he perked up and said brightly, 'But my cousin has one in the village.'

'Then go immediately and fetch it,' Amrita screamed.

The mali came in to check on her. She asked for a cup of tea and tried the phone but it was still dead. Twenty minutes later Ram Swarup was back with a battered tape-recorder. Hastily she slipped in the cassette and switched it on. There was absolute silence for at least five minutes. She was about to switch sides and try her luck when she heard a voice she recognized only too well. It was Minx. But she sounded different. Her low, nearly hoarse voice seemed not so much muffled as amplified. There was also an eerie echo in the background. Transfixed, Amrita listened as Minx spoke sadly, with a finality that was chilling.

'This is goodbye, my darling,' Minx said. 'You will never have to suffer the sound of my voice in your precious ears again. But before I leave you, there is one more mission I have to complete . . . a promise I must fulfil, an oath I have to redeem. You will understand. I know you will. Farewell, my darling, my life, my precious one. Remember one thing, whatever I am doing is all for you, only for you . . . .'

The tape stopped abruptly and Amrita jerked back into reality. She let the tape play on anyway, while she thought desperately . . . why had Minx sent her the tape at this point? Of course it was not a mere coincidence. For one, it meant that Minx was in the vicinity. If that was so, Minx had kidnapped Rakesh. But the blood? Could she have successfully overpowered someone so much bigger and stronger? Amrita's mind was racing wildly. The sound quality of the tape seemed different . . . professional. As if it had been recorded in a studio. Obviously, Minx hadn't done it here, in this god-forsaken place.

The police were expected shortly. The tape was still on, as Amrita clutched her throbbing head and longed for her family to be beside her, now when she needed them so badly. Suddenly, she was jerked out of the semi-reverie she had fallen into by an unexpected sound on the tape that had been running noiselessly so far. It was the muffled sound of a man's voice—Rakesh's. Amrita recognized it immediately. It was hard to tell what he was saying—the words were garbled, incoherent. There were other sounds, of furniture being moved and something large and obviously heavy, falling noisily to the ground.

Amrita strained her ears to listen, Rakesh was obviously arguing and she could make out a stray word or two 'Stop', 'Bitch'.

So he was alive . . . at least when Minx had recorded the tape before delivering it to her. Amrita rejoiced and then stopped, reminding herself that everything could have changed by now. She heard a screech of something scraping against a rough surface. And then nothing. The blank tape continued to run. She waited till she got to the end of it. Optimistically, she flipped it over and played the other side all the way through, but it was empty, as she had half-expected it to be.

The police reacted with surprise when Amrita silently handed over the tape to them. The senior inspector examined it and asked the usual questions, 'How did you get this? When did it arrive?' Tonelessly, Amrita recounted the sequence of events.

'Have you heard it?' the policeman asked.

'Yes,' she said pointing to the battered-up cassette-player.

'What does the man want?' the cop asked, rewinding it.

'Woman,' she answered softly.

'What?' he said.

'I mean it's a woman on the tape.'

The policeman perked up. 'That is something new. A woman! The gang must be using new tactics. They've obviously changed their strategy. Don't worry, we'll catch them. They cannot fool us with such tricks.'

Strange Obsession

'There is no gang,' Amrita all but screamed. 'It's just one woman—one single woman.'

The policeman turned to her curiously. 'How do you know that? What makes you so sure? These people are professional kidnappers. We are on their track. They change their methods from time to time, that's all. But we'll get them.'

Amrita spoke more sharply than she intended to, 'Look, listen to me. I know what I'm saying. This woman is not a stranger. She doesn't belong to any gang. She is known to me.'

'What?' the policeman exploded, 'why didn't you tell us all this before? Were you trying to fool with us? Who is she? What is really going on? Please, madam, we must write down your statement and then you will have to come with me.'

Amrita didn't move from her chair. The tape was rewound. The inspector switched it on, watching her face constantly. Amrita stared into her lap as Minx's gravelly voice filled the room once more. At the end of her message, the inspector switched off the machine and turned to Amrita, 'So, this woman is a close friend of yours. Kindly give us her name and other details . . . but before that, we have to establish a connection . . . some motive. How do you know she is the one who has kidnapped your husband? I was expecting a demand, a threat, something. This woman has said nothing, unless you are a part of the conspiracy. You can stop your dramebaazi and confess straightaway.'

Amrita shook her head fiercely, 'No, no, no. Stop your ridiculous talk. Don't you see, she is the murderess.' She flicked on the button of the recorder, 'Here! Listen . . . listen carefully.'

The inspector concentrated on the garbled noises that followed. 'This does not prove anything . . . not even that the two of you could not have planned it all. For what . . . tell me? His money?'

Amrita broke down and started to weep, 'You are such a fool. You don't understand anything, do you?'

The inspector shut her up rudely, 'Madam, I have understood what I wanted to. The time to understand is now yours. I'm expecting my commissioner shortly. We've also sent a wireless message to Delhi. Whatever explanations you have can be saved for later. I'd like to take down a few details. The name of your accomplice . . . her background and yours. The rest will take place in court. You can take it that you are under arrest as of now.'

Twenty-seven

'Come on . . . I have planned some entertainment for you.'

Rakesh stared at his tormentor with contempt in his eyes. The rough rag gagging his mouth was beginning to hurt. The ropes around his wrists had cut deep welts into his flesh. Minx was standing a few feet away, dressed in her standard black costume. But this time she had strapped on a holster and added boots. He kept staring at her and thinking how utterly repulsive she was. Mercifully, he could not see her mean eyes, hidden as they were behind the large tinted frames. He was being held in a cramped log cabin up on a ridge. Minx had brought him there with a gun thrust into the small of his back as she had prodded him to walk faster.

Rakesh recalled the dawn encounter fifteen minutes away from the bungalow where he had left Amrita sleeping unsuspectingly. Someone had struck him forcefully over the head from the back with some hard, blunt object.

He'd fallen on the dried-leaves-covered ground with a dull thud and hit a rock lying there—before he had lost consciousness, he had recognized the familiar smirk and recoiled at the sound of the hollow laugh. Rakesh remembered thinking in that split second that Minx would probably kill him. When he came to she had succeeded in tying him up. He saw her sitting a few feet away. Smoking nonchalantly and taking swigs from a canteen bottle slung around her shoulder. The gun was in its holster. She also had a jack knife stuck into her boot. Then he passed out again.

A sharp kick in his side had woken him up. The sun was overhead now and it was bright and hot under the trees, 'Let's go . . . we have a long walk ahead of us, hero,' Minx had snarled. Rakesh had tried to get to his feet and stumbled. His head hurt and he could feel blood coursing down the side of his face.

'What the fuck is going on?' he had slurred, his words coming out thick and slow because of the gash near the corner of his lips.

'You'll find out soon enough. Now move,' Minx had snapped drawing out the gun and pushing the barrel into his ribs.

'Where's my wife? Where's Amrita? What have you done to her?' Rakesh asked.

'Shut the fuck up before I kill you,' Minx had ordered and kicked him again. He had staggered, overcome by excruciating pain. Minx had reached for a cloth entangled in a nearby bush and had asked him to bend down so she could tie his mouth up. Very deliberately, she had removed his long scarf and thrown it carelessly away, 'Let your darling wife discover it when she comes looking for you,' she had laughed. 'I'll bet it will cheer her up.'

*

The walk to the log cabin had been long and arduous. Every two steps Rakesh felt as if he'd collapse and never rise again. Minx was there, ready to kick him each time he tripped. She walked behind him, singing tunelessly, taking frequent sips from her canteen bottle. Rakesh was dying of thirst. He was awfully hungry too. But she wouldn't let him stop even for a second.

Once they arrived at the small cabin, she got busy. Rakesh noticed it was well equipped with food supplies, distilled water, rolls of toilet paper, firewood, bottles of rum, imported chocolates, coffee, sugar, detergents. There was even electricity courtesy a large portable generator. Minx pulled off his gag but kept his hands tied. 'We might be here for, let's see—a day, a month, a year . . . maybe forever. That depends on how badly your wife wants you. I thought we should make ourselves at home till then. Relax, I've got music, movies . . . you name it. Beats anything a five-star hotel can offer by way of inhouse entertainment. I'm sure you'll agree with me once the show starts. But before that, we need to talk a little, you and I. Are you ready?'

Rakesh didn't bother to disguise the contempt in his eyes as he regarded Minx silently. She opened a can of imported beer and handed it to him. He drank it down within seconds. Minx came up to him and ruffled his hair. 'You're pretty attractive, you know—great body, great hair, great smile. Pity I don't like men or I'd have gone for you rather than that scrumptious wife of yours.' Rakesh made no response. Minx continued, 'All this nonsense could've been avoided if you'd listened to me and left her alone when I requested you to. I asked nicely, remember? But you, like an obstinate fool, went ahead and snatched her from me. Why? You could've got any other girl. And don't give me that shit about being in love with her or I'll break your jaw.'

Minx unwrapped a Lindt slab and put two squares of chocolate into his mouth. Rakesh clenched his teeth initially, then thought better of it.

'Good boy,' Minx said, her face barely two inches from his. 'No talk? Fine. I'll talk. Amrita was mine and will remain mine. No matter what shit she might have shovelled in your direction, that is the truth. She loved me then and you can be bloody sure she loves me now.' Abruptly, she rose and went towards a low table with a largish covered object on it. 'Voila! Tra-la-la . . . home movies,' she trilled as she removed a grease-stained tablecloth to reveal a gleaming television set with a slim, black VCR. 'Ready to watch some action?'

Rakesh closed his eyes and put his head between his knees as Minx fiddled with the controls. 'Here we go . . . watch . . . it will be very familiar to you.' She turned around and noticed his posture. Two or three swift strides and she was yanking his head up by his hair. Once again he felt the cold steel of the muzzle against his temple. 'Watch,' she commanded. 'If I see you close your eyes or remove them from the screen—bang—you'll be dead.'

Rakesh looked at the images on the small screen impassively. He had known what was in store for him all along. He recalled the night Amrita had told him about those kinky encounters and with what relish Minx used to photograph them. Rakesh had not wanted his wife to 'confess'. But obviously it was important to her to unload her dark secrets in an effort to free herself from her overwhelming sense of guilt. She had gone into such graphic details that nothing he was watching that moment shocked or surprised him. Minx watched his face closely, chain-smoking the while. 'Like my home movies, darling?' she asked.

Rakesh decided to play along. 'Love them,' he replied with a careless laugh, adding, 'in fact I have a few that might interest you. Remind me to send them to you when we get back to civilization.'

Minx rushed at him with the burning end of her cigarette. 'That's for being smart,' she hissed as she stubbed it out on his arm.

Rakesh howled with pain.

Minx laughed.

On the screen, a grotesque close up of Amrita's genitals flickered briefly before Minx abruptly switched off the machine. 'I'll save the best for later,' she announced before walking out of the cabin.

Twenty-eight

'I'm going out on my own,' Amrita told the mali as she buttoned up her blazer. 'Don't worry about me. I'm going to find him on my own.'

The mali tried to stop her. He went shouting for Ram Swarup but the hill-boy had gone to the village. Amrita was out of the garden in seconds, striding purposefully towards the woods.

She found the spot where the scarf had been dangling. She stared at the two stones on which the blood had darkened and dried. The forest smelled fragrant and sweet and the light was perfect. She sat down on a moss-covered boulder close by, listening to the birdsong and absently crackling dry leaves under her boots. She felt strangely at peace. Somehow she knew Rakesh was safe and that Minx would not be able to touch him.

Amrita walked on further up the hill for another forty-five minutes. She spotted a small clearing with four or five huts clustered around a well. She stopped for a drink of water. The villagers were obviously accustomed to strangers. They offered her a charpoy to rest for a while. A young boy struck up a conversation in a dialect she found hard to follow. He pointed towards a hill in the distance and said, 'Friend.' She looked at him interestedly. He spoke in an excited voice and gestured wildly. Amrita vaguely got the impression he had observed city people going there. Amrita was instantly alerted. She showed him a ten-rupee note and asked him to accompany her. He refused to take the money but seemed eager to help her.

They encountered Minx just as Amrita was ready to give up and turn back. The young boy greeted her like an old friend. She recognized him too. The sight of Amrita didn't surprise her at all.

'Hello, beautiful, we've been expecting you,' she said taking her by the arm. With a sharp click of her fingers, she dismissed the boy. He scampered off happily, waving to both of them. They continued to walk in silence. Amrita knew Minx well enough to realize she would not get a straight reply to any of her questions. But something told her Rakesh was unharmed. Minx put her arm around her and kissed her softly in the hollow of her neck. Amrita did not draw away. That would have made Minx furious and led to a forced and prolonged intercourse. Minx launched into a cheerful conversation about the weather and the prettiness of their surroundings. It was like they were on a picnic. Amrita didn't utter a word even when Minx linked her fingers through hers and whispered urgently, 'I can't wait, darling, I need you so badly. I won't be able to make it back to our jungle home unless I have you now. You're looking delicious, marriage suits you.'

Amrita continued walking as Minx reached over and fondled her breasts, slipping her fingers under her bra and squeezing the nipples till they hardened. 'So . . . you still respond to my touch. I see,' she laughed a satisfied laugh. Amrita shut her mind, gritted her teeth, and increased her pace. Minx let her hands travel over Amrita's body freely. It was difficult to keep walking, but Amrita was determined not to react.

They reached a turn-off marked on the magnificent trunk of a gigantic peepal tree. Amrita, caught offguard by Minx jumping in front of her, took in her breath sharply. Minx caught her by the shoulders and pinned her against the tree. 'Now . . . I want you now. Right here,' she said, her face a few inches away from Amrita's, her hands over her breasts. A koel flew noisily away as squirrels ran around, disturbed by the two women. Amrita's body was limp as Minx unbuckled her belt, unbuttoned her jeans and pulled off her clothes throwing them carelessly over the bushes. A ray of sunlight illuminated Amrita's magnificent body, making it glow in the transparent, greenish light of the forest. Minx stepped back and her voice caught in her throat as she said, 'Oh my God! Amrita, how utterly beautiful you are. I could die just looking at you right now. I wish you could see yourself, beautiful. Like a wood nymph . . . my wood nymph.'

She came to her slowly and took her in her arms, dragging her down to the base of the tree. Amrita felt her back being scratched by the bark and she noticed beetles scurrying around while Minx kneeled in front of her.

'Please . . .' she finally broke the silence, 'just don't hurt me. That's all.'

Minx kissed her on the mouth and whispered. 'Why would I do that to you? Why? I worship your beauty.' Amrita waited for Minx to touch her, but was surprised when Minx pulled away suddenly and stepped back.

'Something wrong?' she asked.

Minx had tears streaming down her face. 'I can't . . . you smell different. You smell of a man . . . your man. He is all over you. Everywhere. Between your legs, on your breasts, in your mouth. No, I can't touch you ever again. Get dressed, let's move, it's over.'

Gratefully, Amrita climbed into her clothes. Minx had already walked quite a distance. Amrita caught up with her, panting with the exertion of running uphill. She took her hand in hers but Minx jerked it away. 'Don't touch me,' she said, her voice low and sorrowful. Amrita withdrew immediately. In a way, she understood.

*

Rakesh's eyes lit up when he spotted Amrita framed in the doorway. 'My darling . . . I knew you'd find me,' he cried, struggling against the ropes cutting into his wrists.

Minx came up to him and undid the knots, cutting through the strands with a pen knife. Amrita fell beside her husband and hugged him, while he stroked her hair and face, covering them with kisses.

Minx looked away, smoking, dragging deeply and staring vacantly out of the open door.

Rakesh called out to her from the floor, 'What is your next move?'

Suddenly, she snapped out of her reverie, 'I'm not through with the two of you yet. Shut your mouth and wait . . . .' The gun in her hand silenced them quickly. Minx turned to Amrita and said in a voice that was rapidly regaining its old tone. 'Your dear husband was most unimpressed by your performance on the video. I've been thinking . . . maybe he has something better to offer that might be worth preserving for posterity.'

The two of them exchanged looks, uncertain of what Minx meant. Amrita pleaded, 'I thought you said it was over. I thought . . . .'

Minx cut her off abruptly, 'Fuck what you thought. I am the one who does all the thinking here. Not the two of you. Get that? But to answer your question—yes—it's over between you and me. But it's just beginning between you and him. I can't wait. This is the chance I've been waiting for. Get ready for the performance of your lives . . . and no tricks.

Remember, I'm the one with the gun.' She walked towards them, playing with the weapon in her hand. 'You heard me. I want to see some great action in this dump. I'm giving you two minutes to get organized. Strip! Now! That's an order.'

Minx turned around to fetch her camera. Seeing his chance, Rakesh lunged at her and grabbed her by the knees. Minx fell face forward, but her reflexes were quick. Amrita screamed as the gun went off and a bullet hit a wooden beam on the roof. Another shot rang through the woods as Minx squeezed the trigger again, aiming blindly in Amrita's direction. The bullet grazed her arm and lodged itself in a stack of mattresses in a corner. Rakesh loosened his grip around Minx's knees, afraid that the next one would find its mark. Minx leapt out of his grasp and aimed the gun at both of them, curling her lips and snarling, 'Fools! Just do as you're told. Don't annoy me further.'

Amrita turned to Rakesh, her eyes wide with fear, 'Let's not argue with her, Rakesh. I know what she's all about. She means it. Just do what she's telling you.'

Rakesh stared in disbelief. 'Are you crazy? You want me to take off all my clothes for the benefit of this lunatic? I'd rather die.'

A bullet whistled through his parted legs. 'You won't get away that easily, sweetheart,' Minx said smoothly. 'I'll shoot your balls off and stuff them into your wife's mouth. Next I'll tear off her nipples with this sharp baby here and feed them to the crows. You'll look quite ugly before I'm through with you. And you'll suffer. Oh, yes . . . really, really suffer. Horrible, huh? So cut it out and get on with the show. I'm ready. My film is hooked. This is going to be the best porn film ever made. I even have some mood music to inspire you. Amrita loves bolero. She gives great head to it. I've sucked her off on that one too. Let's see what you can do. Use your imagination. Don't feel shy. Pretend I'm not there. Ignore me. She's your wife after all. No crime involved. You've seen how well she fucks women. I get the feeling she's even better with men. Pull your pants off, you oaf. Let me see what it is you're hiding. Amrita seems to love it. And what Amrita loves, I want to destroy. I want to see how enormous you really are.'

Amrita spoke up quietly, calmly, 'Minx, I beg of you, leave my husband alone. I'll do anything you want me to . . . I always have in the past. You know that. I'll make love to you, you can do whatever you want to me. But let him go. I promise you . . . I'll divorce him. I'll live with you forever till I die. I'll never look at another man. I won't let anybody touch me. I'll be yours, all yours, just yours. But let Rakesh get out of here. He won't tell the police. He won't file a complaint. No hassles. I'll sign anything you want. Do anything you ask . . . .'

Minx pushed her away roughly. 'Stop playing Florence Nightingale for that crumpled up limp wimp. This is a moment I have waited for so don't try and cheat me out of it.'

Minx put the muzzle of the gun through Amrita's shirt and ripped it open. Rakesh attempted to stop her, but she turned on him swiftly and pointed the gun at his gut. 'Naked,' she commanded. 'That's how I want both of you to be. Go on . . . start now.'

Amrita signalled to her husband with her eyes, adding, 'Let's not argue, darling.' She got out of her clothes carefully and waited for Rakesh to remove his.

'It's cold in here,' Amrita complained.

Minx raised her eyebrows, 'So it is . . . silly me . . . I hadn't noticed. Here . . . huddle under this till I tell you when to start.'

She flung two rough blankets at her and yelled at Rakesh, 'Get on with it, mutt, we don't have all day and all night.' Rakesh removed his shirt and stepped out of his trousers but kept his underpants on.

'Wow! Modest are we?' Minx mocked. 'Look at your wife. Two seconds and she's nude—like a well-trained whore—which is what she is, by the way. You obviously need persuasion.'

She whipped around and instructed Amrita, 'Go take off his ridiculous undies.'

Amrita rushed across and pulled them off. Rakesh hung his head refusing to meet her eyes. Minx circled the two of them. 'Pathetic. Look at you . . . like a dead worm,' she said nudging his penis with the nose of her

Strange Obsession

pistol. 'Wait . . . maybe you need music, booze, hash to get you going. Worry not. I have it all.' Bolero came through the speakers as she poured rum for all of them and handed the glasses around. Rakesh threw his away while Amrita took small sips from hers.

'That's better, darling,' Minx said approvingly as she fetched her Camcorder. 'Let's have some dancing. Maybe a slow flamenco. How about it?' She pushed Amrita at Rakesh and said, 'Do it for him like you used to for me. You are so good at it, especially when the tempo goes up.'

Wordlessly Amrita put her glass away and began to whirl around Rakesh slowly, gracefully, as Ravel's immortal music soared. Rakesh looked miserable and shouted, 'Stop this absurd drama. Kill me instead. I can't bear it any longer.'

Minx zoomed in for a close-up, panning the camera from his anguished face to his groin. Amrita continued to dance. She came up close behind him and whispered hastily, 'Just do as she says, darling. Have faith in me. Let's play for as much time as we can. I know the police will get here and save us soon. The villagers will show them this hideout.'

Minx stared at the two of them through the lens of her video camera and exclaimed, 'Pretty good so far. You two should consider doing blue films together.' Reluctantly Rakesh pretended to relax and joined Amrita in her bizarre dance.

'Take him into your lovely mouth now,' Minx instructed. 'Remember, I am the director. Don't stop till I yell "cut".' Amrita knelt and took Rakesh's penis between her lips.

'Use your fingers . . . like you used them on me,' Minx continued. To her surprise Amrita found Rakesh growing against her tongue. She rolled him gently from one side to the other, while Minx bent low to catch the movement. 'He seems ready to fuck now,' she said to Amrita. 'Take him. I want you on top, don't hurry.' Amrita pushed her husband down on the rough floor and climbed over him, slipping in his erect penis easily, smoothly.

'Great, I love this,' Mint said excitedly. 'I feel like I'm back in school watching all those dirty films.'

Amrita moved her hips like a lithe dancer, while Rakesh groaned below her. Minx jumped around, switching the Camcorder on and off, playing with the gun in the other hand and keeping up an incessant stream of remarks. 'What an exciting honeymoon. Bet the two of you hadn't expected anything like this. Go on Rakesh . . . do your thing. Tickle her nipples, caress her . . . enjoy yourself. Let's see some satisfied smiles.'

Amrita increased her pace to match the tempo of the music. The two of them climaxed just as Bolero reached its crescendo. Minx threw down the video camera, flung down the gun and danced around them ecstatically, yelling and screaming obscenities. Exhausted by the effort Amrita lay on Rakesh's chest, while he momentarily shut his eyes. Neither of them noticed that Minx had strewn straw around them and was moving frantically around the room chanting a mantra of some sort. 'This is heaven,' she said, hugging both of them. 'I couldn't have dreamt of a better end to our love story. Darling, I can't tell you how happy you've made me . . . . So happy. I could die right now. This minute. Now, now, now.' They heard the small sharp click of a cigarette lighter and then they smelt the smoke. Rakesh leapt to his feet and dragged Amrita up. Within seconds they were engulfed in flames. Flames that were already touching the beams on the ceiling. They heard Minx laughing, as they threw themselves out of the cabin and fell to the floor heavily. Glancing back they saw Minx's black-clad silhouette outlined against the inferno as she whirled around. Laughing, singing, arms outstretched, head thrown back, 'I'm happy . . . I'm so happy.'

*

Rakesh ran towards a small out-house some distance away. He found rags and gunny sacks which he threw at Amrita. 'Here . . . cover yourself. I'm going in there to pull her out.'

Amrita tried to stop him. 'Darling . . . don't please don't . . .' but he was gone, wrapped up in discarded blankets clutched closely around his body. Amrita prayed like she'd never prayed before. She heard the sound of villagers approaching and cried out for help. A party of ten ran up the incline and she noticed a couple of policemen along with an elderly, distinguished-looking man wearing a steel grey safari suit. 'Help!' she cried out, 'my husband is in there . . . and my friend. Please do something.'

The villagers attacked the flames energetically while the elderly gentleman directed the policemen to go in and help the two people trapped inside. Amrita was relieved to see the flames being brought under control with buckets of well water. Holding the blankets as tightly as she could around her, to cover her nakedness, she walked up to the man who was so obviously in charge. 'Will they be all right?' she asked tremulously.

He answered without looking at her, 'We'll know in a minute.' She stood shivering next to him even though the heat from the subsiding flames was still intense. 'My daughter is in there,' the man said abruptly.

Amrita gazed at him incredulously. 'You mean you are Minx's father?'

'Yes . . . Minx . . . she is my child . . . my only child', he replied.

*

Two limp bodies were carried out minutes later. Amrita could hardly recognize them. She walked up slowly as Minx's father barked orders to the others. She came and stood behind him in silence, her eyes dry, her throat drier. 'They're alive both of them,' he said without turning around. 'They look far worse than they are . . . don't worry we'll be able to fix them up as good as new.'

Amrita stared, transfixed by the sight. 'Oh God! Why did it happen,' she murmured over and over again.

*

Mr Iyengar led her away from the hospital room. 'Come on, you need some rest. We can't have you collapsing on us.' Amrita didn't want to leave. 'He needs me,' she said simply.

Mr Iyengar guided her towards the waiting-room. 'Yes . . . your husband needs you. And that's why you should go back and sleep. He needs a strong woman to sit by his side, not a wreck, which is what you'll end up being if you don't listen to me.'

Amrita sank into the nearest armchair while Mr Iyengar paced around restlessly reminding her of his daughter. 'How is she . . . Minx?' she asked.

'Pulling through, that's all I know right now,' he answered. 'We'll know for sure in a couple of days. My daughter is tough. She isn't one to give up. Your husband seems a strong person too. I expect both of them to make it. The doctors are optimistic.'

Exhaustion was beginning to catch up with Amrita. She had gone without sleep for close to thirty-six hours.

She had not eaten very much either. Mr Iyengar spoke to her slowly. 'Your parents have been informed. They're on their way. Your brothers too. And your husband's people. We've given them a police jeep.'

'Thank you,' Amrita whispered, her voice unable to rise.

'I have to thank you and your husband for saving my daughter's life,' Mr Iyengar said after a pause. 'If he hadn't gone in after her, she'd have been dead today.'

Amrita stared pensively out of the window. 'Does her mother know?'

Mr Iyengar shook his head. 'The shock would kill her. She's in a very precarious condition, as you probably know.'

Amrita looked up at him, 'Minx rarely spoke about her. Is she ill?'

Mr Iyengar shook his head. 'Hasn't Minx told you . . . my wife has been institutionalized for the past ten years. This news would kill her. I don't have the courage. I don't.'

Amrita's eyes welled up with tears. 'I didn't know, Minx never told me. I thought her mother had left her, left you . . . .'

Mr Iyengar gave a short, dry laugh. 'I see my daughter has been spinning tales again. She's very good at that, isn't she? Takes everybody in. Everybody, besides her father. That's what she cannot forgive about me. Poor Meenakshi. Such a wasted life. Such a tragic life. And she had everything a girl could want, everything.'

Strange Obsession

Amrita got up and joined him at the small window. 'You used the word forgive . . . I was under the impression there was more, much more to forgive, apart from your being the only one to see through her.'

Mr Iyengar turned to face her. 'Such as?'

Amrita found it difficult to carry on. 'I don't know how to put it. Minx told me about her childhood. In detail . . . it must have been horrible. Disgusting. How can a daughter who has been through all that ever forgive her father? He cannot call himself her father. He is no better than an animal . . . a beast.'

Mr Iyengar seemed puzzled. 'Did she tell you I beat her? Belted her? Yes . . . I remember doing that when she was very young. I will not justify it now . . . but at that point I had every reason to. She was an impossible child. Impetuous, rebellious, defiant and difficult. I have struck her. Not often, perhaps twice or thrice.'

Amrita interrupted him. 'I wasn't referring to your hitting her, though she did tell me about that too.'

'Then what?' Mr Iyengar was insistent.

Amrita's eyes blazed as she blurted out, 'You know what I'm talking about. Why are you pretending you don't understand?'

Mr Iyengar's face betrayed nothing as he stared steadily straight into Amrita's angry eyes. 'I'm sorry Mrs Bhatia, but I have no idea what you are driving at.'

Amrita spoke in a voice filled with contempt. 'You disgust me. Had I had such a father, I would've committed suicide years ago. What you did to your young daughter can never be forgiven. You used her, abused her, exploited her . . . you low-down, frustrated man. Why didn't you go to a prostitute if your wife couldn't sleep with you? Why did you have to force a child into satisfying your lust?'

Mr Iyengar's face was a mask of revulsion, his voice was stricken when he finally spoke. 'Did my daughter, my own precious child, tell you all this?'

Amrita nodded.

'Poor, poor girl. Poor Meenakshi. I wish I'd realized earlier just how sick she really was. Maybe I would have been able to save her the fate that befell her mother.'

Amrita saw Mr Iyengar crumple before her eyes as he unsteadily reached for a chair. For a few minutes neither of them spoke. She watched closely as the man sat holding his head in his hands with tears wetting his face. 'What crimes must I have committed unknowingly to suffer this! Meenakshi!! My little Meenu . . . how could she have told such loathsome lies about her own father? My God! I curse the day her mother gave birth to her.'

Amrita asked quietly, 'How do I know she's lying and you are telling the truth? How does anybody know?'

Mr Iyengar looked up, his eyes swollen, his voice breaking. 'God Almighty knows the truth. The psychiatrist who treated her mother knows it too . . . but eventually it is up to you, what and whom to believe. My daughter is the severely disturbed child of a disturbed mother. She suffers from delusions, she tells lies, she makes up stories. The number of schools she has been expelled from have their own tales to tell. I tried hard, too hard, to be both mother and father to her. To protect her. But today I realize just how badly I've failed. Yes, there were times in my busy career when I couldn't pay her the sort of attention she needed. But I didn't ever imagine I'd have to face what I just did. Is this the price I must pay for neglecting her when she needed me?'

Amrita hesitantly reached out her hand and placed it over his. 'Please, forgive me, I'm so sorry . . . and so ashamed. I take back my ugly words. Your daughter and I . . . you probably know already . . . we . . . we shared an unnatural relationship. She forced me into it . . . blackmailed me . . . tortured me . . . scared me . . . . And then . . . I began to enjoy it. To respond. I became dependent on her. . . so dependent I thought we'd spend our life together till I met my husband. It was he who saved me from her clutches.'

Mr Iyengar nodded. 'I know everything. My men kept me informed. I was aware of every move made by my daughter. I have detailed dossiers on her activities . . . and incidentally, on yours too. So . . . please don't explain anything. I already know what I need to know.'

Amrita looked at him quizzically. 'As a father didn't it upset you? Her using your name, your influence, your position, for terrorizing people, for getting what she wants?'

Mr Iyengar answered thoughtfully. 'I was always afraid of her . . . scared of her rage, unsure of what she might do if I reacted. I had to put up with a great deal to protect her mother. But my men, the few I trust, kept an eye on her most of the time. But Meenakshi outwitted them also. She is sly and clever when it suits her—as you well know. But let me tell you . . . the only time I got worried, and I know she did too, was when you struck up a friendship with Partha. We had to find some way to shut him up. He'd managed to dig out too much. Meenakshi came to me during that period, I'm sure she didn't tell you that. I'd not met her for some years. She was crying. And I remembered the little girl without friends who used to crave her mother's company. I felt sorry and would've done anything she wanted me to. Meenakshi was mortally afraid of being exposed. She thought Partha was going to do it—strip her naked in public. She begged me to finish him off. Or at least to get all the files on her destroyed. I refused, even though I knew she'd never forgive me for turning her down. And that's when she decided to use her own means and methods.'

Both of them straightened up as they saw the doctor approaching. 'Both the patients are doing fine,' he said cheerfully. 'We'll require to monitor them in the I.C.U. for two or three more days till their condition stabilizes.

I can give you an opinion on corrective surgery after that. Mr Bhatia will require minimal help. His legs got rather badly burnt and his right arm needs some work on it. Ms Iyengar's condition will have to be assessed later. I'm afraid we'll need more time to patch her up . . . the face in particular. I'm also worried about one eye. But we're doing our best.' Amrita and Minx's father discussed a few more details with the surgeon before he left them to go home and get some well-deserved rest.

Mr Iyengar said to Amrita, 'You need to sleep . . . and eat something. We can't have another patient on our hands. Let me drop you back—I have a jeep outside.'

Amrita followed him wordlessly, too exhausted to say anything. They drove through the dark roads in silence, each of them lost—or trapped—in their own strange worlds. Just before she could say a feeble, 'Thank you . . . and good night,' Mr Iyengar touched her arm. 'I want you to know something. No matter what happens in the future, you and your husband will never be bothered again. That is my promise to you. I intend taking charge of my daughter henceforth. Full-time. I won't take any chances . . . never again. She will stay with me and I shall get her the best care possible.'

Amrita leaned her head against his arm gratefully. 'Another thing,' Mr Iyengar continued, 'your secrets are safe with me. I have destroyed them . . . every single scrap of paper, film, photographs or recording.

It's all gone. I found everything when I broke open her flat after she disappeared. She'd given my men the slip very ingeniously this time by leaving the building clad in a burqa borrowed from her neighbour. The man on duty assumed it was that lady when it was actually Meenakshi. We broke into the place when we saw no one entering or leaving for two days. And that's when we stripped it clean—I supervised the entire operation personally. You have nothing to fear, now or in the future. And I give you my word. Meenakshi will not be allowed to come anywhere near you again as long as I live.'

Amrita's tears wet his shirt sleeve. He put his arm protectively around her as he walked her to the gate. 'God bless you, my dear,' he said as Amrita turned to say good-bye. She managed a smile and a small wave as the mali came up to tell her the good news, 'Aggarwal saab, memsaab coming. Dinner is waiting.'

Amrita ran joyfully inside to get the place ready for her parents. It was all right. Everything was all right. She felt safe and protected. The dark didn't frighten her any more.

Epilogue

Amrita's eyes lit up at the sight of the silver tea-tray. A good, hot cup of well-brewed Indian tea was just what she needed to take care of the jet lag. She stirred uncomfortably. Her enormous belly had begun to get in the way already. And it wasn't even five months yet. Twins? Everybody seemed to think so. She got up clumsily and drew the curtains. Rakesh had left for his morning jog. They had just flown in from New York. And here he was, their first day in Delhi after two long years, running around South Extension.

Amrita patted her belly and crooned softly to her unborn child, 'We are home, we are home.'

The servant knocked softly on the bedroom door. 'Akhbar, memsaab,' he muttered and gave her the Hindustan Times. Amrita scanned the headlines disinterestedly. Nothing had changed in her absence. Terrorists, strikes, scams, scandals. She turned the page to scan the classifieds. With a fond smile she recalled how that was a daily ritual in the Aggarwal household. The image of her mother at the dining-table reading out marriage, birth, engagement and anniversary notices to her father floated before her sleepy eyes as they travelled down the crowded columns.

She missed the item on her first reading. Skipped it altogether. Something made her go back to the top of the page. It still did not register. After all, there were thousands of Iyengars in India. Tens of thousands. Amrita assumed it was yet another anonymous Iyengar who had died 'under tragic circumstances'. Then her eyes travelled to the next word—Meenakshi. It took a second or two before the realization struck her. Yes, it had to be. Minx was dead. The announcement was terse, crisp, to the point. None of the usual flowery nonsense—left for her heavenly abode . . . fondly remembered . . . deeply mourned. This was one obit that believed in brevity.

'Iyengar (Meenakshi) passed away on 7th August in Bombay under tragic circumstances. No condolences please.'

Amrita reread it a dozen times. Her tea grew cold. And the hands which held the newspaper even colder. She felt herself shiver involuntarily. Amrita was free at last.

Acknowledgements

Special thanks to David Davidar, my friend, publisher and editor—in that order—for his quiet support and constant encouragement.

PBD 11/1012 BILL 20760